DARK
SECRET

A gripping detective thriller full of suspense

JANICE FROST

JOFFE
BOOKS

Published 2016 by Joffe Books, London.

www.joffebooks.com

© Janice Frost

ISBN-13: 978-1-911021-37-7

To my mother, with love.

Prologue

Two in the morning and minus fifteen outside. Gray Mitchell lay awake, grateful for his down-filled quilt and the residual warmth still lingering from the heating, which had sputtered off at midnight. He'd grown up on the East Coast of America, where winters had been colder, but twenty years in LA had spoilt him. After two years in England he wondered whether he'd ever acclimatise to the capricious British weather.

It wasn't just the plummeting temperature that was keeping Gray awake. He had a lot on his mind, principally his relationship with his partner of nearly a dozen years. Leon Warrior was the reason he had left his homeland in the first place — and why he was now thinking of going back.

Just as he was drifting towards sleep at last, Gray's mobile vibrated on the bedside table. He groped for it in the darkness, knocking it to the floor. Who could be texting at this hour? Gray switched on the light and squinted at the carpet. Predictably, the phone had landed out of reach and so he had to get out of bed. His phone case felt cold in his hand but as he scanned the message, a different sort of chill gripped his heart.

Am on the roof of the
cathedral. Afraid I might jump.
Please come now.

In less than five minutes, Gray was dressed and out of
the house. The fresh snow was ankle deep and a layer of
ice underneath made for treacherous walking. Gray slipped
and slid over the cobblestones as he headed for the
scaffolding surrounding the cathedral's south-west front.
He made for a spot in the hoardings where a couple of
kids had found a gap a few weeks back. They had managed
to scramble up to the roof of the cathedral and had taken
stunning pictures of the city at night and posted them on
Instagram.

The opening in the hoarding had been given a
temporary fix with a plank of wood nailed loosely over the
gap. It was easy enough for Gray to prise it free. The
darkness on the other side was not his only problem —
the ladder leading to the first deck of scaffolding had been
removed. At fifty-four, Gray was slight but strong and
supple. He had done some of his own stunts in the string
of low-budget movies he'd appeared in back home.
Nevertheless, he needed all his physical prowess now to
launch himself high enough to grab hold of the scaffold
and haul his weight up to the first deck.

By the time he managed to pull himself onto the
boarded walkway, the palms of his hands were red and
stinging from gripping the icy steel pole. In his haste to
leave the house, he had forgotten to wear gloves.

Gray scaled the scaffold at a reckless pace, frightened
that he might be too late. His laboured breathing expelled
white clouds of vapour into the freezing night air, along
with any thought for his own safety. Higher and higher he
climbed, conscious of the lights of the city receding below
him.

On the final deck, Gray stepped off the scaffold onto a long narrow parapet running partway along the length of the cathedral's west front. There was no safety rail and the ground was a vertiginous two hundred and fifty feet of empty freefall space below. A short distance away on either side of him, the twin towers of the cathedral's west front rose to a dizzy height, their distinctive, piercing spires hidden behind giddy swirls of snow.

Gray took a few hesitant steps forward. It was treacherous underfoot, ice and snow making the uneven stone walkway slippery. Ahead of him, where the parapet met the left tower, Gray thought he could make out a human form silhouetted against the stonework, but it was impossible to be sure in the swirling snow. It might just as easily be a stone carving. Gray called out, his words muffled and distorted by the wind. No one answered, and the shape seemed to dissolve in the snowy gloom.

Heart racing, Gray inched forward, pinning himself to the parapet wall, at times slip-sliding dangerously close to the edge and the sheer drop to the cathedral's forecourt far below.

As he neared the tower, he called again. All the way along the ledge he had been wondering what he should say. Now, approaching the spot where he thought he had glimpsed the nebulous shape, he worried that it really was too late.

Gray thought he heard a voice calling to him from behind the tower and he called back, "Stay where you are." A step. "I'm coming." Then, "Hold on. Whatever it is, this isn't how to fix it."

Gray shuffled forward, back pressed against the parapet wall, needing something solid to lean against, even though there was now a little more room to manoeuvre. Close up, he could see that the shape was a statue after all. A weathered stone king with a snow-filled crown and an empty, emotionless stare loomed up in front of him. Had the statue witnessed a solitary, despairing figure leap out

3

into the void? For a moment, Gray stood completely still, afraid to move, afraid to know the truth.

Another couple of steps and he was there, clinging for dear life to the crumbling statue. Snow was falling fast around him as he hugged the stony king to edge past it. But there was nothing on the other side, only more snow and a triangle of pitched lead roof sloping steeply away from him. There was no one ahead of him on the parapet and no way that anyone who might have been there before could have gone anywhere but down.

Gray's eyes filled with tears. He stood, holding onto the statue, head bowed, snow settling in his collar and dripping cold down the back of his neck. He did not hear the hooded figure stealing up behind him, or see the arm raised above his head, weapon in hand. He did feel the sudden, agonising pain of a fracturing blow to the back of his skull. His knees buckled, and he sank down on the snowy parapet, perilously close to the edge. Gray Mitchell twisted round and looked up. He saw a familiar face inside a fur-trimmed hood. "You!" was all he had time to say before his assailant's foot sank into the small of his back, sending him over the edge.

No one but the hooded figure was around to hear the shriek that was the last sound Gray Mitchell uttered as he plummeted towards the ground. A gush of warm blood pooled around his head, turning the snow to pink slush where he lay.

The hooded form stood on the ledge looking down before turning and making its way back to the scaffolding. Minutes later, safely on the ground, the figure paused to look at Gray Mitchell lying unmoving on the forecourt, then turned and headed off. Enveloped in snow and darkness, the silent killer disappeared into the bitter night.

Chapter 1

Laurence Brand liked his job better in the summer months. Then he could wear his loose-fitting Roman tunic and a pair of gladiator sandals barefoot (his wife having forbidden the addition of socks). Sometimes, for a flourish, he would wind an aromatic laurel wreath around his head.

Laurence strove for authenticity and this was harder in the colder months because, as far as he was aware (and he was something of an expert on the subject), authentic Roman citizens did not wear thermal undergarments from Marks and Spencer's. It did not matter that he was the only one who knew what was underneath his toga, when he was Caius Antonius, he wanted to get every detail right. But he hated the cold, so in the winter he had to make concessions to the British weather. Today, though, Caius's clothes were left hanging in the wardrobe and it was jeans and a T-shirt and woolly jumper that covered up his long johns.

Business was slower now that the holiday season was behind them. From October onwards, Laurence only did a handful of tours, for just a few intrepid tourists or

5

businesspeople in town for a conference. This time of year most of his earnings came from giving talks at the museum or to groups like the Women's Institute. And there were the school visits, which he always enjoyed. Caius Antonius was popular with the kids, at any rate the primary school ones. He tended not to do secondary, as they tended to take the piss. Even the Latin words he used failed to impress the older ones.

Few state-school kids learned Latin these days. In his former career as a classics teacher, Laurence had loved introducing his students to his passion. At the beginning of the autumn term, face to face with the cream of Year Eight, he had always begun by asking: 'Why study Latin?' Year after year, he would go halfway around the class before some bright spark came up with the answer he was looking for. *To learn about the Romans, sir.* Precisely. In Laurence's opinion it was all about the Romans. Then his school decided that learning about the Romans could be achieved perfectly well within the history curriculum. No one gave a toss about dead languages any more.

Faced with early retirement or finding employment elsewhere, Laurence had heeded the advice of his wife Maxine and embarked on a new part-time career as a Roman tour guide. And so, Caius Antonius had been born, emerging fully grown with an impressive CV that included long years of service as a centurion in the army of the Empire. A veteran of numerous campaigns, Caius had been posted in his later years to the northernmost outpost of the Roman Empire at Hadrian's Wall. Now retired, he was an active and dutiful citizen of Stromford. Immersed in his Roman alter ego, it sometimes seemed to Laurence that they were kindred spirits occupying a single body.

Laurence regularly had imaginary conversations with Caius. A Roman centurion knew as much as anyone whether or not it was a good idea for the Scots to vote for devolution, or for Britain to leave the European Union. On the Scottish question, Caius was unapologetically partisan. *We didn't give them any handouts in our day. They're ungovernable and we don't need their taxes. The wall's there for a reason, by Jupiter.* On Europe, he believed in centralising power in Rome. Whereas Laurence tended towards a left-of-centre bias in political matters, Caius represented the other extreme, more Empire than Republic. Laurence enjoyed their debates. He believed they gave him a balanced outlook on life.

Maxine often referred to Caius as Laurence's 'evil twin.' Even so, she wasn't averse to manipulating the dual nature of her husband's personality to her own advantage.

"That's Caius talking," she would say, or "Caius needs a healthy Mediterranean diet, not that stodge you like to eat." Only occasionally would Maxine side with Laurence over Caius.

Laurence prided himself on seldom being stumped by a question from his tour groups. It meant spending hours doing meticulous research but that was no great hardship. Over the years, he and Maxine had travelled to most of the famous Roman sites in Europe. Maxine did not share his passion. She was happy to wander around the ruins with him for an hour or so, but then she would take off to a beach or the nearest shops. It did not seem to matter that their interests did not coincide. They had rubbed along quite nicely for twenty odd years. What did it matter if, on a trip to Northumbria, Maxine preferred a day at the Metro Centre to a day at Vindolanda?

Having run her own tea rooms for ten years, Maxine had quickly become bored when they moved to Stromford. She had taken a part-time job in the cathedral café and within a year, she and a fellow worker had taken on the catering contract. Now, it seemed, she was busier, and happier, than ever. The café was located next to the chapter house and in the summer months, tables spilled out into the cloisters. Laurence liked to lunch there on slack afternoons, sipping a glass of wine and enjoying the peace and quiet.

Through their jobs, and Maxine's natural sociability, they had quickly acquired a circle of friends in the historic Uphill area where they lived and worked. Maxine's business partner, Helen Alder, was a forty-something disillusioned nurse. She'd discovered a love of baking after watching T*he Great British Bake Off* and enrolled on a course at the local FE college. Helen was Maxine's new best friend.

Helen was one of those larger-than-life characters, nearly six feet tall, with a swimmer's broad-shouldered build, and a loud personality. Laurence was slightly scared of her; she reminded him of the matron in the hospital where he had had his tonsils removed when he was six years old. Matron had ordered his mother to leave at the end of visiting time, and he had clung to her until Matron prised his fingers loose. He imagined Helen telling customers what to order, where to sit. But according to Maxine, Helen's manner was partly bluster. She had another side to her personality. Don't we all, thought Laurence, thinking of Caius. Maxine drew his attention to Helen's wrists, which bore the scars of a failed suicide attempt. Maxine had called it a 'cry for help.' Caius Antonius merely snorted. *Cry for attention, more like.*

Despite his eccentricities, Laurence had made friends too. His visits to the café often coincided with break-time for the craftspeople who worked at the cathedral. The stonemasons and stained-glass experts were working on a seemingly endless series of restoration projects on the magnificent edifice. Until he met them, the only stonemason Laurence had ever come across was the hapless Jude Fawley, from Thomas Hardy's novel. Like Jude, Laurence had dreamed of escaping his working-class background into the giddy heights of academia. Unlike Jude, he had made it to university. With a first class honours degree in classics, Laurence had worked within the comprehensive school system until it closed its doors on the languages of antiquity.

On one of his first visits to the café, Laurence had looked up from the book he was reading as a group of workers in safety boots, navy overalls and hard hats walked through the door. They'd queued up at the counter, talking and laughing with the staff. Laurence had watched Maxine flirt with a pang of resentment. His wife was an attractive, shapely woman, ten years younger than him. In their working clothes, these guys looked big and manly. Laurence was dressed in what was essentially a skirt, his spindly legs and knobbly knees stretched out under the table, one bony shoulder bare and a laurel wreath around his balding head.

As they settled around a long table with their steaming mugs and bacon butties, Laurence noticed that at least two of them were women, and possibly a third, though this turned out to be a slight man with a long brown ponytail. That evening, Laurence had asked his wife about the workers and learned that they frequently came into the café, where they were entitled to a discount.

"You seemed to be on pretty friendly terms with them." Maxine had glared at him. She had never liked his insecurity. But Laurence had never been able to understand what she saw in him. He wasn't exactly god's gift in the looks department and she was, well, perfect. *A goddess*, Caius whispered inside Laurence's head.

The next time he'd popped into the café, Maxine introduced Laurence to the craftsmen and women and somehow he had become part of the group. He soon came to know them as individuals, none of whom posed a threat to his marriage. Laurence hit it off immediately with Vincent Bone. He was the oldest, a sinewy, quiet-mannered black man. Vincent was a devout Christian and had a tendency to refer to God as 'the Boss.' For the first few weeks of their acquaintance, Laurence thought he was talking about a real person. Vincent would signal the end of the break with, "The Boss wants us back at work." Laurence pictured the Boss as a man in a hard hat and clunky boots with a long white beard and a stonemason's hammer.

Laurence had also struck up a friendship with the youngest member of the group, a nineteen-year-old apprentice stonemason. The aptly named Marcus had expressed an interest in learning Latin, and Laurence had been tutoring him one evening a week and on Sunday mornings.

Today was one of those days when he had no tours arranged. Laurence was planning to take a stroll down the Long Hill to see if he could find some inspiration for Maxine's Christmas present. There was a new shop down there that sold the kind of thing she liked to wear — long floaty tops and full, ankle-length skirts. Laurence secretly preferred the figure-hugging black trousers and fitted blouses that she wore to work.

Perhaps he would call in at the cathedral café for lunch and enjoy a chinwag with Victor. Afterwards, he could head across to the Jester for a glass of real ale. He would wear that new winter jacket Maxine had persuaded him to buy at the weekend. His phone buzzed. A text from his wife. Bit unusual, she seldom contacted him during work unless it was an emergency. As he read Maxine's message, Laurence's heart lurched.

> Laurie, don't be alarmed, please come immediately. There's been a terrible accident. PS It's not me. Maxine xx

* * *

As his taxi passed the cathedral, Leon Warrior clocked Laurence Brand scurrying across the cobblestones. Off to see Maxine, no doubt. If ever a man loved his wife it was Laurence. Leon smiled. He knew Brand's irascible alter ego, Caius Antonius. The centurion had left a wife behind

10

in every outpost of the Roman Empire. He was the opposite of Laurence in every way imaginable.

As the taxi pulled into his drive, Leon looked up at the bedroom window, searching for any sign of Gray. Leon felt a pang of guilt, thinking of how much Gray had sacrificed to be with him. The weather was a challenge of course, and his partner complained incessantly about the British climate.

Gray had suggested the move. Career opportunities were dwindling for both of them. They were both tired of Hollywood, and the whole dreary business of endless auditions for bit parts in second-rate movies or TV dramas. Leon's last role had been as a corpse. He had lain still throughout the whole autopsy scene, naked and cold. When it was over, all the other actors had walked away, leaving him lying there, with a lump of dead meat on his chest. He'd had to call on a cameraman to help him heave the bloody, prosthetic carcass off him before he could sit up. There had to be a better way to earn a living.

He had met Gray on the set of a horror movie. They were both playing zombies, awaiting their turn to have their heads ripped off by the hero. Leon and Gray had spent their breaks drinking herbal tea, and appreciatively watching the hero push his beautiful body through a punishing routine of calisthenics. By the time their scenes had been wrapped up, Leon and Gray were an item. "I was yours the minute you opened your mouth," said Gray, referring to Leon's English accent. For Leon, it had been Gray's gentle manner and his kindness and generosity towards his fellow actors. "Keep your ego in proportion to your talent," Gray was fond of saying. Unlike Leon, he had been cured early on of all hubris.

It had taken them a while to work out what else they could do. Leon's career had been slightly more lucrative than Gray's in the early days and he had invested wisely. "Let's face it; we're a pair of old has-queens," he said to Gray one day. "What we need is a complete change."

Moving back to England had been on his mind, but he had not confessed as much to Gray. He hadn't needed to. "I'd move to England with you in a heartbeat, you know," said Gray.

"The weather's crap," Leon warned.

"You can get tired of the sun," said Gray. They were lying on the beach watching a group of golden-tanned youths playing beach volleyball.

London had been the obvious choice. Then, Leon had come across some pictures of his home city, Stromford, in one of the movie magazines. When Gray saw the beautiful Gothic cathedral at the city's heart, he fell in love.

The idea for the ghost tour business had arisen during a visit to England to look at properties. Before travelling up to Stromford, they had done the touristy thing in London, including sightseeing from open-topped buses. They had been standing in the rain, listening to a man dressed in Victorian garb describing Jack the Ripper's antics in salacious detail. "We could do this," Leon had whispered to Gray.

Leon and Gray had bought a sprawling turn-of-the-century house close to the cathedral. Before moving to the States, Leon had played a part in a British sci-fi series which had obtained cult status over the years. Sometimes he wondered if his acting career might have gone better if he'd stayed on this side of the pond. Another member of the cast was now acting in a soap that had been going strong for thirty-five years. Leon had written to him, inviting him on the ghost tour. The press had come along and that had provided some useful publicity. They were thinking of branching out to include medieval tours. Shame Laurence Brand was already doing the Roman one — they could have done a beautiful job of that. Leon had fond memories of his time as a Roman legionary on the set of Gladiator. He had been trampled to death by a horse seconds after the opening titles. Russell Crowe had even offered him a hand up. His signed, framed still as Maximus

Decimus Meridius — surely his finest role — had pride of place amidst the many other photos on the 'wall of fame' in the hallway of Leon and Gray's new home.

The eccentric Laurence Brand had been a tad hostile at first, no doubt concerned that the ghost tour would steal punters away from his tour. In fact, it was quite the reverse. Leon and Gray recommended Laurence's tours and put quite a bit of business his way. Now it was quite common for people to turn up for a ghost tour saying Caius had recommended it to them. Laurence and Maxine had become their friends. They often joined Leon and Gray, along with some of the others in their little social circle, at what Leon rather pretentiously referred to as his 'soirees.'

Leon had accepted that in moving back to the town he had grown up in, sooner or later he would encounter people from his past, acquaintances from his schooldays who had never moved away. Some of them Leon would have preferred not to see again. Back in the eighties, as a teenager questioning his sexuality, Leon had been a target for bullies. He'd seen one of them in Marks and Spencer's a couple of weeks ago with a teenage kid. Leon had stood behind him in the queue at the men's department checkout. This man still made him feel like a frightened fifteen-year-old.

Gray too had suffered bullying as a teenager. He'd seen a therapist of course, that's what people did in L.A. The therapist had told him to let go of his negative feelings. Leon disagreed with this philosophy. He had resolved to confront the man, but as it turned out, it was Gray who lost it on their next encounter.

Leon opened the door and called into the long, empty hallway. "Honey, I'm home!" Then again, "Gray, where are you?" No Gray. But no message and Leon felt a surge of relief. At that moment his phone rang. Maxine's number. Disappointed, Leon ignored it. It rang again. This time he took the call. Maxine's voice was shaky, so he knew instantly that something bad had happened.

"Leon, there's been an accident. You need to come to the cathedral right now."

Chapter 2

Dozens of early-morning commuters must have walked right past the snowy mound near the west-front entrance. It was not the only thing that had been blanketed by the heavy snowfall the previous night. Like furniture draped with dust sheets in a country house, everyday objects had all become formless shapes. Joe Hemswell, the cathedral caretaker, had almost walked straight past it.

Joe wanted nothing more than to hurry inside and put the kettle on for a quick cuppa before he began his morning duties. Instead he veered off the path to the left, the frozen grass crunching beneath his feet. As he drew closer to the mound, his heart began to race. Close up, the mound of snow was looking more and more like the form of a person lying outstretched on the ground. All week there had been reports about the plight of the homeless. A man in Sheffield had been found in a shop doorway, frozen to death.

Joe looked at the mound. It was undeniably human and when he knelt to brush away the snow, he touched something hard and smooth, like leather. He scraped a little more snow away and saw the toe of a man's boot.

Joe stood up and looked around. Not another living soul about. He reached into his pocket and then hesitated. He needed to be sure before he called the police. He moved to where the head ought to be and scraped away the freshest layer of snow. Underneath, he saw pink slush, as if a red drink had been spilt over the snow. But this was no drink. Intermixed with the pink were blobs of grey, like cold porridge or tapioca. Joe deliberated. He brushed more snow away, just to be sure, looking just long enough to see what it was.

He had not expected what was left of the dead man's face to be familiar. He was shocked to recognise Gray Mitchell. Joe took a few steps backwards and vomited into the snow. After a couple of moments, fingers trembling, he called 999.

* * *

Maxine Brand was in the cathedral café kitchen with her business partner, Helen Alder, and their two staff, Hilda Prentis and Chloe Maitland. They were busy preparing for the day ahead. Hilda was spreading margarine from a huge catering tub over slice after slice of bread. Chloe, the work-experience girl, was preparing the fillings. Helen and Maxine were unpacking the morning order from the local baker's, a sumptuous supply of cakes, pastries and savoury snacks. It was a full hour and a half before opening time but there was still a lot to do before their first customers started drifting in. The stonemasons would be in for their morning break. Maxine opened up early for them.

For the past half hour, they had heard police sirens wailing nearby. Helen had tuned the radio to one of the local radio stations to see if there had been an accident on the roads. They were unaware of the drama unfolding outside the west entrance to the cathedral.

Joe Hemswell walked in from the cloisters. His face was white. It was not unusual for Joe, or another member of the cathedral staff to wander in first thing for a chat, or to buy a sandwich or drink to take away. Joe's entrance was usually pretty low-key. But today everyone turned to look at him. It was immediately obvious that something big had happened.

"Joe Hemswell, you look like death warmed up," Hilda said.

"What is it, Joe? Is it Laura?" Maxine asked.

Joe shook his head. The women waited. Work had stopped. Only Chloe carried on mixing mayonnaise into a bowl of tuna. She was sixteen years old and in love for the first time, with a boy called Harry. She hummed along to a song on the radio.

Maxine turned the radio off. "Sit down, Joe. I'll bring you a cup of tea."

Joe nodded and pulled a chair around so that he could sit with his back to the radiator. Maxine placed a mug of tea in front of him.

Joe put his hands around the warm mug. "I found Gray Mitchell lying out front near the west entrance. He was in the snow," he said.

"Oh God! Is he okay?" Helen asked.

Joe shook his head slowly.

Even Chloe was listening. Maxine asked if Gray had had a fall. Helen muttered something about his heart.

Joe cleared his throat. "Suicide," he said.

Maxine and Helen stared at him, then at each other. No one spoke for a moment.

"How?" Helen asked. "Hypothermia?"

"They think he might have jumped from the roof."

Joe's words prompted a stream of 'Oh my Gods.'

"All those sirens — it was Gray," said Maxine, distraught.

"I don't believe it," Helen said. She looked defiant. "Gray wouldn't commit suicide. He wouldn't do that to Leon!"

Maxine stared at her friend, speechless.

Then Chloe said, "Well, if he didn't jump, someone's got to have pushed him then, haven't they?"

Hilda shushed her.

"I'm calling Laurie," Maxine said, expecting a look of disapproval from Helen. But for once, her business partner didn't chide her for telling her husband everything.

At forty-six, Helen was recently divorced after twenty years of marriage. She was finished with men for the foreseeable future, so she said. Her ex, aptly named Dick, was now living with a twenty-eight-year-old and they had just had a baby girl. Maxine suspected that Helen's man-hating phase was temporary. She had noticed the way Helen eyed up the male stonemasons.

"I'm a sucker for men in uniform," a drunken Helen had once confessed. "Especially paramedics — those green trousers and shirts . . . all that rushing around with life-saving equipment." The trouble with Helen was that she liked men too much to hate them. Equally, and not unimportantly, men liked Helen.

So Maxine had called her husband. Laurence Brand arrived to see Joe looking less ashen-faced, revived by the heat from the radiator and the attention of the women still gathered around him.

"What's happened?" he asked.

"Oh, Laurie! Gray Mitchell's dead. They think it's suicide."

Laurence gaped at her. "I don't believe it. I saw him yesterday morning at the farmer's market. He was looking forward to Leon coming back, planning a special meal to celebrate. He was happy."

"We're all saying the same thing," said Helen. "None of us can believe he would take his own life."

"It must have been an accident. It's the only possible explanation," said Laurence.

"But what on earth was Gray doing on the roof?" Helen asked.

"How did he even get up there? It's all locked up at night, isn't it?"

"Those kids found a way, didn't they?" Heidi was referring to the two lads who had climbed up the scaffolding and taken pictures from the cathedral roof. After that, the scaffolding had been secured and signs put in place giving dire warnings about the dangers of attempting to climb the dangerous structure.

"Gray's certainly capable of scaling it. He is — was — a fit man. He used to do the odd stunt in his films," Laurence said.

"Someone could have let him in," Chloe said.

Joe shook his head. "There aren't many people with access to keys for the west tower. I'm one of them and the tower's locked at night. It was still locked up this morning. Climbing the scaffolding's the only way anyone could have got up there after hours."

"Someone needs to tell Leon. He should hear about this from friends, not the police," Maxine said. "He'll be home now, wondering where Gray is."

For a moment, they were all silent.

"They were so sweet together," Maxine whispered. "Leon will be heartbroken."

"Alright, I'll do it," Maxine finally said. She tried twice before she heard Leon's voice. Was it her imagination or did he sound worried already? She couldn't tell him over the phone, but she did want to prepare him a little for the news. She found herself saying, "Leon, there's been an accident. You need to come to the cathedral café right now." She'd tried to keep her tone neutral but she knew Leon would pick up on the fear in her voice.

Chapter 3

Detective Inspector Jim Neal strode over to join the team assembled by the body. One of the cathedral staff had identified it as Gray Mitchell, an American who had settled in Stromford fairly recently, with his English partner. Neal's head was thumping and he wasn't in the best of moods. He'd stayed up half the night drinking with his old friend Jock Dodds, never expecting an early-morning call about a fatality. Then again, he was a copper. *Of all the bloody luck.* It wasn't as if he and Jock had much time to catch up these days. Both had demanding jobs. They managed a couple of weekends climbing in Scotland each year, but other get-togethers were few and far between. Jock had stopped off on his return from a conference of cardiac surgeons in London and Neal had been planning to take him to the train station later in the day. The early-morning phone call had put an end to that. Luckily his sister Maggie was free to take him, and Jock wouldn't complain. He'd always had a bit of a thing for Neal's younger sister.

Despite his hangover, Neal was pleased to see Ava Merry back on the job. It was her first day back after she had been injured on their previous case. She had also had some time off to recover from an operation on her Achilles tendon. At Neal's insistence, Ava had attended a few sessions with the police counsellor. In Neal's opinion, Ava had not fully confronted the feelings that emerge when you nearly kill a person. She had been far too upbeat when he had visited her in hospital after the event. Neal had been annoyed at the way she had handled the Amy Hill case, carrying out her own investigation alongside the official one. But his DS had got results, and results mattered. More to the point she had put a dangerous man out of circulation and for that he was ready to overlook her unprofessional behaviour. Nevertheless, much as he liked Ava, Neal felt that it would take time to trust her again.

Ava had her notebook out and was questioning a rather shocked looking man — probably the caretaker who had discovered the body. She gave no sign of being aware of Neal's approach. The interview appeared to be coming to an end and Ava was putting her pen away. *Poor bloke looks frozen as well as shocked*, Neal thought. Ava turned round and greeted Neal. Perhaps she had been aware of him after all.

"Morning, sir," she said.

A little guardedly, he felt — or was he just being over-sensitive? This first day back on the job together was always going to be a bit awkward. It was going to take time to get into a working rhythm with each other. They'd never really had a chance to find one last time around.

"Morning, Sergeant. Good to see you back on the job. How's the foot?"

Ava jogged on the spot for a couple of seconds. Her injury was a hundred per cent better, she said. She was a fitness fanatic, always out running, or clocking up lengths at the pool. Ava was also beautiful. Even this early in the morning, dressed in jeans, purple polka-dot wellies and an oversized parka, she looked radiant.

"What have we got, then?" He winced slightly.

"You alright, sir? Look a bit peaky this morning."

Neal grunted. Thank goodness it's still half dark, he thought, remembering the bloodshot eyes he'd glimpsed in the bathroom mirror. The very thought of sunlight glinting off the snow made his head twinge.

"I'm fine. Fill me in."

"The bloke I was just talking to is one of the cathedral caretakers. He spotted an oddly shaped mound of snow on the paving stones as he was making his way round the cathedral this morning. He went over to take a closer look, scraped away the snow and discovered the body. He reckons it's a bloke called Gray Mitchell. He's American. Lives uphill with his partner, Leon . . ." Ava searched back through her notebook, "Leon Warrior."

Neal looked up at the twin towers of the cathedral, their spires shrouded in early-morning darkness and freezing fog. He'd been up there shortly after he moved to Stromford. The view from the top was spectacular, but it was a long way down.

"We don't know exactly where he fell from," Ava said, also looking up. "Most likely it was from the parapet near the tower."

"We'll need to get up there, see if we can piece together what happened. The most likely scenario is suicide, but we'll need to treat this as a suspicious death until we know otherwise. How's your head for heights?" Neal asked.

"Okay, I think," Ava answered. "Did a bit of rock climbing when I was doing my Prince's Trust gold medal." Then she added more truthfully, "of course, Brimham rocks aren't exactly the Monros."

Neal smiled, thinking of the oddly shaped rock formations in Yorkshire's Brimham Moor. The popularity of outdoor climbing had mushroomed in the past few years thanks to the ubiquity of indoor climbing walls. You could hardly pass a scar or rock face nowadays without

22

seeing a group of school kids dangling off it. He wasn't sure he liked the trend. Climbing for him meant the vast emptiness of the Scottish Highlands and his own or Jock Dodds's company. He could do without clusters of middle-aged thrill seekers or corporates on team-building exercises. Then again, his ten-year-old son Archie loved indoor climbing walls.

"Let's take a look at the body, then," Neal said. He grimaced. A body that had hit the ground at high velocity was not going to be a pretty sight. Even from a distance, it was obvious that there was brain matter all over the snow.

"Hunt's been delayed. Traffic's at a standstill on the road leading out of his village," Ava said.

It hardly needed a coroner to confirm that Gray Mitchell wasn't going to be getting up anytime soon, Neal thought, but it would be useful to have an approximate time of death.

Judging by the amount of snow accumulated around Mitchell's half-excavated remains, he must have been lying there for several hours. There had been heavy snowfall throughout the night, but according to the weather report, it had stopped around five o'clock. Too late for the snowploughs to clear the roads in time for the morning rush hour. He sighed. There would be plenty to keep his colleagues busy today. The accident toll on the roads had soared since the onset of the cold snap.

"You okay?" He noticed Ava was looking a bit pale.

"Not every day you get to see someone's brains spilled out," his sergeant answered. "It's kind of sobering, isn't it? Everything that made him the person his family and friends loved reduced to a load of . . . minced tofu."

"At least it doesn't smell bad. I suppose we've got the sub-zero temperature to thank for that," Neal said. Crime scenes involving decomposing bodies turned his stomach. He could just about stand to look at even the vilest remains, but the smell got to him every time.

"Two sets of footprints leading to the body. Reporting officer and the caretaker?" Neal asked. Ava nodded. It was the first responder's duty to do what he or she could to secure the integrity of the scene. A couple of police cones marked out the immediate area around the body, and one of the responding officers was at work with a reel of tape.

"At least in weather like this there shouldn't be anyone hanging about gawping," said Ava, stomping her feet. The caretaker reckons he didn't touch the body, just scraped the snow away so that he could get a better look. Probably wishing he hadn't."

"Probably better for us if he'd left well alone. Still, could've been worse, I suppose. I've seen disastrous cases of accidental tampering with evidence." Neal noticed Ava's red nose and stomping. "Come on, let's go inside and speak to Hemswell. It'll get us out of this bloody cold for a bit," he said.

Ava looked like she might hug him.

They walked to the east side of the cathedral, where the café was located.

"I'm sorry, we're not open yet," called out a woman. Neal flashed his ID at the group of people assembled around a distraught-looking man in his fifties. Neal felt a stab of irritation. The investigation was probably already in danger of being compromised by speculation and rumour.

"Detective Inspector Jim Neal, and this is Sergeant Ava Merry. We'd like to have a short word with you, Mr Hemswell," Neal said, looking at Joe.

The other man stood up instead. "Speak to me first, Inspector. I'm Leon Warrior, Gray Mitchell's partner."

Neal was taken aback. He had not expected word of Mitchell's death to get out so quickly. He wondered who else Joe Hemswell had been blabbing to. He looked around at the circle of concerned faces and saw his answer. If everyone present had contacted someone else, it would soon be standing room only in the café.

24

"Mr Warrior—"

The man cut him off. "I just want to say right from the outset. There is absolutely no way that Gray would take his own life."

"Firstly, Mr Warrior, I am sorry for your loss. Secondly . . ." Neal couldn't help glancing at Joe Hemswell when he said it, "the circumstances surrounding Mr Mitchell's death are at present unknown. We will make no assumptions until our investigations get under way and we can start to reconstruct what happened. Until then, no one should be speculating one way or the other."

"I want to see him."

Neal was surprised that these hadn't been Warrior's first words. Then he noticed the group of women forming a kind of protective wall around him. He realised that it was only because of them that Leon Warrior was being spared the sight of his lover's brains splattered in the snow.

"I'm afraid that wouldn't be a good idea," Neal said gently, knowing his words probably only made matters worse. "We will be treating Mr Mitchell's death as suspicious and we need to restrict access to the . . . er . . . to his body, to our forensics people for the time being."

The woman who had said the café wasn't open yet, pressed Warrior's shoulder.

Neal cleared his throat. "In the meantime, my sergeant and I will take contact details from all of you. You may all be asked for a statement in due course."

"What for?" the youngest one asked.

The other women shushed her.

One of them said, "We want to know what happened to Gray more than you do, Inspector. I think I speak for all of us in saying we'll gladly answer any questions you might have." Everyone nodded, except the young girl, who sighed exaggeratedly and rolled her eyes.

I'll let Ava deal with that one, Neal thought.

* * *

An hour later, Neal and Ava left the café. Those who had been closest to Mitchell: the Brands, Helen Alder and Leon Warrior all said that Gray Mitchell would never take his own life. Neal knew better than to draw any conclusions based on their certainty. If there was one absolute in police investigations, it was that people were seldom what they seemed to others, even — sometimes especially — those closest to them.

"What did you make of that lot?" Ava said when they were outside.

"Well, if it does turn out to be suicide, they'll all be gobsmacked. Unless one of them murdered Mitchell and was lying through their teeth, of course."

They passed through a tall, heavy, panelled door and stepped directly into the cathedral's north transept leading to the nave, where they stood silent for a moment, both instinctively craning their necks upwards.

"I brought Archie here in his pushchair once," Neal said, breaking the spell. "He had one of those helium balloons tied to his wrist and he somehow worked it free. It floated right up to the ceiling in the south transept." Archie had howled, one of the guides had tutted loudly and a group of Japanese tourists had laughed and pointed upwards and over at the pushchair, to Neal's embarrassment.

"Wonder what became of it?" he said. It was one of those memories that stick.

They went towards the west entrance of the cathedral, where the final drama of Gray Mitchell's life had been played out.

Outside, the thin pain behind his eyes reminded Neal that he was still hung-over. Cursing Jock Dodds, and his 'just another wee dram for the road,' Neal rubbed his temples and proceeded down the steps.

"Looks like the cavalry's arrived," Ava said. She was referring to the presence of the full forensics team. The scene had now been properly secured with police tape.

"We need to get up there." Neal pointed up at the scaffolding around the west front of the cathedral. It partially obscured the public's view of what was one of the finest examples of medieval Gothic architecture in Europe. Striding across to one of the uniformed officers, he said, "make sure access to that scaffold is cordoned off as well. The last thing we want is a bunch of stonemasons getting up there before us." He glanced at his watch. To Ava, he said, "let's find out where the cathedral works department is located, and we'll need to know who's responsible for health and safety around here."

It turned out that the stonemasons, carvers and stained-glass restorers were based in a workshop across the road from the cathedral, back on the east side. The nearby health-and-safety office was in a timber-framed medieval house that had been converted into offices for administrative staff. They headed for the offices first.

Ava rang the bell. Neal noticed the slight misalignment of her nose caused by a blow from a chair leg, during their last case. She had refused plastic surgery to straighten it, and Neal thought he understood why. Before the injury, she had been perfect; now she had added character to her striking features. Ava had gone out on a limb to prove her suspect's guilt. She had risked her life by becoming involved in a relationship with a man she suspected was guilty of multiple sex offences as well as murder. Her behaviour had been brave but reckless. Neal was uncertain how to handle her. He had no wish to subdue her spirit, or alienate her by being the heavy-handed boss, but her actions had worried him. Neal hoped that the caution she'd been given by George Lowe, their DCI, would have some impact.

Neal slightly envied Ava's passion. His own youthful enthusiasm had been curbed by early fatherhood and the weight of responsibility it entailed. He was aware that many of his colleagues at the station considered him dour, and he did tend towards seriousness and rationality. Perhaps he and Ava might be good for each other.

The woman who greeted them was small, with hair cut sensibly short. She was dressed in jeans and one of those faux-Scandinavian jumpers that were all the rage. Snowflakes and reindeer paraded across her heavy hips and breasts. Neal showed her his ID.

She ushered them in, saying, "Is this about that poor bloke they found in the snow outside the cathedral?"

As if it could be about anything else.

She led them down a long hallway cluttered with Hi-Vis jackets, safety boots and hard hats. The office looked out across the road to the cathedral's east entrance, in view of the café. A double-decker bus outside cast a shadow over the small room. Neal could see the bus passengers straining backwards to see what was going on. It wouldn't be long before word spread around and the city was abuzz with speculation and rumour. No doubt the bloody press will be making an appearance soon, Neal thought sourly.

Ava answered the woman's question. "Yes, we were hoping you might be able to give us some information about getting access to the scaffolding. We need to go up there as soon as possible."

"What happened to him?" asked the woman.

"We don't know yet," said Ava.

"Of course," the woman said. "I'm Geraldine Skerritt. Most people call me Gerry. I'm the acting head of health and safety."

"Acting?" Ava queried,

"Er, my boss had a bit of an accident."

Ava raised an eyebrow. "On the job, was it?"

"Actually, no. He fell off an unsecured ladder and broke his leg while clearing out the guttering on his garage roof."

"Right." Ava suppressed a smile.

Neal, mouth parched and head throbbing dully, was in no mood for humour. He wanted something to drink. He accepted immediately when Gerry offered, asking for coffee, strong and black.

Neal ignored Ava's smirk. He never drank black coffee.

Mugs in hand, they sat around Gerry's desk, enjoying the warmth radiating from the heating pipes.

"If you need access to the scaffolding, I take it you think he fell from there," Gerry said.

"It's a possibility," Ava replied.

"I can't believe anyone else managed to get up there," Gerry said. "After that incident with the kids climbing up and taking pictures, we put secure measures in place to prevent the public gaining access. I thought the scaffolding decks were impregnable now."

"Hardly impregnable," Neal said. "Anyone with enough determination and some basic tools could easily find a way to get in." His customary sensitivity in handling interviewees was sadly lacking this morning. Geraldine Skerritt was irritating him more than she should.

"Where there's a will there's a way," Ava commented. She directed a sympathetic glance at Gerry, but the health-and-safety officer was staring at them wide-eyed.

"You . . . you don't think it could have been . . . murder, do you? I mean that's another possibility, isn't it, besides an accident or suicide?"

"Like we said, we can't say anything much about the cause of death until we begin our investigations," Ava reminded her.

"Do you know who it is . . . was? Or are you not allowed to tell me?"

"Gray Mitchell. Did you know him?"

She sputtered over her tea. "Gray? Are you sure?"

Joe Hemswell had been in no doubt about Mitchell's identity.

"Poor Leon," said Gerry. "I didn't know Gray — or Leon — well. Gray was often in the café when I was passing through — it's a shortcut to the west side. He and

29

Leon were friends with Maxine and Helen who run the café, and with Maxine's husband, Laurence. I'm not that friendly with any of them but I always give the girls in the café a wave when I pass through and I sometimes stop for a cup of tea and a chat."

"We'll be taking brief statements from the people you just mentioned. Was Gray closely acquainted with any of the other cathedral staff?"

"I don't think he was particularly close to anyone else. Leon and Gray haven't been living in Stromford for very long. Laurence and Maxine have been here quite a bit longer. They didn't all get along so well at first."

Neal and Ava exchanged glances. "Why was that?" Ava asked.

"Because of what they do." Neal gave her an encouraging look. "They give guided tours. Laurence does Roman ones and Gray and Leon do a ghost tour — and a medieval one, I think. Or maybe they're just thinking about that. Anyway, Laurence was a bit put out when Gray and Leon set up their business. Thought they'd take trade away from him, I suppose, particularly given their celebrity status." She punctuated the words with air quotes.

Ava suddenly exclaimed, "Oh my God! I've just realised who Leon Warrior is." She looked at Neal. "He played Dr Stephen Troy in *Spacedrifters*, a sci-fi series that was on in the eighties. My brother's a bit of a fan. It was very popular back then. God, he doesn't look anything like how he did in the series."

A polite way of saying he looked old, thought Neal. He cast his mind back to the eighties but had no recollection of the series. Perhaps it hadn't been shown in Scotland, or maybe he'd been out playing. Kids still did that back then, or at least he and Jock had.

Gerry nodded. "The *Stromford Courier* did a piece about their ghost business last year. Leon went to Hollywood when *Spacedrifters* finished but I don't think he made much of a name for himself out there. Still, I suppose he did meet Gray."

"Was Gray an actor too?" Ava asked.

"Yes, but not a very successful one as far as I can gather. He had a small part in *Gladiator*, I think. They both were in it, one of them got trampled by a horse just after the opening credits and the other was gored in one of the gladiatorial games scenes. I forget which was which."

"Coming back to what you said about Laurence being 'a bit put out' about Leon and Gray's business," Neal said, eager to get back on track. "Was there serious rivalry between them?"

"Not for long," Gerry said. "But you'd have to ask someone else about that. I don't always hear all the gossip." Neal nodded. Ava was scribbling away in her notebook. Gerry glanced at her watch, then over the road at the café.

"That's the stonemasons going over for their morning break," she said. A group of seven or eight men and women in overalls and workers' jackets were making their way along the path leading to the café. "They've been in the workshop a lot more lately because of the weather. They normally go over around half past nine."

"We need to take a look at the scaffolding around the west front," Neal said. "Can you help us with that?"

Gerry nodded. "I can lend you some safety gear — boots and hard hats, but it can be treacherous up there in this sort of weather. I'll call Mike Hotter over. He's the site safety foreman. He'll take you up."

"Some of our forensics people will also need access. I'd be grateful if you'd issue them with boots and hats too," Neal said.

* * *

A wind had whipped up by the time they began ascending a series of ladders leading up the scaffolding. They had located the point where Gray Mitchell must have gained access. It had not been hard to find. The splintered gap in the six-feet-high close-boarded fence had most likely been kicked in. A couple of scene-of-crime officers had already inspected the fencing and the area around the gap, taking detailed photographs. They had also dusted the ground-level scaffolding poles for prints and were now ready to start on the next level of decking.

Neal and Ava warned Mike Hotter that he must try to avoid disturbing any traces left by Mitchell or a potential killer. He complained all the way up. He wasn't used to being told what to do in what he obviously regarded as his own domain.

He tutted when he examined the damage to the fencing.

They looked down at where Mitchell had landed. From here they could guess where he must have fallen from.

"You okay?" said Neal.

Ava was gripping the safety rail. "It's a bloody long way down, sir."

All three stood silently, gazing down at the scene below. The police cars and vans and hordes of blue-uniformed and white-suited SOCOs looked tiny, almost invisible against the snow. Outside the cathedral's boundary wall stood a huddle of onlookers and beyond that the rest of the city went about its business.

Any other day they would be admiring the view, Neal thought. The cathedral and the nearby Norman castle were built on a hill that sloped away in a collage of orange pantile rooftops, across farmland, the distant Wolds and finally, the North Sea. None of that was visible today in the grey gloom of early morning and lingering freezing fog.

"Poor bastard," said Hotter. "At least he wouldn't have known what hit him."

"Not strictly true," Neal said. "He would have had a few seconds of falling through empty space. Plenty of time to see the ground rising to meet him."

"And see his life flash before his eyes. I suppose he would have thought of Leon," Ava added.

In the silence, Neal wondered what his own last thoughts would be. It was a no-brainer. The face of his son Archie would follow him into eternity.

"If he didn't come up here with the intention of killing himself, why did he come up?" Ava said. "He must have had a compelling reason, particularly on a night like last night with a blizzard blowing. Did he come to meet someone? Not up here on a snowy night, surely? Or did he come to help someone? Maybe someone phoned him? Did they have an argument?"

Ava was thinking like a detective, asking the kind of questions that might help reconstruct the last hour of the dead man's life. Neal's own brain was still too befuddled with alcohol to think clearly.

"That's for you lot to puzzle out," Hotter said. "The sooner the bleedin' better. The last thing this area needs is negative publicity just before the Christmas market. A lot of people's livelihoods depend on the extra trade it brings in." It was true. Shops, cafés, restaurants, hotels, stallholders, all had a stake in the market. "All it wants is for people to believe there's a killer on the loose and visitors will stay away in droves."

"Nobody's saying there's a killer on the loose. That kind of talk breeds unnecessary panic," said Neal.

"Can't stop folks talking."

"Think about the victim's loved ones," Ava chipped in. "It's bad enough for them not knowing what's happened, without listening to half-baked stories."

Hotter stared at her for a moment, then nodded.

Neal smiled to himself. He had noted the way Hotter had watched Ava climbing up the ladder. He couldn't blame him. His sergeant was a pretty sight.

They were all shivering now. The icy wind was blowing flurries of snow into their faces. When they spoke, their breath condensed in the air. It was going to be another bleak day. The three of them began the long descent down the scaffold.

Back on solid ground, Neal turned to Ava. "Take one of the constables with you and collect Leon Warrior from the café, if he's still there, otherwise head over to his place. I want you to take a look around, but make sure you don't disturb anything. The SOCOs will be going in there when they're finished here. Look for notes, messages, and any signs of disturbance. We need to recover Mitchell's mobile phone as soon as possible. If it's not on him, make it a priority when you search his place."

"Sir, Leon Warrior's already been home. He could have hidden or destroyed any evidence he found there — including a suicide note."

"I'm aware of that, Sergeant, but we still need to be thorough."

"Yes, sir," Ava answered. She went over to ask the scene-of-crime people whether they had retrieved Mitchell's phone.

The SOCO held up a polythene bag that contained a smartphone. Ava nodded. At least they had something.

Chapter 4

The café staff were still preparing sandwiches.

"Everyone's going to be coming in here to find out what's going on," said Maxine.

"Don't you think we should close as a mark of respect?" Helen said. She glanced over at Leon sitting in the window recess. Laurence was with him.

"I'm not sure it would be appropriate. Gray wasn't connected with the cathedral in any way and besides, we can't afford to let all this food go to waste." Maxine nodded across to the kitchen area. "And we're contracted to be open, remember?"

"I suppose you're right. But I feel for Leon and, to be honest, I'm feeling a bit emotional myself."

"We're all feeling emotional, but we need to keep it together for Leon's sake."

"Laurence should take him home."

There was a sudden draught from the door to the cloisters.

"It's that young sergeant. Ava something, wasn't it? Looks more like a model than a copper," said Helen.

* * *

The atmosphere in the café was heavy with grief, but to Ava it was a relief after the tension of the past hour in Jim Neal's company. She had been dreading the return to work after her convalescence. She had seen Neal only twice in that time — first when he had visited her in hospital after her ordeal, and then when he had called her into his office while she was still on sick leave, to give her a dressing down about her handling of the case. She shivered when she thought of Neal's words, and his cold stare. She regretted that she'd let down a man whose integrity she'd grown to respect.

Neal had vouched for her, she knew, when questions had been raised about her own conduct. After all, she had slept with a man she suspected of serious sex offences against very young women. Ava could not explain it. In a warped way, she had been attracted to Taylor. But she was ashamed, unsure whether that made her behaviour more, or less, reprehensible.

This morning she had been unassertive, deferring to Neal, being his silent partner. It was not in her nature to be submissive and she was finding it exhausting. Their respective ranks inevitably defined their professional relationship but, as far as Ava was concerned, in all else they were equals. Ava knew she was inclined to be impulsive, even reckless at times, but she couldn't help trusting her instincts. If she was going to succeed in the job, she knew she would have to deal with this.

Ava knew Neal was concerned about her lack of remorse. She had nearly killed Taylor. Neal had stared at her open-mouthed when she said, "It was a fight to the death, sir. Him or me." Neal, she suspected, was a man given to deep introspection. He had killed someone once, and suffered long agonies about it. But he shouldn't expect her to be the same. You acted and moved on. Life was too short for regrets and recriminations. Ava's approach to life was not to look back.

Ava had protested when Neal insisted that she see the police counsellor. She had endured three sessions with the kindly and well-intentioned woman. Ava was proud to have emerged from the therapy unshaken. Not that she'd have revealed this to Neal. He was convinced that the sessions would help her re-evaluate her perspective.

Ava watched Laurence Brand consoling Leon Warrior. The men were both in their mid-fifties, with greying hair. Warrior was a bit of a silver fox. He was of medium height, lean and muscled, a man who obviously took a lot of care with his appearance. He was impeccably dressed in a well-cut suit, and a fine woollen trench coat was draped over the arm of his chair. Brand, on the other hand, was one of those men of a certain age who are invisible in a crowd. He was average-looking. He had a bit of a gut, and was dressed in loose-fitting jeans and a navy Berghaus jacket.

"I'm sorry to interrupt, but we need to search your house, Mr Warrior. I have your partner's keys but I'd be grateful if you would accompany us. You may be able to advise us if anything is out of place or doesn't feel right."

"Nothing feels right," Warrior said.

"I'm sorry for your loss," said Ava. Her fingers twisted around the strap of her handbag, leaving sweat on the leather. Why was she feeling so nervous? This wasn't the first time she had dealt with a murder victim's nearest and dearest. Then she realised that she was not nervous at all, but impatient to get to work. She was also rather guilty that it was this that was uppermost in her mind, not her concern for Leon Warrior's loss. She felt that Leon Warrior must see right through her hollow sympathy. Well, if the post-mortem revealed Gray's death to be suspicious, then this was a murder investigation and every second counted.

"I can see you're eager to get on with your job, Sergeant," Leon Warrior said, and Ava blushed. He rose stiffly from the table, waving away Brand's offer of support.

* * *

The house was a rambling, late-Victorian pile in the Uphill area of the city, all jutting gable ends and period features. It was located at the end of a quiet cul-de-sac about five minutes' walk from the cathedral. With the snow slowing them down, the walk took a bit longer and Ava's feet were numb inside her wellies by the time they reached the latticed wood entrance porch.

Ava and PC Dale entered an impressive entrance hall with faded floor tiles in a geometric design, and a sweeping oak staircase. Leon led them into a high-ceilinged room with two tall windows that stretched almost from floor to ceiling. The room must have been bright on a sunny day. This gloomy morning, Leon switched on the light.

Ava's eyes flitted around the room. The antique furnishings gave an impression of a room suspended in time. A grandfather clock stood between the two windows. There was a grand piano, glazed bookcases, a chesterfield sofa. Ava wouldn't have expected a couple of ex-Hollywood actors to feel comfortable in a place like this.

"Gray and I love old things," Leon said. "The old couple who were selling the house threw in a lot of the furniture. The stuff we had in our condo in the States would have looked out of place here." Ava looked around the room, nodding at PC Dale to do likewise. Both wore gloves to avoid leaving prints.

In the kitchen, they found the charger for Mitchell's phone still plugged into the wall socket.

"Mr Mitchell had his phone with him," Ava said. "Our forensics people will examine it. His last messages might provide an insight into why he left the house in the middle of the night."

"What do you mean?" Leon asked. "Are you suggesting he went to meet someone?"

"I'm not suggesting a rendezvous with a lover, Mr Warrior. I'm sorry if that's what you thought I meant," said Ava.

"But it's a possibility, isn't it?"

"Everything's a possibility at this point in time. Mr Mitchell might have been lured to his death by a threat, a lie, even a cry for help."

"A cry for help. Yes, that would be in keeping with Gray's character."

"That's just the sort of insight that's useful to our investigation, Mr Warrior."

Next, Leon led them up the sweeping oak staircase to a galleried landing and into the master bedroom, a large en-suite overlooking the back garden. On a clear day, it would have had a nice view of the cathedral's towers.

As they progressed from room to room, Ava asked Leon to look carefully and tell her if anything was missing, or out of place.

"Take your time. Try to get a sense of anything that's not right."

"Everything's exactly as it should be," Leon said.

Except for one thing, of course. Gray wasn't there. All too soon the dead become no more than a memory, Ava thought. Suddenly she remembered her long departed grandmother.

Their search brought them back to the room they had started in.

"I apologise for the cold," Leon said. "We haven't got around to double glazing yet. We both love the sash windows so much. This house is rather expensive to heat, so we heat the rooms selectively. We wouldn't normally use this room in the morning."

He was rambling, speaking about Gray in the present tense, Ava noted, obviously still in shock. She hoped Leon would suggest moving to whatever room did hold some warmth, for she was still chilled to the bone and Leon was visibly shaking. Instead he sank onto the velvet sofa and sat with his head in his hands.

"How long had you and Gray been together?"

"About twelve years. We met on the set of a low-budget zombie movie. Did you know we both acted in *Gladiator* and *Master and Commander*? Russell said we made a great couple, bless him. Do you know the movies?"

"No. I've heard of them, of course." Ava wondered briefly why the grief-stricken man would bother to name drop. Nostalgia maybe.

"Aren't you going to ask me the usual questions, Sergeant? I've been on the set of enough crime dramas to know the routine. Did Gray and I have a fight before I left for London? Did he seem any different from usual? Did he have any enemies? And the big one — can I prove where I was last night?"

Ava smiled. "All of the above."

"Gray and I parted on the best of terms. He's been a little quiet lately, but that's his nature." He paused. "I suppose you're going to find out sooner or later, so I might as well tell you now. Gray is — was — bipolar. But please don't go leaping to the conclusion that he was suicidal. It simply wasn't the case. I know all the signs, believe me, and Gray was not in the depressive cycle of his illness. And he was assiduous about taking his medication."

Ava nodded. Gray Mitchell had been an actor, even if not a very successful one. Was he good enough to hide the extent of his illness from those closest to him? It would be necessary to verify what Leon had just revealed. Dr Hunt would be aware of it soon anyway, toxicology reports were a routine part of autopsy examinations. A little voice in Ava's head whispered *suicide*. She pushed it away. She wouldn't allow Mitchell's illness to prejudice the outcome before the investigation had even begun.

"Enemies?"

"No. Gray had no enemies here. All he's made is friends since arriving in England."

"I heard that Laurence Brand wasn't happy about the competition from your ghost tours," she said.

"Ah. Someone's been talking. Well, it's true that Laurence was a bit put out when we first set up, but that didn't last for long. Our tour is very different from his. It attracts a different clientele."

"Still, it must have riled him. After all, he'd had it all his own way for a while. If a Roman tour was all that was on offer, surely that was better for him?"

Leon looked piqued. "Maybe you should speak with Laurence."

"I will. Mr Warrior, since your return to Stromford, have you or your partner met with any hostility from the local people?"

"Gay bashers, you mean?"

Ava winced, but nodded.

"I grew up in Stromford in the seventies and eighties, Sergeant. Those were much less enlightened times. I didn't come out until I was in my late twenties but by then I had suffered my share of homophobic abuse. Young people have a sort of radar for anyone who's different. I just wish I had had the courage to come out and be counted sooner. It's one of my greatest regrets in life."

"In those days it wouldn't have been good for your career, I suppose?"

"That's right." A hint of bitterness crept into Leon's voice.

Ava asked the question again. "Have you experienced any homophobic bullying recently?"

Leon didn't reply.

"Mr Warrior?"

"It's hardly worth mentioning. Just a stupid incident, but Gray was very angry about it."

If this did turn out to be a murder investigation, no detail was irrelevant. Ava waited for Leon to continue.

41

"Gray and I were strolling around the farmers' market one afternoon back in the summer. We were looking for a stall that sold a local cheese we both liked . . ." He began to cry. "Sorry. There are going to be a lot of moments like this, aren't there? Perhaps when they stop making me upset, I'll learn to treasure the memories."

Ava nodded. She had very few memories of her dead grandmother now, but all were suffused with a sense of kindness and warmth. It made her feel happy and sad at the same time. "Bittersweet," she said absently.

"Yes, bittersweet. Anyway, we were at a stall selling local cheeses and a man came up to us accompanied by his teenage son. I recognised him immediately, though it must have been over thirty years since I last saw him."

"Who was he?"

"My school nemesis, Ray Irons. School bully extraordinaire. Anyone he didn't like was labelled 'poofter.' He *really* didn't like me."

"And how did he react when he saw you at the market?"

"Rather predictably, I'm afraid." Leon mimicked, "'*Well, well, well, Leo Warrior. Always knew you was a fucking poofter.*' To his credit, the young lad seemed embarrassed by his father's comment."

"What happened?"

"Gray took a swing at him."

"Seriously?" Ava was impressed, forgetting to be professional for a moment. She cleared her throat. "Did Gray do that sort of thing often? Did he have a temper on him?"

Leon shook his head, "I think it was because I'd told him so much about Ray Irons and his bullying ways. He always said if he ever met the man, he'd deck him."

"Did he injure this Ray Irons? Did Irons report the incident to the police?"

"Irons had a bloody nose. I was surprised he didn't retaliate — he would have done in the past. Perhaps it was because his son was with him. We didn't hear anything about it, so I guess Irons didn't report it."

"Any witnesses?"

"The guy on the cheese stall and a couple of other customers. And Irons' son, of course."

Ava made some notes. Next to Ray Irons' name she wrote 'Hate Crime?' She looked up to see Leon Warrior studying her.

"You have perfect symmetry of features."

"Not quite." Ava smiled. She tapped the bridge of her slightly misaligned nose.

"Hardly noticeable. Adds character. You could have been an actress — or a model."

Ava snorted. "Not me. I'd rather be doing something that makes a difference to the world than prancing around on a runway."

"Or strutting and fretting an hour upon the stage, then heard no more?"

"Oh, I didn't mean acting." Warrior's quote had made Ava suddenly realise that she might have caused offence. She was often guilty of opening her mouth and shoving her foot inside.

Leon Warrior leaned towards her and Ava sensed a change in his demeanour. He spoke in a low voice. "Make a difference in this case, Sergeant Merry. Gray did not take his own life and I want to see whoever pushed him from that scaffold brought to justice."

His words were uttered with a dramatic — or melodramatic — flourish. Ava found herself entranced for a moment. She found herself replying in an overly solemn voice. "Justice is my business, Mr Warrior. I will do my utmost to . . ." She stopped. Coughed. "I can assure you that we will do our outmost to investigate Mr Mitchell's death."

"I'm cold," Leon said, suddenly himself again. "And you look positively blue, Sergeant Merry. "Would you like a brandy to warm you up?" He stood up and walked over to a drinks cabinet.

"Thanks, but no. I'm on duty." Ava was already working out in her head where the nearest warm coffee shop might be.

Leon saw Ava and PC Dale to the door. He was holding it together well, Ava thought, considering his grief was still raw. Then again, he was an actor. Was he good at feigning grief? It was not until they were halfway down the street that Ava realised they had not discussed Leon Warrior's alibi.

Chapter 5

Neal hoped that by not accompanying Ava to Warrior's house, he was demonstrating that he still had confidence in her ability to do her job. Besides, it was imperative that any suspects be identified quickly. There was no time to lose.

Neal approached the group of workers who maintained Stromford Cathedral's magnificent stone and glasswork. They were a small workforce. Eight or nine people sat around a table for their morning break in the window alcove of the cathedral café. All of them were sombre-faced and subdued.

He showed his badge and drew up a chair. "I'm Detective Inspector Jim Neal. I'm assuming you're now all aware of the tragedy that occurred here in the early hours of the morning?"

Heads nodded, glances were exchanged. Neal's ten-year-old son, Archie, often asked him what superpower he would most like to have and Neal always gave the same answer: "The ability to read minds. It would make my job so much easier."

"First of all, I'm sorry. I know that some, perhaps all of you were acquainted with Gray Mitchell, and some of you may have known him as a friend." So formal, Neal thought. Over the years, he had offered his condolences to many strangers. The job required him to keep a certain distance, but sometimes he felt that aloofness was not just inappropriate, it was also counterproductive. He was aware that Ava struggled with the whole issue of professional detachment and he had no great wisdom to offer her. "Think of it as a shield, not a shell," he had said to her once, thinking of the consultant who had delivered the news of his father's impending death. He had been clinical, almost cold.

There were expressions of disbelief and head-shaking, some of them had tears in their eyes, others looked stoical. Who was genuine? Who wasn't? How to tell? Neal cleared his throat.

"It's important to build up a picture of Gray Mitchell's movements and state of mind in the days before his death. I'd be grateful if any of you who knew Gray well could tell me something about him."

A grey-haired black man in blue overalls took the lead.

"I'm Vincent Bone. Supervisor and master stonemason. We all knew Gray by sight, of course. He was often in here with his partner, Leon Warrior or with his friend, Laurence Brand." He looked over to the food preparation area behind the counter. "Leon and Gray are friends of the Brands, and Helen Alder. Out of our little group here, myself, Marcus and Clare and Angie knew Gray best." He nodded at each person as he spoke.

The youngest member of the group was a slight lad. He kept stroking his soul patch, either from nerves or out of habit. His brown hair was tied back in a ponytail, a navy paisley bandana knotted at his neck. He was wearing a cross-shaped earring. Neal guessed he would have at least one tattoo. Archie thought tattoos were cool. Ava had one on her hip. He had caught sight of it once at a social gathering of coppers at the pub. Neal wasn't sure what he thought of it, but he had long ago stopped associating body art with the criminal underworld.

"Marcus is our apprentice stonemason," Bone said.

"I got to know Leon and Gray through Laurence," Marcus said. "Laurence is teaching me Latin."

Neal nodded. He looked around at the other people Vincent Bone had singled out. One of the women introduced herself as Angie Dent. She said that she worked in the cathedral gift shop, and was sorry Gray was dead. She described him as "a lovely bloke." Angie had a peculiar accent that Neal couldn't quite place. It wasn't local. Neal prided himself on his ability to pinpoint a person's home county when they spoke. Angie Dent had him puzzled.

Next to Angie sat the only other female member of the group. Angie introduced her as her mate, Caitlin Forest. Caitlin looked utterly miserable. She sat with her head bowed, and only nodded as Angie spoke.

"Last time I saw Gray was at his and Leon's place last week," Vincent Bone said. "Probably the same for all of us, am I right? It wasn't exactly a party. Leon and Gray referred to these gatherings as their 'soirees.' There were about eleven of us there: me and Marcus, the Brands, Helen Alder, Angie and Caitlin and a couple of people Leon knew from before he went to the States. I can't remember their names. Can you, Marcus?"

The young apprentice shook his head. "You'd have to ask Leon . . . or Maxine and Helen might remember."

"Did Gray seem himself?"

Marcus nodded. "Seemed okay to me."

"How about Leon? Did he seem alright? No problems with their relationship?"

"They were sweet," Marcus said. He nodded solemnly.

Vincent agreed, then said, "there was a bit of an argument about a fellow they'd come across at the farmer's market. From Leon's old school. He used to bully Leon, and Gray . . . well Gray sort of confronted the fellow. Leon thought he should've left well alone. A bit of a reversal there. Gray's normally the placid one."

"Confronted?" Neal could tell the man was holding back.

"Gray might have thrown a punch, but maybe I remember that wrong. I had a few beers that night."

Marcus was less subtle. "No, I remember. Gray smacked him one."

"Are you going to treat this as a hate crime, Inspector?" Angie Dent asked.

"We don't know if it's a crime, yet, Ms Dent." But the idea had already occurred to Neal. Angie Dent was around his sister Maggie's age, he estimated, in her early to mid-twenties and with a similar build. She was slim, almost boyish, but unlike Maggie she had bubblegum pink hair. Her eyes seemed cold to Neal. Perhaps that was owing to their rather washed out shade of blue — or the dim light.

"Gray wouldn't have jumped," Vincent said.

"No one can be sure of that, Vin."

Bone looked at Angie. Neal caught the slight twitch at the corner of his eyes. Neal suspected that Vincent Bone was not a big fan of Angie Dent.

"Well *I'm* sure," he said.

"How about you, Caitlin?" said Angie. Caitlin was still looking abject.

"I . . . I agree with the others," she said. "Gray was a kind man. I don't think he'd commit suicide because he would care too much about the people he left behind, especially Leon." She looked at Angie, as if seeking approval.

"Why's that, Caitlin? Because he didn't have, 'I'm bipolar' tattooed across his forehead?" Angie said.

No doubt the others had been hesitant to mention this fact in case it prejudiced his judgement, thought Neal. He would have to be careful. Mitchell deserved not to be defined by his condition.

"Leave her alone, Angie. She was only giving her opinion," Marcus said. Caitlin was looking flustered.

"Thank you for your time," Neal said. The clock on the wall told him it was only midday, but already he felt like he'd done a full day's work. There was little hope that his hangover would be letting up any time soon.

Neal stood up, aware that everyone in the room was watching him. Outside, in the exposed cloisters, a biting wind cut through him, stinging his face and bringing tears to his eyes. His boots crunched over the grit-scattered path. Neal paused for a moment. The cathedral walls towered above him, touching a low sky swollen with snow.

The door of the café squeaked and Vincent Bone stepped outside. He was wearing a brown leather Australian-style bush hat and a fur-trimmed sheepskin coat falling all the way to his workman's boots. He tipped his hat as he approached Neal. "Peaceful spot, isn't it? You can feel the Boss's presence all around you." Neal's hungover brain took a few moments to catch Bone's meaning. As Bone walked past him, Neal wondered where 'the Boss' had been in Gray Mitchell's hour of need.

* * *

Laurence Brand stood on the pavement outside Leon's house, looking left and right though the street was a cul-de-sac. It ended in a high wall, overhung by yew trees from the graveyard on the other side. Two of the bedrooms in the house overlooked the graveyard and Leon often made jokes about the 'neighbours.' A terrible thought occurred to Laurence — soon Gray might be buried there. Perhaps he'd asked Leon to scatter his ashes somewhere in the US, where he had grown up. Or Leon might be one of those people who keep their loved ones in an urn on the mantelpiece. Laurence wondered what he would do with Maxine's remains, should she die before him. Would it be weird to carry some of her ashes in his inside pocket so that his wife would always be close to his heart? As always, the thought of losing Maxine made Laurence tremble. All his married life he had lived with the fear that one day he would lose her.

Over the past year Laurence had grown accustomed to the little social group that revolved around Leon and Gray. It consisted of him and Maxine, Helen Alder, Vincent Bone and the young people who worked with him — Marcus, Angie Dent and Caitlin Forest. Would Leon continue to host his little 'soirees' now that Gray was gone? Laurence felt a pang of guilt for thinking of his own pleasure, with Leon so recently bereaved. Then he had an even guiltier thought. Would Leon carry on his ghost tour business without Gray? Would he be looking for a new partner? Surely Laurence was the obvious choice?

As he approached the cathedral, Laurence caught sight of the police vans still parked around the west front. He thought of calling in at the café to see Maxine, but he knew he would be in the way. There was no chance of Vincent Bone being there at this time either, so Laurence made his way to the Long Hill. As he walked along the cobbled street, Laurence began to relax. This was Caius's territory. Two thousand years ago, they would have been standing in the heart of the Roman city. With his tour group, Caius liked to pause at this spot. He would point out the circles of stones along the road, marking where the columns of the forum had once stood. Then Caius would relate stories about his life in the city. Depending on the audience, he would embellish these with bawdy references to the brothels he liked to frequent.

Though he was no actor, Laurence regarded his immersion in Caius's persona as a kind of performance. His pithy depictions of his Roman's life and times were, hopefully, entertaining, though occasionally he caught sight of someone stifling a yawn or rolling their eyes. At such times he could hear Caius uttering a long chain of expletives, of which *Futue te ipsum (go fuck yourself)* was the least offensive.

It was no secret that Laurence had not taken to Leon Warrior and Gray Mitchell at first. He and Caius had regarded them as pillagers. He wondered who would be the first to tell the police about that. Laurence was suddenly uncomfortably aware that if Gray Mitchell had been murdered, he might be a suspect. *Stercus accidit (shit happens)*, Caius whispered. Laurence's Roman alter ego was not a timid man.

Chapter 6

"Mitchell's injuries are consistent with a fall from a considerable height," Ashley Hunt said as he walked into the inspector's office. The pathologist stifled a yawn. From Hunt's dishevelled appearance it appeared he had worked through the night to arrive at this conclusion.

"Multiple fractures of the upper and lower limbs and ruptured internal organs."

A pause.

Neal leaned forward in his seat. "And?"

"It wasn't a suicide, Jim."

"Go on."

Hunt slid a photograph across the table. Neal stared at the mess that was Gray Mitchell's face and head on the dissecting table. Hunt then handed him a second photo, taken at the crime scene. Neal thought he knew what Hunt was going to say next.

"Mitchell landed face down, yet there are two planes of injury, front and back of the skull," Hunt said, pointing to the crime scene picture. "As well as an injury from the impact of hitting the ground, the victim has a laceration and depressed skull fracture to the back of the scalp. This injury isn't consistent with his fall. It must have come from an assault. A blow to the back of the head administered with significant force, I would guess. No doubt the assailant was counting on the injuries being disguised by the fall. I'll save the finer details for my report. Just thought you'd like to know what you're dealing with."

"Thanks, Ash. I appreciate your getting this done so quickly."

"Business is a bit slow at the moment. Expect it'll pick up over Christmas. That's when the real suicides tend to peak. Not to mention the road-traffic fatalities."

As soon as Hunt had left, Neal called Ava Merry into his office.

"Poor bloke. When I spoke with Leon Warrior yesterday, one of the reasons he gave for relocating to the UK was the high crime rate over there. Pretty ironic, isn't it?"

Neal nodded. "This is now officially a murder investigation. Horrific as that sounds, it will probably come as a relief to Mitchell's partner and friends. They were all convinced Mitchell couldn't have taken his own life."

"I got the impression Leon would have taken a suicide verdict as a kind of betrayal. And I think he would have blamed himself for being away, or for not having seen that Mitchell was depressed. Still, he won't get any rest now until we find out who murdered his partner. Assuming it wasn't him, of course."

It was true, Neal knew. For a person bereaved by a murder, there was no comfort. Even the ritual of the funeral would bring no sense of closure. Only justice could do that.

"*Is* Warrior a suspect?" Ava asked. "Yesterday morning, when you saw him at the cathedral, he said he'd just got back from London, didn't he?"

"Yes. I assume you questioned him about his alibi when you went to his home yesterday?" Neal said.

Ava avoided his eye. "Er . . . kind of . . . He was very upset and . . . well I didn't really get the full details."

"I'll take that as a no." Neal didn't even try to hide his displeasure. "For God's sake, Merry. I know you've been on sick leave for a few weeks but I don't expect to have to retrain you on the basics. Now Warrior's had plenty of time to rehearse his story. And you've lost the opportunity of seeing his initial reaction when he's questioned about his whereabouts."

As soon as he said it, Neal wondered why he was suddenly feeling so hostile towards Ava. He'd been glad to see her back on the job yesterday, even though it felt a bit awkward. Now, her first oversight had him rankled. Was it because he wanted her to be as good as he knew she could be? Because he didn't want her to risk her career, making any more mistakes?

Ava glared at him. She was making him feel like some kind of tyrannical eighteenth century naval commander. In truth, he hated all that stuff about rank. Neal wasn't even keen on being addressed as 'sir.' But this was a serious omission. He didn't apologise. Ava stomped out of his office. She didn't exactly slam the door but she closed it with more than necessary force.

Neal stared sourly at the door for a few moments. No doubt Ava was now talking with PJ (the nickname everyone used for PC Polly Jenkins) about his bad humour. All the previous day he had been hung-over. His ill-humour had no doubt confirmed their view of him as a dour Scot. The truth was that he had been feeling miserable lately. Jock Dodds had more than hinted that Neal needed a woman in his life. Neal couldn't disagree. In his last case he had fallen a little in love with a suspect's mother, Anna Foster, but only at a distance. He had seen her a few weeks ago near her bookshop. She had smiled at him and he'd smiled back. They had not stopped to talk. Then Maggie told him she had seen a 'For Sale' sign on the bookshop. Neal was sorry to see a bookshop go. That was all.

He sighed and looked through the pane of glass on his door. Ava was stooped over PJ's computer. He opened the door and walked over to join them.

PJ and PC Dale had been assigned the task of checking through CCTV footage of the area around the cathedral on the night of Mitchell's death. Neal had also instructed PJ to locate Ray Irons and run a check on his record. Irons was apparently a bully and a homophobe, and bullies did not take lightly to being publicly humiliated, particularly by gay men. Perhaps he had wanted to get even. Enough to lure Mitchell onto the cathedral roof and push him off? Surely, knifing him in the street would have been more his style

"Grab your coat," Neal told Ava. He made an effort to keep his tone neutral, even friendly. "We're going to visit Laurence Brand."

Neal had caught Ava exchanging glances with PJ and he was sure he'd heard PJ snigger. Probably discussing his sex life. No doubt they all thought his mood was down to needing a good shag. Neal couldn't really disagree with them.

* * *

"You drive," Neal said.

Ava slid into the driver's seat and turned the heater on while Neal scraped ice off the windscreen with the edge of his credit card. Ava was wearing one of those ridiculous woolly hats that looked like an animal's head — a fox, Neal thought, or was it an owl? He hoped she intended to remove it before they met Laurence Brand.

As Ava pulled slowly away from the kerb, Neal mused aloud, "A murder investigation involves known knowns, unknown knowns and unknown unknowns."

"Sorry, sir?"

Sometimes Neal felt the gap in their ages widen. "I was paraphrasing. Donald Rumsfeld? Iraq?" A pause.

"Say it again," Ava requested. Neal quoted the former US Defence Secretary: "There are known knowns. These are things we know that we know. There are known unknowns. That is to say, there are things that we know we don't know. But there are also unknown unknowns. There are things we don't know we don't know."

"So the stuff we know, like Gray didn't commit suicide, he was murdered, that's a 'known known,' right?"

Neal nodded.

"And stuff like who the killer is and why he or she did it, would be known unknowns? Because we know someone killed him and we know there must be a reason but we don't know what either of these are yet." Another nod.

"And the unknown unknowns are kind of like the things we don't know we don't know? Like, maybe a secret we couldn't even guess at?"

"Agreed." Neal was impressed. "The unknown unknowns are the worst because no matter how much we uncover, however much we think we know, there can always be something we could never have accounted for. We can't predict them or even see them coming."

"It's a bit of a slippery one that last category, isn't it? I thought I knew what I meant when I said that just now, but now I'm not so sure. It's kind of like one of those things you think you've grasped only to find it slip away again and the more you think about it the more you get in a muddle."

Neal smiled. "I know what you mean. Perhaps we should stick to the things we know and the things we know we don't know and hope like hell there aren't too many unknown unknowns lying in wait."

"So, what else do we know for sure?"

Neal suddenly thought of a snowy day in Edinburgh. He was gallantly lifting Archie's mother, Myrna, over the deep slushy puddles on Princes Street. He was wearing suede desert boots and the freezing water soaked his socks and made his feet numb and painful, but he didn't care. Myrna was all he cared about in those days.

"Sir?" Ava's voice jolted him back to the present.

"What did you say?"

"I said we know that Gray Mitchell and Leon Warrior disagreed over how to deal with Warrior's school bully. We know that Mitchell and Warrior upset Laurence Brand when they started up a business rivalling his . . . Actually, I didn't say that last bit. I was about to, only you didn't seem to be listening."

Neal smiled, suddenly no longer angry with his sergeant. He replied, "You're right, Ava. Sorry . . . I was distracted by something I saw."

Calling her by her first name seemed to thaw the ice between them, if not on the road outside. The car veered suddenly to the right and began spinning into a skid. Instinctively, Neal moved to grab the wheel, but Ava barked, "I've got it," steering expertly into the skid.

"I was in control of the vehicle," Ava said, but without rancour.

"I know. It was just an automatic reaction. I'm sorry. I never doubted your ability."

"Thank you."

Laurence Brand's home was just north of the popular Long Hill area around the cathedral and castle. The house had a long entrance hall with plenty of pictures on the walls. These were mostly photographs of classical sites from around the world, some featuring a smiling Laurence or Maxine. Neal recognised the Parthenon, and made a mental note to take Archie there one day.

Predictably, they were offered coffee. Neal asked for tea. Ava smiled with pleasure at the state-of-the-art coffee maker.

Brand said, "I'm not sure how I can help you, officers." These were the words most often heard at the beginning of an interview with a potential suspect. Brand was edgy. Most people were. Neal wondered whether it would make a difference if his interviewees had any inkling that he was often just as nervous. He looked at Ava. Did she feel it too? He thought not. Her eyes were darting around the room, taking everything in. No doubt she was hoping he'd let her take the lead.

"Please try not to worry about this interview, Mr Brand. It's customary for us to speak with people who have a connection to the victim. It doesn't mean you're a suspect, just that you might have information that could be useful to us. You and your wife were guests at a social gathering Mitchell and Warrior held at their home last Wednesday, weren't you?"

Laurence Brand nodded.

"We are eager to speak with all the guests who were at the gathering that evening. It was the last time your group of friends was all together before Mr Mitchell's murder."

Brand sputtered over his tea. Ava handed him a tissue from a box on the coffee table.

"Sorry . . . that word just brings home how horribly real all this is," Laurence said. "What do you want to know, Inspector? The usual crowd was there, plus a few others. Maxine and I, Helen Alder, Vincent Bone, Marcus Collins, Caitlin Forest and Angie Dent."

"And the others?"

"Colin and Eloise Sergeant. A couple Leon had kept in touch with since his acting days. They'd been out to visit him in LA a few times over the years. They don't live in Stromford. Travelled down from York, I think.

"How late did everyone stay?"

"Most of us left around midnight. The Sergeants were staying the night at a Premier Inn, I think. Caitlin and Angie left earlier — around eleven, I would say. Angie felt unwell and Caitlin took her home."

"What did you talk about?" Neal asked. Laurence Brand shrugged. Ava looked up from her notebook.

"All sorts of things. It was a social evening, Inspector. People chatting, a bit of music and entertainment.

"Does anything stand out?"

"Not particularly. Leon and Gray did some comedy sketches. Had everyone in stitches. Maxine sang — she's got a great voice. We all played charades."

"What was wrong with Angie?" Ava asked.

"Oh, she fainted. I saw it happen. She'd just been speaking with Caitlin — don't quote me on this but I think they were having a bit of a disagreement. Caitlin stomped off and Angie went over to stand by the window. Gray was the perfect, considerate host, always making sure everyone was included. He went over to Angie when he saw her standing alone and began speaking with her. I was watching them and at first everything seemed fine. Then, suddenly, Angie just passed out. Fell into Gray's arms, actually."

"Did you hear what Angie and Caitlin were quarrelling about?" Ava asked.

Brand shook his head. "I was too far away. There was music in the background and several different conversations going on around me. I probably wouldn't even have heard Angie raising her voice if I hadn't been concentrating on the pair of them at the time."

"Concentrating?" Ava said.

Neal nodded to himself. It was an odd choice of word and he'd expected his sergeant to pick up on it.

Brand seemed flustered. "I just meant I was people watching. I was standing with Maxine and Helen and they were chatting about some cupcake recipe or other. I was bored, so my eyes strayed around the room and I suppose they just came to rest on the two of them."

Laurence Brand began to ramble on. "Leon and Gray were great hosts. Very down to earth people considering they've mixed with some of the greatest actors of their generation. They were both in *Gladiator*. Did you know?"

Neal nodded, suppressing a smile, remembering Geraldine Skerritt's comments about Warrior and Mitchell's demise in that particular movie. It amused him that Laurence Brand was impressed by Mitchell and Warrior's minor celebrity. Perhaps he just couldn't resist a bit of namedropping.

"I imagine Angie caused a bit of a stir, passing out like that?" Neal asked.

"Oh yes, everyone was concerned," Brand replied. "Everyone's fond of Angie — and Caitlin."

"Did Caitlin take Angie home immediately?" Neal asked.

"More or less. After Angie had had a glass of water she said she felt better, but Caitlin insisted on taking her home. She can be quite bossy, Caitlin can. To tell the truth, Angie did look like death warmed up, so to speak."

"And apart from that one incident, nothing memorable happened at Leon and Gray's party?" Neal said.

Brand shook his head. "It was a delightful evening, as I said."

"One more thing, Mr Brand. Did anyone else see Angie and Caitlin having a quarrel?"

"I don't think so. Everyone was chatting or dancing. I just happened to look their way." A pause. "There was one thing, though. I saw Caitlin grab Angie by the arm. Quite firmly too, I think. I expect they were just rowing over some lad or other."

Brand knew of no reason why anyone would want to kill Mitchell, although he did mention the incident involving Ray Irons. He was not aware of any problems in Mitchell and Warrior's relationship and he hadn't noticed anything unusual about their behaviour in recent weeks, except that perhaps Gray had seemed a little subdued.

Neal brought the interview to a swift close shortly after that. He had asked Brand the day before where he had been when the murder took place. Brand had been in bed, alone. His wife Maxine had been spending the night with her friend, Helen Alder.

Brand saw them to the door. The inside of his house was very warm — clearly the Brands didn't worry about heating bills. Then again, who did, in temperatures like these? Neal was grateful that his coat had been hanging over the radiator. As soon as they stepped outside, he felt the chill creeping back into his bones.

Safely out of earshot, Ava said, "So what do you reckon Caitlin and Angie had a falling out over? Or was that just a load of bull?"

"Why would he make it up?"

"Just putting it out there."

"I'm inclined to believe, like Brand, that it was nothing important." Neal glanced at his watch. "You take Angie Dent. I've a feeling she might relate better to you than me. I'll take Warrior. Diana Lenton's been assigned as Leon Warrior's Family Liaison Officer and she's been with him since last night. By now, Leon will be fully aware that Gray Mitchell's death is being treated as a murder investigation."

Ava nodded approvingly. She knew Diana quite well, though they weren't friends. Having an FLO was an asset to an investigation. She would gather information from Warrior about his partner's activities in the weeks leading up to his death. His lifestyle and interests, places he'd frequented, people he'd seen, changes to his daily routines or behaviour, any worries he'd had — anything that might help to build up a picture of why Gray Mitchell had become the victim of a violent crime. She would also support Leon emotionally and keep him informed of any progress being made.

It was all too easy to lose sight of the other victims of a crime — close family members or friends. In these days of funding constraints the need for efficiency often eroded the time for compassion. The FLO could step in to help fill the gap. It was an important role, but not one that attracted Ava. She needed to be more involved.

"She'll be brilliant at it. She's a real people person."

Neal and Ava parted a few moments later. Neal headed along Shelton Road, the main arterial route to the north of the city, and Ava to the cathedral.

* * *

Diana Lenton answered the door to Leon Warrior's sizeable house.

"Morning, Inspector Neal. Still cold out there, isn't it?"

"Morning, Diana. Yes, it's not getting any warmer."

"S'pose you're used to it, aren't you? Being from Scotland."

Neal wished he had a penny for every time someone had said that to him. He had grown up in a village near Edinburgh and could remember few occasions when the weather had been as bad as this. He smiled politely. It was easier just to agree.

"How is Mr Warrior?" he asked.

"Pretty good, considering. Not sure if it's shock or denial, or just natural resilience kicking in."

"Or acting, perhaps?"

"Never thought of that."

Leon was sitting watching TV, glass of scotch in hand. It was not yet noon and Neal wondered at Diana Lenton's definition of 'coping well.'

"Inspector Neal's here, Mr Warrior."

Warrior looked round, nodded at Neal and reached for the remote.

"I spoke with your charming sergeant yesterday. You're a lucky man having her on your team, Inspector."

Neal glanced at Diana standing in the doorway. She was a plain woman, dowdily dressed.

"I'm not sure what I could possibly have to tell you that I haven't told Sergeant Merry and Diana already,

Inspector." Warrior ushered Neal forward with a wide sweep of his arm.

"I won't take up too much of your time, Mr Warrior. I understand that you must be tired of all these questions, but as you know, your partner's death is being treated as murder. It's important to gather as much information as possible right from the outset."

"You can count on my cooperation, Inspector."

Warrior poured himself another drink. He was already slurring his words. Not only that, but Neal noticed that his very Standard English of the day before had suddenly become Northern. Perhaps the real Leon Warrior emerged under the influence.

"I need to ask you about your whereabouts at the weekend."

Warrior sighed. "I drove down to London on Friday afternoon. The weather was frightful. Gray insisted that I take a shovel and a blanket and a flask of hot coffee with me in case I got stranded somewhere on the way. He was always very thoughtful."

Neal nodded. "What was the purpose of your trip? Couldn't it have waited until the weather improved?"

"I was attending a sci-fi convention at a London hotel. The show I appeared in during the eighties still has a sort of cult following and I'd been invited as a star guest. You'd be surprised how much people will pay for a photograph with someone from the cast of *Spacedrifters*."

Neal gave a polite smile. He had no idea what the going rate would be for such a thing. He asked Leon for the name of the hotel hosting the convention. It would be easy enough to check out his alibi.

"A few nights before you left for London, you and Mr Mitchell hosted a party here for a number of friends. How did that go?"

"It was a great night — good company, good wine. Only downside was Maxine Brand and her bloody awful singing. Whoever told that woman she's got a good voice should be shot. Laurie, no doubt. The silly man's besotted with her."

"Did your partner enjoy the evening? Did he seem himself?"

"Yes. Gray always enjoyed our soirees. That night was no exception."

"Were either of you aware of an argument — or a disagreement — between Angie Dent and Caitlin Forest?"

"No. You've heard about Angie fainting, haven't you? Poor lass. She seemed really shaken. Caitlin took her home. She's a talented girl, Caitlin. She did some work for us, the stained-glass window on the staircase, perhaps you noticed it? It casts a beautiful mosaic of coloured light across the hall on a summer's day."

"No. Not much sun to scatter the light at the moment, is there?"

"It's a lovely feature. Have a look on your way out."

Neal didn't miss the hint, but he sat on. Warrior poured himself yet another scotch. Neal wondered if there was much point proceeding with the interview. Nevertheless, he asked a few more questions. Warrior's answers threw up no surprises, no leads. His tone became increasingly maudlin.

"Do you drink a lot, Mr Warrior?"

"No. Hardly ever these days."

"These days?"

"I was a bit too fond of the bottle once, Inspector, but this . . ." He held up his glass, miraculously full again, "This is just grief."

Neal nodded. He had a brief memory of himself lying wasted on his bathroom floor after Myrna left him. Alcohol was always the first resort.

"What can you tell me about Mr Mitchell's activities in the weeks leading up to his death?" Neal directed a sideways glance at Diana Lenton.

"I've been over all that with Mr Warrior, Inspector. I've got a list of places Mr Mitchell frequented, and his

64

movements in the weeks before his death. I can email you my notes this afternoon," she said.

Neal nodded. "We need to start building up a picture of who Mr Mitchell spent time with, and where, over the past few weeks. Every detail's important. At this stage, practically anyone he's been in contact with recently could be a suspect." Another thought occurred to Neal, but he couldn't think of any way to ask without causing offence.

"When you and Mr Mitchell decided to move to England, were you in any kind of trouble over there?"

"What the hell d'you mean by that? We're the bloody *victims* here, lad. Nothing really changes, does it? Not so long ago you lot were throwing us in prison for expressing our love in public. Why the hell did I think Gray's murder would be treated with any kind of seriousness by a bloody copper?"

Diana intervened. "Mr Warrior, I can assure you the inspector didn't mean anything . . ."

"It's alright," Neal said. "Mr Warrior's upset. He's just lost a loved one. Mr Warrior, you're right. Laws change but attitudes linger. I hope you'll believe me when I say that I will attach no less importance to your partner's murder than I would to any other murder investigation. That's how it always should have been."

* * *

Laurence Brand could not settle. The interview with the detectives had made him uneasy. He wasn't sure why. For several minutes he wandered around the house, trying to decide whether to go out. He had been planning a trip to the county archives after the interview. Maxine had suggested he consider genealogy as a hobby for the winter months when business was slow. He found he was enjoying researching his family tree.

Assisted by a pile of self-help books with words like 'Idiots' or 'Dummies' in the title, Laurence was unravelling the mysteries of social media. He had 'friended' distant relatives on Facebook, who had faces that were sometimes astonishingly familiar. "Oh, my God!" Maxine had exclaimed on seeing a ruddy-faced woman with bushy eyebrows and a sneering countenance. "She's the spitting image of your aunt Marge."

Laurence had Norse blood, he was sure. The surname Brand was thought to have been introduced to England from Old Norse, but its origins were Germanic also. It had associations with words like 'sword' and 'steel' and 'flash' and 'fire.' Laurence pictured some hulking blond, bearded Viking ancestor, wielding a mighty sword as he burned and pillaged his way along the east coast of England. "Barbarians," whispered Caius.

Laurence decided that he would never be able to concentrate with so much else on his mind. Perhaps he could wander along to the cathedral café and see if Maxine would take a break for a bit. More than anything, he wanted to see his wife. Just looking at Maxine had a calming influence on him. Laurence checked his watch. She might be able to spare him ten minutes.

Maxine was going to be interviewed today as well, Laurence knew. They had discussed their alibi the night before. It was unfortunate that Maxine had been at Helen's. They spent most evenings at home together, reading, watching TV — a documentary or one of those baking shows that Maxine adored. Laurence found them depressing and stultifying. He watched them with her out of a sense of duty, and, he supposed, love. He couldn't even think his own thoughts because Maxine was the kind of person who watched TV in an interactive way. Laurence had to concentrate so that he could respond to her comments. It pained him that Maxine was not as attentive whenever there was something on that he was watching. She always seemed to have something more pressing to do, or she simply informed him that the show didn't interest her.

Laurence had told the police he had spent the evening reading. The police hadn't asked him what — did they ever do that nowadays? Laurence had volunteered the information anyway, but they were more interested in the fact that Maxine had spent the night at Helen Alder's and could not back him up.

Laurence regretted telling the police about that non-incident between Caitlin and Angie. Neal and Sergeant Merry had seemed so desperate for information. Now Laurence worried he'd made too much of what he'd witnessed. Or *thought* he'd witnessed.

Like most people over fifty, these days Laurence had trouble remembering where he'd left his glasses. Maybe he'd imagined the whole thing? Factor in the three delightful cocktails he'd knocked back and the wine at dinner, and it was a wonder he could remember being at the soiree at all. One detail he remembered very well, of course. The dress Maxine had been wearing. It was a favourite of his, which she wore rarely now — probably worried it made her look fat. It was red with a fitted waist that emphasised the voluptuous curves she tried so hard to hide.

* * *

Laurence entered the cathedral café, glad of the sudden welcome heat and the chance of some respite from his own thoughts.

"I'll just take a few minutes," Maxine said to Helen. She poured two coffees and put them on a tray alongside a couple of croissants. She hesitated a moment over butter and jam. "Come on, petal, let's sit in the alcove," she said to Laurence. He took the tray and followed his wife.

"This business is really getting to you, isn't it?" Maxine said.

"I suppose it is. Gray was one of the good guys."

"Leon's one of the good guys too," Maxine said. "Isn't he?"

"I didn't mean . . ."

"I know. Leon's still with us."

"It won't be the same."

"Things change," Maxine said. "What did the police ask you?"

"Just what you'd expect. How well we knew Leon and Gray, whether Gray seemed different lately, what we were doing the night Gray disappeared. They seemed very interested in Leon and Gray's soirée."

"Well, no one there would harm Gray, surely? We were all close friends."

"I think I said something a bit stupid," Laurence blurted out. "I might have landed Angie and Caitlin in it, without meaning to."

"Why, what did you say?" Maxine paused, croissant in hand.

"I told them I thought Caitlin and Angie had a bit of an argument and Caitlin stomped off in a huff."

Maxine stared at him. "You didn't say anything to me about it."

"Exactly. It wasn't that much of a big deal. I think I sort of . . ."

"Bigged it up?"

"For want of a better phrase."

"Oh, Laurie. You'll be worrying about this for days now, or at least until the police realise it's not important."

"I don't want to get Angie or Caitlin into trouble." Laurence sighed. "I've got a lesson with Marcus this evening. I think I'll have to cancel it. I won't be able to concentrate."

Maxine looked exasperated. "No, you won't, Laurie. Listen to me. This is just you getting things out of proportion again."

Laurence glared at her. "It's not the same," he said. Maxine covered his hand with hers.

"I like it here, Laurie. Stromford's good for us. We've made friends, our businesses are doing well. I don't want to have to move again."

Laurence looked down at his wife's hand gripping his. Could Maxine feel the sweat on his palms? She was leaning forward and he could see her round breasts straining at the buttons on her white blouse. White blouse, black trousers or skirt, and sometimes a black apron with thin white stripes, like butchers wore. The women in the café all dressed the same. Maxine was a shapely size fourteen and her hair was dark brown, eyes chocolaty velvet. In describing his wife's looks Laurence couldn't help resorting to cliché. At work she tied it back in a loose ponytail. Why did she stay with a pathetic man like him? She had moved once to accommodate him. Would she be prepared to do it again? How could he expect her to when she was so settled here?

"Laurie!" His wife's voice startled him back to reality. She looked worried.

"I'm sorry, love."

"I have to get back to work. Helen's due a break."

Laurence looked over to the food preparation area behind the counter, where Helen was piling sausage rolls onto a plate. He felt a stab of jealousy. Sometimes it seemed his wife spent more time with her colleague than with him. He sighed and she let go of his hand.

"It's going to be alright," Maxine whispered as she pecked him on the cheek.

As he was leaving the café, Laurence caught sight of Sergeant Ava Merry standing at the zebra crossing on the road along the cathedral's east side. No doubt on her way to question another suspect — another of his friends. Laurence touched the spot on his cheek where his wife had kissed him. She had told him everything was going to be alright. He wished he could share her optimism.

Chapter 7

Angie Dent had not turned up for work in the cathedral shop that day. According to her supervisor, she had called in sick. Unwilling to waste time now that she was there, Ava sought out Vincent Bone at the stonemason's yard.

Vincent Bone showed her into his tiny office. Its door was propped open with a sleeping pig carved out of stone. The office was situated off a large workshop where stonemasons were busy working. Bone took Ava over to where Marcus Collins was chipping away at a lump of rock with a hammer and chisel. He was learning the skill of 'boning in,' Vincent Bone explained, creating a flat surface on a piece of quarried stone. According to Bone, this was the first skill anyone wishing to become a stonemason needed to master.

Ava watched Marcus for a few minutes. Finally Bone touched the boy lightly on his arm. Marcus removed his protective goggles and smiled at his supervisor. "Nice job, son," Bone said, running his hand along the flat surface of the stone. "Your mason's eye is improving. Listen, Marcus, the detective sergeant here wants a word. We'll go to my room. Can't hear much out here."

"Hey, cool gargoyle," Ava said as they passed another stonemason. He was working on a rather revolting-looking stone figure, its face blunted featureless by pollution and weather.

"It's actually a grotesque," Marcus said.

"Never heard of that. Is that just another word for a gargoyle?"

"No. Gargoyles are essentially waterspouts designed to carry rainwater away from the side of a building to protect the stone or brickwork. Grotesques have an architectural purpose. Bearing weight's one example, but often they're purely ornamental."

"Scary ornament."

"That's because they were originally intended to remind people of the existence of evil," Vincent said. "Though in your line of work I don't suppose you need reminding. This is what evil looked like to the medieval mind. I guess in reality the bad guys are harder to spot, eh?"

"Yeah, just a tad."

Bone led the way into his office and closed the door.

"You're an apprentice stonemason, aren't you?" Ava asked Marcus. "What attracted you to it?"

"I've lived in Stromford all my life and I always liked visiting the cathedral. Over the years I just got more and more interested in the stonework."

"Marcus used to hang around here so much that we ended up giving him jobs to do," Vincent said, smiling.

"You have to train for four years to become a qualified stonemason. I go to college too," said Marcus. He seemed to be quite at ease.

"Marcus, I know you were acquainted with Gray Mitchell. I'd like to ask you a few questions, if that's alright?"

"Gray was sound," he said, his voice a little shaky.

"You met Gray Mitchell and his partner Leon Warrior through Laurence Brand, didn't you?"

71

"Yes. Laurence's been teaching me Latin. He's a really interesting guy, knows loads about history and that kind of stuff."

"I did a bit of Latin at school," Ava said. "*Puella, puellam, puellae, puellae, pulla . . .*"

"Awesome."

"That's kind of all I remember. So, what's Laurence Brand like?"

"He's a pretty good teacher."

"And as a person?"

"Sweet. For an old guy, you know?"

She smiled. It was exactly the kind of thing Sam would say. Nearly ten years younger than her, Ava's brother regarded everyone over thirty as ancient.

"He's not a suspect, is he? Seriously, Laurence wouldn't hurt a fly," Marcus said.

Ava wondered how many times she'd heard those words. People were seldom what they appeared.

"How well did he get on with Leon Warrior and Gray Mitchell?"

"They were friends," he replied, a little guardedly.

"I heard they didn't all get along at first. Didn't Laurence see them as rivals when they started up their business on his patch?"

Marcus shrugged. "I don't know about that. I only met them this year, when I came to work at the cathedral. They've all been pretty good to me."

Ava turned to Vincent Bone. "That's past history," he said. "Laurence, Leon and Gray settled their differences amicably."

"You were both at Leon and Gray's party, weren't you? The one they held a couple of days before Leon went to London?"

Marcus nodded. "It was a cool night. Leon and Gray did some funny sketches."

"Angie Dent and Caitlin Forest were there too, weren't they?"

"Yeah. Caitlin and Angie were there. Angie felt sick so she and Caitlin left early. Lucky them — they missed Maxine's singing."

"Was that before or after they had an argument?"

Marcus and Vincent exchanged puzzled looks. "What do you mean?" Bone asked.

"Laurence Brand thought he saw Angie and Caitlin arguing about something.

"Can't say as I noticed," Bone said, and Marcus agreed.

"What was wrong with Angie?"

"What? Oh, like at the party?" Marcus blushed. "Er . . . women's problems, I think . . . you know — her period?"

"Right," said Ava. "Thanks, Marcus. You can go back to work now."

Marcus stood up and crossed to the door.

Ava always found this part of an investigation challenging. She chafed at the sheer plodding nature of questions that often yielded few results. "Nice kid," she said to Vincent Bone.

He nodded. "If you think anyone around here killed Gray, Sergeant, you're on the wrong track. Everybody liked Gray. He was the sort of person you'd instinctively trust with your life, know what I'm saying?"

* * *

Ava was feeling deflated. Returning to work and landing a murder case on her first day back was a big thing, and the day before she had been jittery with excitement. She was the sort of person who rushed headlong into things. At school, her teachers were always advising her to stop and think before she spoke. She was full of nervous energy, hence the gruelling fitness regime.

Neal was the contemplative one. Despite their differences — and there were quite a few — they would complement each other nicely if they could find a way of working together. *That'll be the bloody day,* Ava thought. She recalled her boss's — in her opinion — disproportionate anger when she failed to check Warrior's alibi. Her phone rang. Neal's number.

"You finished with Angie? Thought you'd be a bit longer," he said.

And your interview with Warrior? Ava thought.

"Anything?"

"Not really. We're going to have to cast our net wider with this one, I reckon," said Ava.

"Well, we can't cover everyone ourselves. Meet me at the Stag in fifteen minutes?"

The Stag was only ten minutes' walk away. Neal was already there when Ava arrived, standing at the bar, pint glass in hand. He rarely drank on the job, and the day before he'd obviously been hung-over. Was this a new development? They moved to a quiet table and exchanged information on their recent interviews. It wasn't a lot to work with.

"Angie Dent might have been on the right track the other day, suggesting we could be looking at a hate crime, although luring someone to a high place and pushing them off doesn't really fit with what we know about that type of crime," Ava said.

"Aye," Neal said, slipping into his native vernacular. "I'd find the hate crime angle more convincing if Gray had been stabbed or beaten to death. Obviously, at present, our likeliest suspect for a hate crime is Ray Irons. If what Leon said about his bullying behaviour at school is true, he might easily have matured into a violent offender."

Neal glanced at his watch. "I've got a mountain of paperwork to catch up on this afternoon and a meeting with George Lowe. We'll speak with Irons tomorrow. In the meantime, liaise with PJ. Find out if she's run a background check on him yet and if not, do it yourself."

Ava nodded, thinking of her own paperwork. Barely two days back on the job and already it was piling up. It was the bane of every cop's life.

"Did your friend enjoy his weekend in Stromford?" she asked Neal when their food arrived.

"Jock?"

"PJ told me."

"How the hell did she know?"

Ava tapped her nose. "Sorry, can't reveal our source." In fact, PJ had bumped into Neal's sister Maggie the previous week.

"Aye. He enjoyed his weekend well enough. Not that he'll remember much about it."

"Like that, was it?"

Neal scowled. Her boss evidently wasn't in the mood for teasing. Sometimes she felt like telling him to lighten up. Then she reminded herself that he had had to bring up his son alone. She bit her tongue. Working the hours she did as well as coping with a child was something she didn't like thinking about. Her biological clock could tick as loud as it liked. She would ignore it.

They left the Stag and returned to the station, neither of them saying much. It was unusually quiet in town for the first week in December. The weather was keeping Christmas shoppers at home, they were going online instead. With only a week to go until the Stromford Christmas market, the local traders were becoming jittery. Ava had lived in the city long enough to know how important the market was to the local economy. For some small businesses it meant the difference between staying afloat and going under.

Neal headed for his office as soon as they reached base. Ava was pleased to see PJ at her desk, staring at her computer screen. As Ava neared, she saw that PJ was online-shopping. She peered over her shoulder.

"You're a bit of a sneaky sneak, aren't you?" PJ said.

"How'd you know it was me?" Ava asked.

"I sense things," PJ answered.

"Saw my reflection in the screen, more like. Seriously, Peej, you should be more careful. That could have been

Neal creeping up behind you." Then she caught sight of what was on the screen.

"Oh my God! Is that top really only twenty-five quid? It's gorgeous!"

"Uh huh. And it's available in your size. Want me to buy it now and you can owe me?"

Ava looked over her shoulder. "Oh, go on then. There's only two left. They'll be gone by the time I get home."

PJ smiled smugly and clicked. "Done! And by the way, it's my lunch break. I'm shopping in my own time."

"Sorry, girlfriend. I'm not your boss. I was just concerned about Neal getting the wrong impression. I've just had a bite with him at the Stag and he's in one of his moods."

PJ snorted. "Just for a change. Want to know what I've come up with so far?"

Ava pulled up a chair. "Start with Ray Irons if you've checked him out."

"Mr Irons is a bad man." PJ reeled off the evidence from Irons' record. "Fifty-four years old. Embarked early on a career of hatred and violence against minorities. Excluded from school for verbally abusing a female black teacher; arrested for participating in a 'fight' outside a gay bar when he was eighteen; joined the National Front at twenty. Here's a picture of him at a rally in the eighties."

Ava hardly needed to look. The picture on the screen only confirmed the stereotypical image of a white male skinhead in Doc Marten boots and rolled-up trousers. Nevertheless, it was unsettling to see the young man on the screen. He stood in a group of them, his face contorted in hatred, Union Jack emblazoned on his T-shirt. Most chilling of all, his arm was raised in a Nazi salute.

"Lovely chap. Bet his mum's proud." Both women stared at the image on the screen, then PJ made it disappear.

"Moving on. Arrested and charged with AGBH in his twenties. Served two prison sentences, the longer one for an attack on a gay man. It left his victim in a coma for a couple of days. Released in 1994. That's it."

"Really? Nothing in the past twenty years?"

"Nada."

"Did he simply grow up? Maybe he got married, settled down a bit."

"It's a possibility, I suppose. Doesn't necessarily mean he's modified his views though, does it?"

"He was less than complimentary to Leon Warrior, so I'm guessing he's not become a nice, cuddly character. Neal and I are paying him a visit tomorrow. Should be fun."

"Rather you than me. Mind you, at least people like Irons are up front about their views. I was in a club once, on a first date with a bloke I'd fancied for ages. We were getting on well until he spotted two guys kissing on the dance floor and he went berserk. Didn't actually do anything, it was just his language — you know, "effing faggots . . .""

"What did you do?"

"Told him my brother's gay," said PJ.

"Is he? You never told me that."

"You never asked."

"When you told me your brother lived with his partner, I just assumed . . . sorry, Peej."

"No need to apologise. Most people would make the same assumption. I would myself if I didn't have a gay brother."

"Do you worry about him? I mean, with arseholes like Irons out there?"

PJ grinned. "Matt's a six-feet-four fighting machine. The arseholes worry about him."

"Okay. So what else have you got?"

"Not a great deal so far. PC Carr is still looking at CCTV footage from the streets around the cathedral."

Ava nodded. Carr would be noting vehicle registration numbers and observing the comings and goings in the area. He'd look for patterns and anomalies, anything that might throw up a lead. He would also be checking for potential witnesses — a vagrant, someone returning late from work or after a night out.

"PC Hughes and PC Winters have been showing Mitchell's photo around in the Long Hill area. They haven't called anything in yet, so I'm assuming there's nothing interesting to report. Tomorrow they're going to go farther afield."

Ava nodded. It was still early days in the investigation. There was no reason to expect results to pour in yet. The initial days of an investigation were an anxious but exciting time. The case lay wide open and you needed to be aware of all the possibilities, all the tendrils reaching back from the act of murder to the victim's life. No aspect of Gray Mitchell's life could be discounted. Nothing and no one, not even those who claimed to be his closest friends.

PJ had little else to offer for the time being. Ava sat down at her desk and began sifting through her paperwork.

It was past four when she looked up, head aching from close concentration and caffeine withdrawal. It was already dark outside. Ava yawned and stretched, then yelped as a sudden cramp seized her calf. "Ouch!" She jumped up and hopped around.

"Cramp?" PJ asked, unnecessarily.

"Bloody painful," Ava said. "Think I'll call it a day and go to the gym. I can work at home this evening."

"Didn't you swim this morning?"

"Only for an hour. Ollie was with me. I dropped him off at school afterwards."

"Rather you than me. I'll stick with my Zumba sessions twice a week."

Ava grinned. Zumba was the latest in a long line of keep-fit activities her friend had signed up to. None of them lasted for long. Ava's zeal for exercise bordered on fanaticism. It had nothing to do with body image and everything to do with being in control. She needed to know she could rely on her strength.

* * *

By the time she had finished at the gym, Ava was feeling energised. She contemplated leaving her car at work and jogging home, then thought of her morning routine. With her younger brother Ollie living with her, she was responsible for someone other than herself and her lazy cat, Camden. She enjoyed their chatty breakfasts and driving into town together for an early-morning swim. It was good for Ollie. He was a geeky boy who would otherwise be spending long, lonely hours studying or gaming.

Ollie had once been described as 'borderline autistic' by a concerned teacher. He was inclined to be reserved and solitary and a little awkward socially. Ava considered that her brother fitted somewhere near 'normal,' on the autistic spectrum. He was never going to be sociable or outgoing, but he would get by.

Ava's cottage was one of a small number of others scattered in the woods on the edge of a former country estate. A wonderful, spicy aroma greeted her as she walked inside.

"Chicken curry? Smells amazing."

Ollie was an excellent cook for a sixteen-year-old. He said he found it relaxing. Now Ava hardly cooked a single meal.

"It's ready when you are." Ollie looked up from his schoolwork spread out in front of him on Ava's huge oak table.

"Give me ten," Ava called, running upstairs to change. She was back in five.

"How was your day?" she asked Ollie as he placed his latest culinary masterpiece before her.

"Good. How was yours? Found the bad guys yet?"

"Not yet," Ava answered, scooping some chicken curry onto a piece of naan bread.

"Any leads?"

"Nothing productive."

"Any suspects?"

"One or two."

"Who? His partner?"

"You know I can't tell you that."

"Bound to be though, isn't it? Most people are murdered by their loved ones, aren't they?"

"We don't make assumptions," Ava said. This wasn't strictly true.

"Are you still thinking it might be a hate crime, then?"

"It's one possibility we're pursuing."

"Guy in my class's dad used to be a skinhead. Actually did time for beating up gay people," Ollie said.

Ava stared at him. "What did you say?"

"George? You know. In my chemistry class. I told you about him last week? He's living with his aunt because he fell out with his dad. What's up, Ave? You look like you've seen a ghost."

"What's George's surname?"

"Irons. Bloody hell, Ave, is his dad a suspect?"

Ava stared at Ollie for a moment, deliberating. Was it such a whopping coincidence? Stromford wasn't a big place, after all. Ollie was at the town's only grammar school. She had never considered that a man like Ray Irons would have a son at a grammar school. Was she being prejudiced?

"Ava? He is, isn't he? He's done time for that sort of thing in the past — well not murder exactly, but he put someone in a coma once."

"Ollie, you can't breathe a word of this outside of here, you understand that, don't you? Especially not to George."

Ollie passed a finger across his lips. "I promise. George's not like his dad. He's really into human rights."

Ava nodded. George Irons must be an exceptional person if he'd resisted his father's conditioning.

"If I happen to be talking to George about his dad, would you be interested in hearing what he says about him?" Ollie asked. Ava hesitated.

"This isn't a game, Ollie."

"He doesn't know you're a cop."

"You didn't tell him what I do?" Ava said.

"I told him you were a civil servant."

"Are you embarrassed about my job?"

"I wasn't sure if people would think it cool or not. Sorry, Ave."

"It's okay," Ava said. Ollie's self-confidence was pretty low. If keeping quiet about his sister's job helped him make friends, it was fine by her.

"So?"

"So what?" Ava said.

"George. Is there anything you want me to like, ask him?"

Ava sighed. What harm could it do?

"I'll think it over," she said at last. "But again, I stress, this isn't a game and you're not to say or do anything without my say so. Understood?"

"Yeah. You can trust me, Ave. I'll be uber-subtle."

"Hmm . . ." Ava ruffled her brother's blond mop. When she took her hand away, he looked like the mad scientist he was probably destined to become.

Chapter 8

The couple sat on a bench in the grounds of the Applewhite Museum, beneath an impressive statue of Augustus Applewhite. This eminent Victorian industrialist and philanthropist was one of Stromford's most famous sons. The grounds of the museum were beautiful at any time of year. Today, in the snow, they were enchanting. And cold.

Marcus Collins and Caitlin Forest seemed to be huddling together for warmth, rather than anything more intimate.

"Aw, come on, Caitlin. I know you don't really want to break up with me. What's this really about?" Marcus said.

Caitlin sighed deeply. "Please don't make this harder, Marcus. We've been over it again and again. I just don't think things are working out between us."

"But two weeks ago you told me you loved me. Nothing's changed since then, has it?" Marcus said. "Has it, Caitlin? Are you seeing someone else? Is that it?"

"Don't be stupid, Marcus. I wouldn't cheat on you. If you can't understand that, then maybe you really aren't mature enough to be in a relationship at all. We have to stop seeing each other." Her voice lacked conviction.

"Please, Caitiekat . . ."

"Don't call me that. It's stupid."

"Is it the age thing? Are you embarrassed because I'm so much younger than you? Because . . ."

"What? No! I told you. It just doesn't feel right anymore."

"That's bullshit. I know you're lying. There has to be a proper reason. People don't just break up over nothing."

"I can't take any more of this." Caitlin stood up. Marcus grabbed hold of her arm and she stared at him.

"It's her, isn't it?" Marcus said. "Angie. She's jealous, isn't she? Why do you always let her boss you around, Caitlin? You're like her little pet. I know the two of you are best friends, but—"

"Shut up! You don't know what you're talking about, Marcus. Angie's my mate, and for your information, she doesn't boss me about. She looks out for me. That's what friends do. Let go of my arm. You're hurting me!" Marcus loosened his grip. He had not realised how tightly he had been holding on.

"Read my lips," Caitlin said. "We're finished. Get over it." With that, she turned and walked away.

Marcus sat for a while longer, feeling miserable. Caitlin wasn't his first girlfriend, but she was the first woman he'd had sex with. Although he wasn't exactly in love with her, he was enjoying the regular sex and he was genuinely fond of her. From the beginning Caitlin had said, "I'm so much older than you. We both know this isn't for keeps. We'll have a good time and then we'll both move on." It wasn't as if she'd deceived him.

Being ditched was more of a blow to his pride than his heart. Still, a break-up was a break-up.

Marcus looked at his watch. He should have been at Laurence Brand's house for his Latin lesson ten minutes ago. He dragged himself to his feet, brushed the snow off the back of his greatcoat and stamped his numb feet to bring them back to life. Next payday he really needed to buy a decent pair of shoes. At least there had been no more snow since the heavy fall the night of Gray's death, but it was still cold.

Poor Gray. He hadn't deserved to die like that. Marcus's mood had been a bit low ever since he heard the news of Gray Mitchell's death. He'd got to know the American through Laurence Brand. Despite the difference in their ages — Laurence and Gray were older than his dad — Marcus had taken to both men immediately. Unlike his father, whom he loved dearly, they were educated. Both were easy to talk to, but Leon Warrior was different from Gray. Marcus liked him well enough but he was less generous and more . . . affected? Was that the word, or was it vain? And he was much less approachable than Laurence.

* * *

"Sorry I'm late," said Marcus when Maxine Brand opened the door. She always made a bit of a fuss of him and he didn't mind. Laurence was in the kitchen, which was even warmer than the entrance hall. Maxine had been baking and the oven was still on. Marcus felt his toes and fingers begin to tingle.

"No wonder your hands are cold. Don't you have a proper pair of gloves?" Maxine said. "Laurence, you must have a spare pair of gloves somewhere that the lad could have. I'll look some out while you're having your lesson." As she talked, Maxine was slicing up a lemon drizzle cake — Marcus's favourite. He was grateful for the hunk of cake and mug of steaming tea she handed him as he left the kitchen to follow Laurence to the study. The Brands were a bit of an odd couple. Maxine was an extrovert, big and bubbly — and sexy too, Marcus thought, thinking of skinny Caitlin. Marcus was not normally capable of seeing Caitlin as anything less than perfect, and he experienced a prick of hope. Maybe there was a cure for his lovesickness after all.

"Have you managed to pick up a copy of that primer I told you about?" Laurence asked, settling into a high-backed leather chair at his desk. Marcus sat in an armchair next to the radiator. He pulled a tattered paperback from his pocket.

"Got it on Amazon for one pence plus postage," he said. "Not in mint condition, but it's readable."

"Excellent," Laurence said. "I thought we'd take a look at the Pliny again today, then ablative absolutes. That okay with you?"

For the next half hour pupil and teacher worked at translating one of Pliny's letters.

"Your heart's not in it today, is it?" Laurence said. Marcus had just failed to translate a straightforward sentence for the second time.

"Sorry."

"Is it a girl?" Laurence asked.

Marcus looked down, miserably.

"*Qui tacet consentire videtur, ubi loqui debuit ac potuit* (Silence means consent). Anyone I know?"

"Caitlin Forest."

"Caitlin? Pretty girl. But isn't she a bit older than you, Marcus?"

"So? You're ten years older than Maxine, aren't you?"

They sat in silence for a moment. Marcus's misery permeated the room until even the radiator felt lukewarm.

"Far be it from me to advise you, Marcus, but—"

Marcus cut him off. "It's no good. She doesn't want me. I wasn't even that into her, it's just that . . ."

Laurence understood all too well. When he first met Maxine he had fallen hopelessly in love at first sight, but Maxine had scarcely noticed him. Even now, he couldn't believe that she had agreed to their first date, never mind a marriage that had lasted twenty years. His courtship of her had been a campaign of attrition. "A man pursues a woman until she catches him," Maxine had said. Even now Laurence couldn't bring himself to believe it.

"I'm truly sorry, Marcus. But you're a good-looking young lad. Plenty of girls would love to go out with you, I'm sure. That young lass in the café for one. I've seen the way she looks at you."

"Chloe? She's just a kid and she's not my type."

"Well, she's not as pretty as Caitlin, but she is kind of cute . . ."

"Then why don't you ask her out?" Marcus's impatient sweep of the hand knocked the tea tray off the table, and an angle-poise lamp went with it. Laurence stared in dismay at the mess on his Persian rug.

"I'm . . . sorry," Marcus stammered.

"It's okay. I wasn't being very helpful with my comments, was I? I'm afraid I'm not very good at this sort of thing. Maybe you should speak with Maxine. She always knows the right thing to say in these situations."

"It's alright," Marcus said, hastily picking up the items he'd knocked over. "I probably shouldn't have come this evening, straight after seeing Caitlin."

"Look, Marcus, don't go off feeling upset. Come and have a glass of wine in the kitchen. Maxine's made chilli. She always makes too much and you look like you could do with a good meal."

"No, I . . . I'd rather go. Thanks, Laurence."

Marcus stumbled into the hallway and retrieved his coat. Maxine popped her head out of the kitchen. "Has Marcus gone already?" She held up a pair of woollen gloves. "I looked these out for him; I was going to give them to him before he left."

"I'll drop them off at the workshop tomorrow if you leave them out, love," said Laurence. He crossed to the kitchen door and pulled Maxine into his arms.

"What's this for, you silly man?"

"Just wanted you to know how much I love you," Laurence said, and ducked as Maxine flicked him with his old woollen gloves.

* * *

Marcus walked down the street from Laurence's house, slipping and sliding on the icy pavement. He had one thought in mind — to get wasted as soon as possible. He stepped through the door of the nearest pub, intending to stay until last orders. After an hour of sitting in a lonely booth, a noisy football crowd cheering at the wide-screen TV above the bar, he'd had enough. He gulped down his fourth pint of 'purple' and stumbled outside again. The alcohol had hit the spot, and the snowy world looked glittery and beautiful in the streetlights. Marcus began humming the classic Slade hit, "Merry Christmas, everybody's having fun." Laurence was right, he thought. He wasn't a bad-looking guy and Caitlin wasn't the only fish in the sea. Tomorrow he'd make a new start. First, though, he'd tell Caitlin exactly what he thought of her. He took his mobile out of his pocket. Slowly, because his fingers were freezing and his mind unclear, he texted a stream of angry, hurtful words. Then he hit the send button.

On his way back to his flat he stopped at an off-licence and bought a few beers. By the time he crashed out, he no longer cared whether he would regret his actions the following day.

* * *

After breaking up with Marcus, Caitlin had intended to go home. It had been a long day and the scene at the Applewhite had been more difficult than she'd anticipated. Marcus had no idea of her real feelings. Once, a long time ago, she had done something bad. Since coming to Stromford and finding pleasure in her work, she had half-believed it might be possible to put it behind her and lead a 'normal' life. But there was a darkness inside her that couldn't be ignored.

Instead of going home, Caitlin had caught a bus out of town and taken a walk over a frost-hardened field to a small parish church. She had discovered it when she was driving around the county to look at the stained glass in old churches. It reminded her of one she had visited as a teenager, attending a wedding with her parents. It had been there that Caitlin had discovered her vocation. Standing in the congregation, bored by the ceremony, she had let her eyes wander. They came to rest on a small stained-glass window. She had gazed at it for the rest of the service. She had been fascinated by the extraordinary juxtaposition of lead and light, the colour contrasting with the sombre scene it depicted.

As soon as she'd come to live in Stromford, Caitlin had visited the cathedral. She had joined a tour and listened to a nervous middle-aged man with a lisp and a red bowtie talking about one of the windows. He explained how to read it the way an illiterate person of the twelfth century might have done, seeing the stories in pictures instead of words. Caitlin immediately wanted to know more. How had the window been created? What techniques had been used? How had the whole astonishing effect been assembled piece by piece with coloured glass? From that moment, she knew that her future lay in learning those techniques. She finished art college and took up an apprenticeship at the cathedral. She had been working there for the past two years.

Caitlin entered the church and stood for a while looking at the window. It was late afternoon now, and in the gloom the glasswork looked dull and faded with age. Caitlin wondered if she would have been so moved by her window, had she first seen it like this. It was in need of rescuing, she thought. When she restored a piece of stained glass to its former glory, lovingly replicating the work of the original masters, it was like turning back the clock. She was making something true again.

Caitlin left the church and walked back across the field to the bus stop. A woman, who was pulling a small child on a sledge, informed her that she had missed the last bus. There was no alternative but to walk three miles to the next village to catch a connection. It was a long, dispiriting walk in the snow, and the bus, when it eventually arrived, was chilly. It broke down on the way to Stromford and it took a full hour for a replacement to arrive. Caitlin was chilled to the bone.

When she stepped off the bus in Stromford, her first thought was to find somewhere to warm up. She found a pub and ordered the soup of the day and a glass of wine, and then another. When a group of students invited her to join their quiz team, she accepted. She would order a taxi later. She left the pub at closing time. Twenty minutes later, she stepped out of her taxi outside the block where she shared a flat with her friend Angie Dent.

Caitlin fumbled for her keys outside the entrance to the block. It was late and she didn't want to use the intercom. Angie might be in bed and she didn't want to wake her up.

Suddenly, someone gripped Caitlin's arm firmly. She swivelled round to see a familiar face peering at her from inside a hoodie. She was about to speak when the first thrust of the blade pierced her neck. Surprise, then shock, followed by a huge adrenaline rush that came too late, as the knife struck again, and again. And, finally, though its work was done, one more time.

Chapter 9

Neal broke the news to Ava when she walked into his office. It was eight forty-five, two days after Gray Mitchell's body had been found outside the west front of the cathedral. As Ava plonked a takeaway coffee cup on his desk he greeted her with the words, "Don't take your coat off. Night shift called in a homicide this morning. Darkwoods Avenue." They had another body.

"That's where Caitlin Foster and Angie Dent live, isn't it?" she said.

Neal nodded. A pause.

"Caitlin or Angie?"

"Caitlin."

"Are we taking the case?"

"I don't think we have a choice. It may be connected to Gray Mitchell's murder."

"Cause of death? I'm assuming she wasn't pushed off a roof."

"She was stabbed. That's all I know."

"A robbery, maybe?" Ava said.

"No, I think we can rule out robbery. The victim was apparently found with a wad of tenners in her purse."

"You really think the person who killed Caitlin also killed Gray Mitchell, sir? The methods are completely different."

Neal merely looked at her. He tossed over his car keys.

"Let's go take a look."

"Sir . . . the interview with Ray Irons?"

"It can wait. Get PJ to contact him and meet me at the car in five." Ava turned to go and he called her back. "Forgot your coffee," he said. Her smile of gratitude lifted his mood. He took a sip from his own cup and composed a couple of quick emails before grabbing his coat.

"It's still bloody freezing, isn't it?" Ava said, slipping into the passenger seat.

"Snow's had a bit of a fright though," Neal commented, putting the car in gear.

Darkwoods Avenue was in a part of town known as South Darkholt. It had been a large village, incorporated over the years into the Stromford urban sprawl. The dark wood that had once been the source of its name no longer existed. The avenue, at least, was tree-lined, Neal recalled.

"You'd think Angie and Caitlin would have moved to the centre of town, wouldn't you?" Ava commented. "They both work in the city and there's not much out this way for a pair of twenty-somethings."

Neal thought this an odd comment for someone who lived in an isolated woodland cottage four miles out of the city. He was glad Ava was no longer living there alone, and that her brother Ollie was a dog person. He was badgering Ava, a cat lover, to take in a rescue dog. People thought twice about breaking into properties when they heard a dog.

Nearly every garden along Darkwoods Avenue had outdoor decorations. These ranged from the subtle — a string of silver lights in a fir tree, to the tacky — a whole garden full of inflatable snowmen, flashing Santas and reindeer with glowing noses.

"Waste of bloody energy," Neal grumbled.

"Where's your Christmas spirit, sir?"

Neal ignored her comment. He wasn't looking forward to the annual Christmas get-together at work. The expectation nowadays seemed to be to turn up in a ridiculous festive jumper. He had no desire to be seen with a carrot sticking out of his chest attached to a bloody knitted snowman.

"This is it," Ava said.

Neal hit the brake, causing them both to jerk forward in their seat. The dregs of Ava's coffee cup splashed over her jeans.

"Sorry."

Angie Dent and Caitlin Forest lived at the very end of the street, in a small block of flats set back from the pavement. The front was landscaped, the rear backed onto a wooded area. A police patrol car was parked at the side of the block and the shivering duty officer greeted them with a nod and a wave.

"Who found her?" Neal asked.

"One of the residents, sir. He's a nurse at the county hospital. Came off a twelve hour shift at six this morning and cycled home. Took him about twenty minutes. Stopped off at the recycling shed to get rid of a plastic bottle and caught sight of a rat. It was scurrying away from what he thought was a spilt bag of rubbish until he got a closer look."

The PC's eyes travelled to the body slumped against some blue wheelie bins, its head drooping lifelessly against its chest. His voice wavered. Neal and Ava looked away, giving him a moment to recover. Neal covered his nose with a handkerchief as he bent to take a closer look at the body. Mingled with the stink of rotten food was the sour smell of fresh vomit.

"My partner, sir," the PC explained. "Brought up his breakfast. I sent him down the road to the café to get a cuppa. He's a newbie and this is a bad one."

Ava bent beside Neal. For the second time that week, they were looking at blood on snow.

"Her coat's all but ripped to shreds," Ava observed. "Looks like she's been stabbed repeatedly."

Neal nodded, regretting the bacon-and-egg buttie he'd had for breakfast. He wondered at Ava's constitution. Maybe she'd skipped breakfast? She was already looking beyond the body at the crime scene, focusing on the way forward. He was doing it too. Solving a crime was an intellectual challenge, Neal thought. It was a creative act that required both intelligence and imagination. He wished his gut would back him up.

They were disturbed by a sudden scuffle. A bold rat poked its head round the side of the recycling shed. It disappeared, leaving a bad taste in Neal's mouth. Rats had no respect for the dead — they'd rummage through the pockets of corpses for food and gnaw at the flesh itself. They often went for the eyes first. Caitlin Forest's clothes or even her exposed flesh would probably show traces of their activity. Neal shuddered.

Neal stood up and scanned the immediate area.

"Nothing obvious at the scene, sir," the PC said.

"Good work, Constable." The older man looked tired. He had probably been nearing the end of a long shift when the call came through. Now he'd be stuck at the scene until reinforcements arrived.

"We'd better speak with Angie Dent, if she's home, but let's keep it short," Neal said to Ava.

Neal tasked Ava with breaking the news to Angie, once the other PC had returned and could accompany her. "Radio down to say what situation you find up there," he said. He wished he could go himself, but he had to remain at the scene.

* * *

The block of flats had a secure entry system and Ava waited a few minutes until Angie's voice asked who was

93

there. She told Angie that she needed to speak with her. Then she let Neal know Angie was okay.

Angie and Caitlin's flat was up two flights of stairs. The stairs and corridors were carpeted, Ava noted, and well cared for. This was not a cheap let. Angie came to the door wearing jersey shorts and a camisole top. She looked from the PC to Ava, her eyebrows raised. Ava showed her badge and asked if they could come in.

Angie nodded and showed them into the living room, saying she'd be right back. She returned a few moments later wearing jeans and a hooded top.

"What's this about?"

"It's about your friend, Caitlin Forest."

"What about Caitlin?" Angie glanced at a clock on the mantelpiece. "She'll be on her way to work by now. It's my day off today, so I asked her not to wake me."

Ava was surprised that Angie didn't seem concerned. Most people confronted by two police officers this early in the morning, would be fearful. Then again, Angie had obviously just woken up. Maybe she wasn't firing on all cylinders yet. Then, suddenly, she was.

"Has something happened? Has Caitlin had an accident on her way to work or something?"

"I'm sorry, Angie. Maybe you'd like to sit down?"

Angie sat. "Oh my God," she said, hand over her mouth. "Just tell me what it is."

"Caitln's dead. I'm sorry," said Ava and sat down beside Angie. The PC stood behind the sofa, pale and awkward. Ava asked him to fetch a blanket and make some tea.

"Did Caitlin come home last night?" Ava asked, wrapping a throw around Angie's shoulders — all the PC had been able to find.

"Keep it round you," she told Angie. "For the shock."

"I . . . don't know. I had a stomach ache — my period — and had an early night. I went to bed around nine o'clock and I slept all night. What happened?"

Ava took a breath. "There's no easy way of telling you this, I'm afraid, Angie. Caitlin was murdered."

Angie stared at Ava, pulled the throw around her and buried her face in it. Ava touched her shoulder, then went to join the PC in the kitchen. He had managed to boil the kettle and was opening cupboard doors, searching for teabags. Ava went over to a tin on the worktop, took out three tea bags and held them out to him. "Hope you're not applying to take your detective exam any time soon," she said.

She looked out the window. It was on the side of the building, giving a view of some trees and a sloping grassed area. Then there was a high wooden fence, behind which lay the garden of the last house on Darkwoods Avenue before the block of flats. The living room was at the front of the building, looking out onto the road. The other side of the block, where Neal had parked the car and where the recycling shed was located, was windowless.

Ava took the cup of tea to Angie. "Did Caitlin often stay out late, or not come home at all?"

Angie shrugged. "Sometimes. She didn't have a regular schedule."

"Did she have a boyfriend?"

"She was seeing Marcus Collins, but it wasn't common knowledge. I'm not sure why they were making a big secret of it, maybe cos they worked together." She took a sip of tea. "What happened to Caitlin? Was it — you know — quick?"

It was what people always wanted to know, of course. Ava understood why people asked, but the answer was never going to be good — or even truthful. Police officers, like medics, had to be circumspect with the facts. Ava suspected that most people wanted reassurance, rather than the truth.

"Caitlin was stabbed. In the neck and chest. She would have lost consciousness quickly," Ava said. To her relief, Angie seemed satisfied.

"You need to find who did this," Angie said. Her eyes were red-rimmed and bloodshot. She certainly didn't look like someone who had slept all night, but Ava knew shock sometimes did that to a person. She also knew not to make promises she couldn't be sure of keeping.

"We'll do our utmost to ensure that whoever did this to your friend is brought to justice," Ava said, ashamed of the cliché.

"Like you brought Gray's killer to justice?" Angie said.

"The investigation into Mr Mitchell's death is still receiving high priority. We're not miracle workers, Angie, but we don't give up."

"Sure you don't," Angie said.

Ava cleared her throat, knowing her next question would hurt. "I need to ask you about your whereabouts last night, Angie. I'm sorry. It's a routine question."

"Yeah, right. I was here, alone. Caitlin was supposed to be coming straight home from work. We were going to watch a movie, but she must have changed her mind."

"Did she seem upset last time you saw her? Was it unusual for her to stay out without telling you?"

"No and no. We do our own thing. We don't usually tell each other what we'll be doing."

"But you were planning on watching a movie?"

Angie sighed. "Only if neither of us had anything better to do. Caitlin obviously did."

"Thank you. Think about having someone to stay with you for a bit," Ava said. "We'll see ourselves out. You should get some rest." She and the PC left.

* * *

"That wasn't much help," she said to Neal. "Angie's feeling hurt and bitter. Vulnerable too. Can't blame her, really."

Neal agreed. He looked at the small unassuming block of flats where Caitlin Forest had lived with her friend.

There used to be a shop there, he remembered. The site had lain vacant for a while after it closed, attracting the usual spate of low-level criminal activity — vandalism, graffiti, kids swapping recreational drugs, the odd bit of soliciting. The reasonably priced flats had been snapped up quickly by first-time buyers. Angie and Caitlin were tenants, he knew. The flat was managed by an estate agency on the owner's behalf. He hoped that Angie would not now be made homeless.

The entrance to the flats was at the rear of the building, out of view of the street and overlooked by bedrooms whose curtains would probably have been drawn by the time Caitlin returned the night before. The refuse and waste recycling shed, which was more of a three-sided timber shelter, also at the rear. It too was out of sight of the street, its open side facing away from the flats. Had someone followed Caitlin home or lain in wait for her here? Either way, killing her out in the open would have invited risks. But not from the CCTV, Neal noted. The camera had been installed purely to survey the residential parking spaces.

"And get someone to find out who to contact about looking at the CCTV footage . . ." he heard Ava saying to one of the PCs. Well, maybe it had caught something.

"What do you reckon this time, sir?" Ava said. No doubt her mind was racing like his. "Angry lover, colleague, friend, knife-wielding maniac . . ?"

"Whoever it was, he or she was brutal if not very efficient," Neal said. "Stabbed in the neck. No doubt aiming — not very successfully — for the jugular, hence the repeated stabbings. The wounds to the chest look like they were frenzied."

"Complete overkill. Gray Mitchell's murder was so different. It's hard to see how there can be a connection between them, other than the fact that the victims were acquainted."

"Aye," Neal said. He looked at his watch. "When were we supposed to be seeing Ray Irons?"

"He's at home all day."

"Let's go, then."

* * *

Even though the main roads had been clear for a couple of days, they made slow progress through the city centre. Shortcuts would have taken them through side roads that would still be icy. With a sideways look at her boss, Ava turned the stereo on. It was on CD.

"Hey! One Direction. This is sooo not your taste in music," Ava commented. "Has Maggie been in the car recently?"

Neal didn't answer. He had spent a lot of time in his teens with a guitar-playing uncle who'd been heavily into singer-songwriters of the sixties and seventies.

"Who's that old man you listen to a lot, again?"

"Leonard Cohen," Neal said. He felt under no obligation to apologise for his taste in music.

"I downloaded a couple of his songs a couple of weeks ago but I thought they were a bit depressing. I prefer something a bit more upbeat. Have you heard any . . . ?"

And she was off, talking about groups she liked, concerts she'd been to, the contents of her iPod shuffle. Archie wanted one of those for Christmas. He would have to ask her advice.

The voice of the SatNav brought them both back to business. "*In a quarter of a mile, take the left turn.*" As they curved round a bend, a wintry urban landscape unfolded before them: half-cleared pavements and white gardens, snowmen and churned-up snow.

"*You have arrived at your destination,*' the disembodied voice announced.

"Not quite," Ava said. "It's a bit further along, sir. Number sixteen."

Neal parked opposite Irons' house. It was a thirties-style semi with a concreted front garden sporting two cars, one half-covered with tarpaulin and missing its rear wheels.

The house itself looked reasonably well-maintained. A flagpole extended out from an upstairs window, but today, at least, there was no fluttering Union Jack. From somewhere inside the house came the sound of a dog barking. A couple of slats in the vertical blinds at the front bay window moved as Neal and Ava walked up the path to the front door. They didn't need to knock.

"Inspector Neal and Sergeant Merry," Neal said. Irons was in his fifties, Neal knew, but he looked slightly younger. The one-time skinhead now had a surprisingly full head of hair for a man his age, though it was pure white. He was heavily built and looked like he worked out, though his sizeable gut was probably more fat than muscle. Neal thought of Gray Mitchell's slender frame and decided he'd shown courage in taking on the bullish Irons.

"May we come in?" Neal asked when no invitation was forthcoming.

"Do I have any option?" Irons was looking at Ava. Most men tended to do that.

Neal raised an eyebrow. Irons jerked his head backwards and they stepped into the hallway. The barking started again, coming from a closed door that probably led to the kitchen.

Irons showed them into a back room. They all took a seat at the old-fashioned dining table that dominated the room.

"The girl on the phone said you wanted to talk to me about that fag, Leon Warrior," Irons said. Neal and Ava both winced. "I could have had his poofter friend arrested for assault, you know. Don't know why I didn't. Must be getting soft in me old age."

"Tell us about the assault, Mr Irons. Did you do anything to provoke it?"

"I was standing at a cheese stall at the farmer's market when those two queers came over. I recognised woofter Warrior straightaway — he ain't changed much and I'd seen him already in Marks and Spencer's a couple of weeks before. I said hello, next thing I know Warrior's 'friend's' trying to deck me."

"Mr Warrior claims that you called him a derogatory name and that's what provoked the assault. That and the fact that Mr Warrior's partner was aware that you'd bullied Warrior for years at school."

Irons feigned astonishment — or perhaps his affront was genuine. "Typical, innit? Bloody political correctness gone mad. I get attacked and you lot side with the perpetrator just cos he's a fuckin' fag."

"I think you're missing the point," Ava said dryly.

"That's how it seems to me, duck," Irons said. "But who cares what I think? Bloody straight white *English*man. We're an endangered species."

Irons' stress on 'English' wasn't missed by Neal, whose accent was unchanged from the day he'd left Scotland. He cleared his throat. "Did you see Mr Mitchell or Mr Warrior again after the incident, Mr Irons?"

"Nope, though I suppose you're going to accuse me of stalking him or something."

"No one's accusing you of anything, though we would like to know your whereabouts on Sunday night through Monday morning."

Irons threw his hands in the air. "I knew it. I've had a clear record for twenty years but every time a fag gets beat up or a Paki gets a brick through his shop window, you still come knocking at my door." He stood up and slammed his fist into his palm.

"That's enough," said Ava.

"Mr Irons," he said. "I advise you to modify your language and your behaviour."

Irons snarled and sat down, shaking his head in mock disbelief. "I was here all night," he said. "Alone. Except for Ripper."

"Your dog?"

"Yeah. Little white Staffie," Irons said. The affection in his voice took Neal by surprise. "We was watching a movie. *The Expendables*. Ripper likes a good action film. Or a bit of porn." He looked at Ava and she met his gaze without flinching.

"I ain't done nothing wrong, Inspector. You ain't got nothing on me. I could easily have taken that American prick on but he weren't worth the bother. And I ain't in a hurry to go back inside. Got my own business now and I'm doing okay. All that political shit I used to be into don't interest me no more."

"Do you know a woman by the name of Caitlin Forest?" asked Neal. Irons shook his head.

"Never 'eard of her. You after pinning something else on me? I ain't no rapist."

A salacious look in Ava's direction accompanied his words. Neal experienced despair.

"Thank you for your time, Mr Irons," Neal said.

Irons shrugged. He did not get up.

"We'll see ourselves out, then." As they walked to the door, Irons called after them, "Sergeant Merry! You can come back anytime, duck."

Ava paused in the doorway, then walked out behind Neal, without looking back.

Outside, she gave vent to her feelings, in language fouler than Irons'. Neal listened to the torrent, nodding approvingly.

". . . pathetic, shit-headed, lowlife, arsehole . . . bastard!"

"You didn't like him, then? Funny, I thought I picked up a hint of something, you know, sexual chemistry between the two of you . . ."

Ava stared at him, then burst out laughing.

"You couldn't make him up, could you?" she said.

"Is he capable of committing a hate crime against Gray Mitchell, do you think?"

"Seriously? You really have to ask?"

"Hmm. Did you take much notice of his house? He's comfortable. When he said he wasn't into politics anymore, I think he meant it," said Neal.

"But his views—"

"Haven't changed; he's still a racist, sexist, homophobic brute. And seeing Leon Warrior again, coupled with the humiliating blow from Mitchell might have reawakened the beast in him."

"And he doesn't have an alibi," added Ava.

"We'll need to get the foot soldiers to do more legwork. Maybe they can tie Irons down to places Mitchell visited shortly before his murder." Neal put the car in gear.

"He didn't bat an eyelid when you mentioned Caitlin Forest, and he thought we were after him for rape, not murder. Or he pretended he did," Ava said. "Was he just on his guard, do you think? Ready for anything we were going to throw at him?"

"It's possible, though I think the mention of rape was for your 'benefit.' I have a feeling that these days, Irons' bark is worse than his bite."

As they drove along, Neal's thoughts drifted to Archie and his current obsession with super powers. "Shame we can't read minds, though I suppose it would be considered unethical. Teleporting to the past might be useful too, though you'd still have to be able to prove what you observed back in the present or no one would believe you . . ." Neal became aware of Ava looking at him and he concentrated on his driving all the way back to HQ.

* * *

Ava arrived home later than usual that evening, having visited the gym again after work. Ollie was busy studying. Camden, Ava's fat tortoiseshell cat, was curled up on the table near his laptop.

"Ready to eat?" he asked Ava. "It's fish and chips tonight, I'm afraid. I've got an essay to write."

"You carry on working for a bit. Even I'm capable of sticking frozen fish and chips in the oven."

Ava poured herself a glass of wine while the food was cooking and sat down with her laptop at the kitchen table. She put *Spacedrifters* in a Google search and spent the next fifteen minutes reading about the show and its stars. It had been on before her time. Ollie was a bit of a sci-fi geek and he assured her that in certain circles the programme had almost attained cult status. Leon Warrior's role had not been a starring one but, according to Wikipedia, he had appeared in nearly every episode of *Spacedrifters'* first two seasons. Then he was dropped from the show.

The concept was pretty simple: a group of people in some far-flung future, exiled from their home planet for plotting against an evil dictatorship, somehow manage to appropriate a spacecraft and escape their home world. They are then pursued by government agents bent on stopping them finding an ally somewhere in the galaxy. A total of thirty episodes had been made, and then the show was cancelled following a sharp fall in the ratings. Fans had launched a campaign to have it resurrected but their enthusiasm had quickly fizzled out and it never resurfaced.

Warrior had played the part of Stephen Troy, an idealistic young doctor who had been arrested and sentenced to death for opposing his planet's harsh euthanasia laws. His character had been widely ridiculed for his tendency to express everything in medical metaphors. He was predictably included in plots in which one of the main characters was seriously wounded or ravaged by a deadly disease which Troy alone could fix.

Looking at Warrior's bio, Ava saw that, after his move to the US, he had appeared in a number of daytime soaps and sitcoms. He was always a minor character, who was often dropped after one or two episodes. The character he had played in *Gladiator* had not lived long enough to warrant a name.

Information on Warrior's personal life was sparse. Ava was interested to read that prior to coming out, Leon had dated an aspiring model and had even been engaged to her for nearly a year. From the early nineties, he had been out.

Ava clicked on a hyperlink to see what she could learn about Gray Mitchell. His working life was similar to Leon's, with the exception that Gray's background had been in the theatre. He had spent some years travelling from state to state with a repertory company, performing Shakespeare in far-flung rural communities in the Midwest.

Ava didn't think Mitchell's apparent lack of partners was significant. He had probably been discreet in the days when to be openly gay in the acting business was career suicide. There was only one photograph that she could find of Mitchell and Warrior together — an image of them in a Gay Pride parade in LA. Ava sighed and closed the lid of her laptop. Then she sorted out the fish and chips.

She and Ollie sat together over their meal, chatting companionably. Before Ollie came to live with her, Ava had been in the habit of eating in front of the TV, more often than not with a microwaved meal and a bottle of wine. Playing big sister was forcing her to be civilised.

"What's your essay about?" Ava asked.

"The Russian revolution. It's due in tomorrow but I've nearly finished. Shouldn't be too late a night." Ollie was doing science and maths A levels. The history was an optional extra subject. He seemed to be enjoying it.

"So, I saw George Irons today," Ollie said.

"And?" Ava answered. She'd half-hoped Ollie would forget their conversation about George Irons.

"I asked him about his dad."

"Oh yeah? I hope you didn't mention the case."

"Course I didn't! What do you take me for? Anyway, I've already told you George doesn't know you're a cop, never mind working on the Gray Mitchell case."

"Okay, sorry for doubting you."

"You'd have liked the way I kind of, like *segued* it into the conversation."

"Word of the day?" Ava asked. Ollie was boosting his vocabulary by learning a new word every day.

"Anyway, it seems that his dad, Ray, was in the National Front in the eighties. You've heard of the NF, right?"

Ava nodded. Ollie often seemed to think she was completely uneducated.

"Tell me something I don't know already."

"Well, George's old man went off on one when he heard that Leon Warrior was back in town."

Now Ollie had her interest. He feigned a yawn. "Suppose we'd better load the dishwasher and get back to work then."

"I know you're bursting to tell me something, so drop the act. Or you'll be back living with Mum before you can finish that essay."

"You got me. Okay. George told me his dad went ape-shit when he read about Leon Warrior and his partner starting a ghost tour business in town. There was an article in the *Courier* about it and he ripped the paper to shreds when he read it."

"Did George say why?"

"When he asked, his dad just went on about effing fags."

"Ray Irons bullied Warrior all through secondary school," Ava said. "Your typical sort of bullying to begin with, then what would now be called homophobic bullying."

"He's not all bad," Ollie said unexpectedly. "Apparently he looked after George's mum for years before she died."

105

Ava raised her eyebrows, "What did she die from?"

"Motor neurone disease. She was diagnosed just after they met."

Ava wondered whether she was going to have to revise her image of the thuggish Irons. He had stood by a woman with a debilitating illness and looked after her for years. He was also a dog lover. But monsters often have redeeming features, she thought. It was all about compartmentalising. What had Neal said? Irons' bark was probably worse than his bite nowadays.

"Finish your essay," Ava said to her brother. "I'll sort out the dishwasher."

As she loaded plates into the racks, Ava was thinking of Leon Warrior's bio on Wikipedia. "There's something I forgot to mention."

Her brother's voice made Ava jump. She had been absorbed in what she was doing and he had crept up soundlessly behind her. Before she knew what she was doing, Ava had grabbed a knife from the draining board and jumped back, in an attack pose.

"Flipping heck, Ava!" Ollie exclaimed, backing away.

"Sorry! Sorry. It was instinct."

Ollie shook his head. "Most people scream when you startle them."

"I . . . it's my martial arts training kicking in," Ava said. She wasn't about to tell Ollie the history behind her reaction. "What was it you forgot to say?"

"I'll tell you if you teach me some of your moves," Ollie said.

"Okay." It was a good idea. Ollie had been bullied at his last school, and a bit of kick-boxing or karate would boost his self-esteem — and keep him safer.

"George said that Leon Warrior got sacked from *Spacedrifters* before the series ended. He was involved in a scandal."

"What sort of scandal?" Ava asked.

"Sorry, that's all George said. He remembers his dad mentioning it to his mum years ago when *Spacedrifters* came out on DVD. George wasn't all that interested at that time."

"Thanks, Ollie. All this info's really useful."

Ollie beamed.

"But no more probing, okay? You've done enough. Oh, you don't happen to have the *Spacedrifters* box set, do you?"

"No, but I could stream it for you really easily."

"You do realise that's illegal, don't you?"

"Everybody does it."

Ava was about to give him a lecture, but let it go.

Ollie went back to his homework. Ava returned to her laptop and ordered the DVD of *Spacedrifters*. She was annoyed that she had to pay an inflated price for something she most likely wasn't going to enjoy.

Chapter 10

Laurence Brand was still reeling from the news of Gray Mitchell's murder. When he learned about Caitlin Forest's fate, his sanity began to lurch sideways. Maxine had called him with the news the minute she heard it from Helen Alder. Vincent Bone had told her. She had failed to show up for work and he was worried she might be ill. And now everyone knew. Young Chloe was so scared she wanted to go home. She was convinced a serial killer was taking out the staff at the cathedral, one by one. Maxine had assured Laurence that there could be no connection between the murders. Laurence asked himself how she could possibly know that.

Since his early twenties, Laurence had suffered from mood swings that nowadays placed him somewhere on the bipolar spectrum. His symptoms were not severe or frequent enough to affect his day to day functioning. Laurence liked to view his moods as just part of his personality. There had been occasions in the past when he had, as he put it, 'lost it.' The last time it happened, he had lost his job and they had moved to Stromford.

Maxine referred to these lapses in judgement as 'episodes.' Laurence was worried that Mitchell's death was about to trigger another one. He was aware of the anxiety gnawing away inside him.

Like the cataclysmic forces below the Earth's crust, Laurence's emotions could overwhelm him, erupting to the surface and creating new landscapes of unrestrained behaviour. Only Maxine and a few close friends knew about his condition, including Gray Mitchell, Leon Warrior, and Vincent Bone. Laurence suspected that Maxine had told Helen Alder. There were few secrets between those two.

Laurence suddenly felt that someone should let Leon know about Caitlin. So he made his way to Leon's house. As he walked, he thought over his conversation with Marcus the previous evening. As far as he knew, he was the only person Marcus had confided in. Laurence hadn't even told his wife about their talk, and he told her everything. Things might look bad for the boy if his relationship with Caitlin Forest became common knowledge. Laurence wondered what he should say if the police questioned him. What would Marcus say? Perhaps he should wait until he had had a chance to talk to the boy before he spoke to anyone else.

Laurence felt the familiar tendrils of anxiety curl around his chest. He reached into his jacket pocket, reassured by the bottle of pills resting there.

Poor Caitlin. Laurence hadn't known her that well, but whenever he visited the cathedral café, Caitlin had been there with the others. She was hard to miss in a group that included only one other woman, Angie Dent. With her bubblegum-pink hair, she reminded him of Cyndi Lauper, an American singer he'd fancied back in the eighties. He began to hum one of her songs, something about girls and fun. Hadn't Leon and Gray met Cyndi once?

Laurence walked up Leon's drive to the front door. When Leon answered, Laurence understood that he had called at a bad time. Leon was in his dressing gown. His hair had a damp, sweaty sheen and his face was flushed. Leon stood just inside the door and Laurence sensed that he wasn't welcome.

"Er . . . this isn't a good time," Leon said. He glanced over his shoulder towards the elegant staircase.

Laurence looked up, saw a movement at an upstairs window and caught a glimpse of naked torso and fair hair. Laurence stared at Leon in disbelief.

"Did Gray know? You always said he was the love of your life." Laurence's voice shook. "Where were you really, at the weekend?"

"Laurence, dear chap. It's not what you think . . ."

Laurence stumbled back down the path. He was in turmoil. He needed to see Maxine but she was at work. He couldn't turn up at the café in a state like this.

He crunched along the newly gritted pavement. All the old, exaggerated feelings about Leon Warrior rumbled inside him. Leon had threatened his tour business, his very livelihood. Laurence was angry, bitter. Leon had betrayed Gray. How could he do this? By the time he reached home and the sanctuary of his study, Laurence was barely in control. Maxine mustn't see him like this. He reached for his bottle of pills and prayed for calm.

* * *

The morning after his lesson with Laurence, Marcus had been late for work. His clock radio woke him, pounding out rock, and he punched it off. His head was throbbing and any movement made him feel sick. He couldn't bear the thought of getting out of bed. He visited the bathroom and took a leak that seemed to go on for ever, and smelt strong and unpleasant. Marcus returned to bed. Maybe if he skipped his shower and breakfast, he could sleep for another hour or so, and he would only be an hour late for work. He'd think of an excuse later, when his head was clearer.

As it turned out, no one had seemed to notice when he walked into the workroom an hour and ten minutes late. Vincent wasn't even around, and a couple of the others were missing too.

"Vincent's talking to the police," said Darren, one of the stonemasons.

"Is it about Gray Mitchell again?" Marcus asked.

In the ensuing silence everyone in the workshop looked at Darren.

"There's been another murder," Darren said.

"Jesus! No kidding? Who is it this time?"

"Caitlin Forest. She was stabbed. Not here — outside her block of flats. They think it happened in the early hours of the morning."

Marcus's heart raced. Someone, possibly Darren, asked if he was alright.

"I . . . er, I'm hung-over," Marcus said.

"We're all in shock, lad. We all saw Caitlin in the café yesterday afternoon and now . . . well. Who knows what happened to her after that? Most likely some madman attacked her. I can't see it being connected to Gray Mitchell," Darren said. "Go on and get a cup of coffee. You look like you need it."

Marcus escaped into the small kitchen. Nobody knows I was seeing her, Marcus thought. In the crime dramas his mother loved to watch, the police were always anxious to know this sort of thing. Then, when the caffeine reached his fuzzy brain, he recalled his conversation with Laurence Brand.

He took out his phone to text Laurence. Then a second memory almost floored him. He realised it didn't matter what Laurence told the police. The last person Marcus had texted was Caitlin. As soon as the police got hold of Caitlin's mobile they would read the angry, abusive diatribe he'd texted her the night before. It would lead them straight to Marcus. It was a very sobering thought.

* * *

Neal walked into the incident room dedicated to the Mitchell murder investigation. He did a quick scan of those present. It was Neal's role as senior investigating officer to coordinate the findings of the different members of the team. Ava Merry was present, of course, as well as PC Polly Jenkins, better known as PJ. She was managing the collating and sharing of information. There were two other police constables who had been doing much of the foot-work in the investigation so far. It was their job to knock on doors, show Mitchell's picture around, call on neighbours, and find out if he'd been seen anywhere he wouldn't normally go. Neal was also expecting the pathologist, Ashley Hunt, to put in an appearance. Dan Cardew from the scientific team, a young forensic science graduate who allegedly had the hots for Ava, was sitting near her. He looked as if he was trying to think of something to say, but Ava was looking the other way.

"Evenin' all," Neal said, in a poor imitation of a Cockney accent. There was a polite laugh. He was never going to be the office joker. "As you know I'm the SIO on this case, but I'm reporting to DCI Lowe and he's taking a keen interest. He's already had the mayor and a host of other city dignitaries on his back, asking whether we've got a serial killer on the loose. There was a stupid, uninformed 'article,' if you can call it that, on the *Courier's* website this morning. Everybody's getting excited about the bloody Christmas market coming up. They want the case wrapped up in Christmas paper with bows on by the end of next week. I don't need to emphasise that, as far as the media's concerned, what's said in this room, stays in this room."

A low murmur of agreement came.

"Right. Let's get started. Dan, can you give us an update on what forensics have managed to come up with so far?"

Dan Cardew stood up and crossed to the front of the room. He was obviously nervous about talking in front of people, and his hand shook visibly as he set up his PowerPoint. As the first slide appeared on the screen a titter spread through the room. It showed an image of Russell Crowe in full gladiator regalia, Jim Neal's head photo-shopped onto Crowe's body. A speech bubble contained the famous lines, "I will avenge his death — in this life or the next."

"S-s-sorry. Wrong slide." Dan cast a nervous glance in Neal's direction.

Neal gave an impatient shrug. A series of photographs followed, and a short film offering a panoramic perspective for those who had not been present at the crime scene. Dan talked them through the slides, describing in meticulous detail how the scene had been processed.

"As you are aware, Mr Mitchell's body was pushed from a great height and stayed where it . . . er . . . landed. The killer disabled him with a blow to the head and would have had little contact with Mr Mitchell's person. There was little chance, therefore, of finding trace evidence around the scene, or on Mr Mitchell's body."

Dan spoke haltingly. The atmosphere in the room, which had been buoyant to begin with, then slightly bored, was now downright despondent. There was no real evidence that might throw up a lead.

"As you'd expect after heavy snowfall, there were no footprints at the scene other than those made by the caretaker who discovered the body."

Dan droned on, saying nothing of any significance. Neal glanced over at Ava. She was twitchy. She'd already twice dropped her pencil. Now she was looking as though she was about to spring to her feet and wind poor Dan up to make him talk faster. Hunt arrived and the pathologist slid silently into a chair next to Neal. Was it Neal's imagination, or did Hunt just give him an encouraging nod?

Dan paused for a moment and looked around the room.

"That lad needs to work on his presentation skills," Hunt whispered to Neal.

Neal nodded, feeling a pang of sympathy for Dan, who was now having tech problems. There was a sudden bustle in the room. Everyone used the hiatus as an opportunity to stretch, talk, or go to the water cooler.

"Have you tried turning it off and on again?" asked PC Dale, and someone else chipped in, "have you tried shoving it up—"

"Alright. Thank you," Neal said. "Dan, was there anything else of significance you had to run us through today?"

"Well, I was just about to sum up."

"Thanks, Dan. Perhaps you could liaise with PJ about circulating your slides to the team?"

"Yes, sir." Dan gave a sigh of relief that seemed to come from his shoes.

Hunt stood up. "Just as well I brought my own equipment," he said, holding up his laptop case. He fumbled in his pocket, "Dammit, where's that bloody memory stick?"

Neal rolled his eyes.

"Gray Mitchell died of injuries resulting from his fall, or more precisely from the impact with the ground," Hunt began.

An inventory of the damage to Gray's internal organs followed that made gruesome but compulsive listening. No one slept through a medical report, and Hunt was an engaging speaker. Neal soon realised that the nod must have simply been a greeting. Hunt, too, had little to offer. The victim had received a blow to the head prior to being pushed, evidenced by a fracture to his skull not sustained in the fall. This much Neal already knew, as did everyone else on the case. Did they really need to see the graphic details?

Hunt speculated that the blow might have been administered by a blunt instrument, most likely a hammer. He advised against immediately suspecting the stonemasonry staff. The weapon was just as likely to be an ordinary household hammer. Unless the actual murder weapon could be retrieved, knowing what it might be was not much help.

Gray, the pathologist concluded, had been a fit man, in good shape and could have expected to live a long life. He had been taking his medication and was likely to have been in good mental health, although it was impossible to say this for certain.

Hunt was a busy man and he wrapped up his contribution quickly.

Neal thanked him and he left. Neal addressed his colleagues. "So, it looks like it's dogged police work that's going to move us forward," he said. He turned to PJ. "Can you give us a rundown of what's been unearthed so far, PC Jenkins?"

"PCs Hughes and Winters have visited a number of venues provided by Leon Warrior and shown Mitchell's photo around. Most people seemed to recognise him. The manager of Costcutter remembers him buying a jar of lime pickle on the Sunday afternoon at around half past three, and he collected an Indian takeaway for one from the Happy Chapatti at seven p.m."

"And prior to Sunday?"

"He'd been seen in many of his usual haunts. Seems Mr Mitchell was quite regular in his habits. Visited Stromford Central Library once a week on Tuesday afternoons, and had afternoon tea at the Tower Café on Thursdays, sometimes with Warrior or another friend, sometimes alone. PC Hughes used receipts found in Mitchell's wallet to retrace his steps and Warrior confirmed that there was nothing unusual in his spending or anything unusual on his credit record over the past few weeks."

PJ scrolled through her notes on the screen. "He kept all the appointments he'd made in advance . . . I'm sorry, sir, there's just nothing so far to suggest that Mitchell was involved in anything that might have precipitated his death."

She carried on. "As we know, Warrior received a text message in the early hours of Monday morning, saying, 'am on the cathedral roof and fear I may jump. Please come,' or words to that effect. The message couldn't be traced. It was probably sent from a disposable."

There was a silence after PJ's words. A sigh was almost audible. Sometimes even dogged police work wasn't enough.

"The person who texted Mitchell left no name, yet it was enough to make him leave the safety of his home in heavy snowfall in the early hours of the morning. The obvious conclusion is that he thought he knew who the call was from. He had answered what he thought was a cry for help and instead it was a death summons." Neal's words only added to the gloom. "Let's wrap it up, then."

Then PC Winters raised her hand. "Just one thing, sir."

"Go on."

"I was out with a friend last night and showed her Gray Mitchell's picture. She'd been to the Barley Inn with her husband for an anniversary dinner last week . . ."

Neal nodded.

"She saw Mitchell there with a young man. She remembered because at one point the young lad was in tears."

Suddenly, all eyes in the room were fixed on PC Winters.

"Could she describe the young man?" Ava asked.

"About five-ten, slight, fine-boned, blond hair. Full lips. Karen, that's my friend, described them as 'kissable.'"

As descriptions went, this was pretty good. They should be able to obtain a decent artist's impression. This Karen would need to come to the station soon. Neal wondered if he should congratulate Winters on doing good work or take her to task for discussing a case out of work. She had been tasked with showing Mitchell's photo around, so he opted for thanking her. She rewarded him with a broad smile. Against all expectations, the meeting ended on an upbeat note.

Neal barked out some instructions. PC Winters was to contact her friend Karen to see when she could come in and sit with a police artist. Someone would also need to call at the restaurant and ascertain whether Gray had in fact been there, how often, and with whom. Hell, if they were lucky, someone might even be able to name the young man he'd been seen with. Neal and Ava went into his office.

"Warrior's going to be upset when we tell him his lover was seeing a younger man," Ava said immediately. "I know there's no evidence yet but it looks suspicious, doesn't it, sir? The Barley's a popular choice for couples. It's in a very romantic setting by the river."

"It's also a way out of town — the sort of place you might go to if you wanted to avoid being seen," Neal said. He wondered if Ava had personal experience of the Barley. "We need to find out who this young man is, as a matter of priority. Contact Leon Warrior and see if you can meet him this afternoon. Find out what, if anything, he knows about Mitchell and our mystery youth."

"What if Leon Warrior lured Mitchell to the roof because he'd found out about an affair? Wouldn't be the first time jealousy provided a motive for murder," Ava said.

"No. But jealous rages are more likely to result in a spontaneous act of violence."

Ava rambled on. "What about Caitlin Forest? Had she found out somehow and taken Gray to task over it? Or told Leon? Though I doubt Leon would murder Caitlin for that reason, especially after Gray was already dead. What reason would Leon have to kill Caitlin, really? It's possible there's no connection and we're looking at two different killers."

There was a knock and PJ popped her head around the door. "Just had a call from Dan in forensics. Caitlin Forest received a text message from Marcus Collins late last night. You're going to want to know what it said."

Chapter 11

Laurence Brand sat in his study for a couple of hours, staring at the walls and attempting to calm his nerves. Not since his final weeks of teaching had he felt so angry. He thought of Gray, the man Leon Warrior had once told him was 'the love of his life.' Laurence had christened Mitchell 'The Quiet American.' Graham Greene was a favourite of Laurence's. He empathised with the moral ambiguities in 'Greeneland,' and his flawed, but human, characters.

As a fellow sufferer from bipolar disorder, Gray had been interested in Laurence's problems. He had cheered Laurence by pointing out that a condition such as theirs was an integral part of their personality. It added depth to their character. It wasn't something that labelled or limited them, but was liberating.

The longer Laurence sat trying to be calm, the more agitated he became. Once before, a perfect storm of circumstances had combined to tip Laurence over the edge. That was back in Maxine's social work days, before she had given all that up in favour of cupcakes and afternoon teas. They had met when she was working cover in the mental health team. Laurence was at a particularly low point in his illness, which had culminated in a suicide attempt. Maxine had baked him a fruit cake — how apt — and brought it to the hospital psychiatric wing where he was on suicide watch for a few weeks. She seemed to like him, something he could never quite fathom. Their eventual marriage had provided the stability he needed to stay one step ahead of his condition. Still, there were the occasional lapses and Gray's murder was triggering one of these now.

Finally, Laurence had to do something. He found himself, only an hour after leaving Leon's house, standing back on the pavement outside it. A brick was in his hand.

If only Maxine had been around to counsel him. Instead, Caius was directing him. Caius had a way of popping into Laurence's head whenever he was conflicted. Unlike Laurence, Caius had a strong character. The centurion was never paralysed by doubt. Rome had risen to greatness on the shoulders of men like him. "*Carpe diem*," Caius whispered in his ear. Laurence's hand tightened around the brick.

He strode towards Leon's front porch. Just short of the entrance, Laurence veered off the drive to face the window looking in on the sitting room. Leon and Gray had held their soiree in this lovely room only a couple of weeks ago. He could see Leon inside, sitting alone at the grand piano. His head was bowed and his hands moved across the keys. As he drew nearer, Laurence could hear that Leon was playing one of Chopin's nocturnes and he paused to listen. He had heard Leon play before, but never music like this. He hadn't realised Leon had it in him. For a moment his grip on the brick relaxed, Caius retreated and a sort of calm came over Laurence. But it was short-lived. The music stopped abruptly and Leon pounded on the keys. The harsh, angry sound brought Laurence's rage surging back. He drew back his arm and hurled the brick at Leon's window, Caius's triumphant whoop ringing in his ears.

The window smashed and the brick flew across the short distance to the piano. It skimmed across the polished surface to hit its target on the side of the face. Then it fell to the carpet with a thud. Laurence launched himself at the shattered window, punching out the remaining shards of broken glass with his bare fists. He hauled himself onto the windowsill and kicked his way through.

Leon stumbled backwards, blood streaming down the side of his face. He fell over his piano stool and landed awkwardly on the carpet. He lay there wheezing.

"Get up, you coward!" Laurence bellowed at him. He stood over Leon, fists up.

Leon raised his hands as he shuffled along the floor, backing away from Laurence.

"L-L-Laurie, what the fuck is wrong with you?" Leon spluttered out between wheezes.

"You know what's wrong with me!" Laurence boomed.

"Is . . . is this about Godfrey?"

The name sounded so unlikely that it took Laurence aback. Godfrey?

"It's about you betraying Gray, you cradle-snatching bastard! How long, eh? Did the pair of you work together to get Gray out of the way?"

Leon groped towards the brick, struggling for breath. An inhaler sat on top of the piano. He moved quickly, launching the brick at Laurence, then crawled across the broken glass.

For the second time, the brick impacted with human flesh and bone, though it only grazed Laurence on the cheek. Leon had thrown it from a prone position and it had little momentum. Nevertheless, Laurence was stunned for a few moments. Leon grabbed the inhaler.

Laurence came at Leon again, but this time he was outclassed. Leon had trained with the best fight choreographers in the business. He danced around his opponent and then took Laurence out with a single blow.

At that moment a siren blared from the road outside and a police car pulled up.

Chapter 12

"Marcus Collins and Caitlin Forest were going out together?" Ava stared at PJ.

"Have Marcus brought in for questioning," Neal said. Then PC Winters knocked on the door.

"Sir, I thought you'd like to know that a patrol car answered a disturbance call from Leon Warrior's neighbour about an hour ago. Laurence Brand's been arrested for chucking a brick through Warrior's window and assaulting him. Both Brand and Warrior were injured. They've been taken to the county hospital for treatment."

"It's all happening," PJ said cheerfully. "I take it you two are off to the hospital? I'll arrange for Marcus Collins to be brought in."

"Thanks, Peej," Ava said, and reached for her coat.

The county hospital lay to the north-east of the city on a sprawling site that had housed a hospital in one form or another since the eighteenth century.

Ava parked in the visitor car park. She and Neal entered the accident-and-emergency waiting area. Both had been here many times before and the receptionist recognised them.

"Mr Warrior and Mr Brand are both in treatment rooms," the receptionist informed them. "I'm sorry, I don't have any information on their condition, but if you take a seat I'll find out for you."

"Let's sit over there away from the TV screen," Neal said. He pointed to a row of chairs off the main seating area. Ava was happy to follow him. The screen was showing one of those property programmes that seemed to be on all the time. Further from the TV screen, they had a little bit of privacy.

They sat waiting. A couple of paramedics wheeled past a young woman on a stretcher. There had been little time to talk on the short journey to the hospital.

"I just can't picture Laurence Brand chucking a brick through Leon's window and attacking him," Ava said. "He seems such a mild-mannered person, gentle almost. Not that you can ever really tell, of course."

"You're right though. Brand didn't seem as though he'd have it in him to run amok. Mind you, he does seem a nervous type. Perhaps there's some underlying condition we don't know about," said Neal.

"You mean a mental health issue?"

Neal nodded.

"If so, something must have pushed him over the edge. Grief over Mitchell's death? They were good friends, Brand and Mitchell. You don't think Laurence Brand thinks Warrior killed Mitchell, do you?"

"Mmm . . ."

"Fancy a coffee?" Ava asked. "There's a little WRVS café just along the corridor."

"No thanks. But you go ahead."

"I won't bother. Probably only got instant."

"How is it working out, having your brother to stay?"

Neal's question took Ava by surprise. In the past couple of days all their conversations had focused on work. Neal seemed to be awkward with her, and it wasn't all to do with her behaviour on their last case.

"All good, so far. Ollie's pretty easy going. He went through a bad time at his last school and living with Mum was getting to him a bit. Now that he's less uptight about things, he's really coming on."

"What school is he in?"

"Er . . . actually, he's at Montgomery Carstairs — you know, the grammar school out on Burnley Road."

"Ah."

"I know you're not keen on grammar schools, sir. It's just . . . Ollie's really bright and . . ."

"Who said I was against grammar schools?"

Ava coloured. "Well, it's just that you're always going on about private education and how unfair it is. And everyone knows your views on the Tories, sir."

Neal actually laughed. "Everyone seems to know my views on a lot of things. Perhaps I should be more careful about airing my opinions."

"Well, you are Scottish, sir. Maybe people just make assumptions. A Scottish Tory's a bit of an oxymoron, isn't it?"

"It's certainly that. For the record, if your brother is happy and thriving at his choice of school, that's all you need to be concerned about."

"He is."

"Good." They were quiet for a few moments, then Neal said, "Ava, there's something I've been meaning to ask . . ."

Ava tensed.

At that moment, a young doctor walked towards them and held out his hand. "Dr Joel Agard. I've been looking after Mr Warrior and Mr Brand. Would you like to come with me? There's a room where we can talk privately."

Dr Agard led them to a small consulting room. He perched on the edge of a trolley bed, leaving two seats free for Neal and Ava. Ava thought he was very easy on the eye, as PJ might say. He was a tall man, dark-skinned and well-toned in his crisp white shirt and tailored trousers.

"Mr Brand's injuries were not serious. He required three stitches to a cut on his cheek and stitches to cuts on his hands. There were also a number of other minor cuts to his hands, which we've cleaned and dressed. As for his mental condition, he's told us that he suffers from a mild form of bipolar disorder — his description, not mine — and that sometimes he gets things out of proportion. I'm not really qualified to comment on that, but we can have a psych evaluation carried out if it proves necessary."

Neal nodded.

"Mr Warrior's condition is not serious either. Again it's a case of cuts and scratches from crawling over broken glass, but he did take a nasty blow to the face from the brick thrown by Mr Brand. Additionally, Mr Warrior suffered an asthma attack and we'd like to see him stabilised prior to discharge. He'll probably be in overnight."

"We'd like to question them both as soon as possible," Neal said. "Is that convenient?"

"You can speak with Mr Brand now. One of your officers is still with him. Apparently Mr Warrior has said that he doesn't intend to press charges. He said it was all a misunderstanding."

"Right," Neal said. "Shame their 'misunderstanding' couldn't have been resolved without resorting to violence." He turned to Ava. "Let's speak to Brand now."

Dr Agard took them to the emergency treatment room. In a curtained cubicle Laurence Brand was sitting up in bed, looking drowsy. A police constable was standing nearby, chatting with a nurse. Neal and Ava gave him a nod as they entered the cubicle.

Brand looked like he had been in a bare knuckle fight. His face was cut and bruised, his hands bandaged and he was clearly woozy from the effect of painkillers. Ava felt a stab of sympathy for him. She was still unable to reconcile her impression of this soft-spoken man with the brick-wielding menace he had become.

"Mr Brand," she said. He opened his eyes. "DS Ava Merry and DI Neal. We'd like to ask you a few questions."

"I'm ashamed," said Brand quietly.

"We're aware that you have a . . . mental health condition," Ava began.

"That doesn't excuse my behaviour. I don't know what came over me. You must believe me, officers. I'm not a violent man."

"Mr Warrior isn't going to press charges," Ava said, "but we'd like to know what was behind your actions this morning. Have they anything to do with Mr Mitchell's murder?"

"I . . . I made a discovery about Leon this morning that upset me greatly. What I don't understand is why it made me act the way I did." Brand sighed. "Leon betrayed Gray. That dear, gentle man who thought Leon loved him as much as he loved Leon. Gray left his career and his country to be with Leon . . ."

"Are you saying Leon was seeing someone else?" said Ava.

Brand nodded. "A young man. I saw him at Leon's bedroom window this morning. He was quite obviously naked. He was hiding behind the curtain, but I saw him plain as day. And Leon . . . when he answered the door, he looked so . . . guilty."

"Do you have any idea how long Leon had been seeing this young man?"

Brand shook his head. "I don't know. But it hardly matters, does it? Gray's hardly been dead a fortnight. It's . . . it's shameful."

"It's possible it was a one-off, that Mr Warrior was seeking solace."

"You're very young, Sergeant. Perhaps you don't understand what it is to love . . ."

"Love isn't the issue here," Ava said, briskly. "I'm old enough to have seen that love can very easily turn to hate.

I'm not a naïve young girl, Mr Brand. You can't be in my line of work."

Brand looked utterly miserable. His eyelids drooped. "Marcus . . ." he suddenly said, as if awakening from a dream.

"What about Marcus?" Ava looked at Neal.

"Nothing. I was dreaming," Brand answered.

"Is there something you need to tell us, Mr Brand?" Neal asked. "Was Marcus Collins the young man you saw at Mr Warrior's window?"

Brand stared at Neal. "Of course not. Marcus isn't gay. As a matter of fact, he was seeing . . ."

Neal completed the sentence, ". . . Caitlin Forest."

"How did you know that? I thought I was the only one who knew."

"Never mind. Mr Brand, are you aware that this morning Caitlin Forest was found dead outside the building she lived in?"

"Yes, I heard. Poor girl," Brand said. Then he looked from Neal to Ava. "No . . . you're not thinking Marcus had anything to do with that! That's preposterous. I'm teaching him Latin!"

Ava tried to suppress her smile.

"Marcus only told me last night. He kept getting his declensions muddled up. I knew something was on his mind and when I asked, he told me about Caitlin. She'd broken up with him earlier in the day and he was taking it badly. I told him there were plenty of other fish in the sea, but I think I upset him."

Ava looked at Neal. Laurence Brand was obviously exhausted and emotionally wrung-out. Perhaps it was time to leave.

"Was there anything else you'd omitted to tell us, Mr Brand?" Neal asked.

Brand bowed his head, shaking it slightly. He was beginning to drift off again.

"Maxine . . ." he whispered, and then he was asleep.

"Let's go," Neal said. "We're clearly not going to get anything more out of him."

Outside the cubicle, Neal went to speak with one of the PCs who had brought Brand and Warrior to the hospital. Dr Agard joined Ava as soon as Neal left her side.

"Mr Brand's wife just phoned to say she's on her way here," he said. Ava thanked him. "Did everything go OK in there?" Agard asked, nodding at the cubicle.

"He was pretty spaced out," Ava said. "What have you been giving him?"

"Painkillers and some tranquilisers. He needed to calm down. I've checked with my boss and he's advised doing a psychiatric assessment. It looks like Mr Brand will be staying in after all, just until we verify his diagnosis and reassess him."

This seemed like a sensible precaution to Ava. There was no real reason for Agard to linger, but he seemed reluctant to move away. Ava could tell he was attracted to her. She wasn't in any hurry for him to leave either. She glanced over at Neal. He was still talking to the PC but he looked up and caught her eye, then looked at Agard. Then he looked away. Ava felt conflicted for an instant, but she didn't feel like analysing her feelings. Neal was her colleague. Agard was not, and he was clearly interested.

"Are you working the late shift?" she asked him, pointedly.

"No. I've been on for more hours than I can remember. I should be off by nine."

"I guess you'll be pretty tired by then, but if you're not, I know a great place to unwind," Ava said.

Predictably, he greeted her words with a smile of pleasure.

"The Cock and Spire? It's on Maitland Street," she said and tore a sheet from her notebook. "Call me when you're free." A quick glance in Neal's direction told her he had not missed any of this.

129

Neal finished his conversation with the PC and strode back to join Ava and Agard. Agard looked embarrassed. He turned over a sheet on his clipboard, stammered something about having a patient to see and headed off towards an empty cubicle.

"See you later?" Ava called after him and the flustered doctor smiled and nodded. He hot-footed it in the direction of the treatment board.

"When you've finished sorting out your social life, we have Leon Warrior to question," Neal said, dry as dust.

Ava followed behind him to a side ward, where Warrior was sitting up in bed. He was patched up just like his attacker. A nebuliser mask covered his nose and mouth, puffs of white mist clouding around his face.

Leon lifted it up. "Can you give me a couple of minutes? It's almost finished."

Ava brought a couple of orange plastic chairs from the corridor, and then disappeared again, returning with two cups of machine coffee. "Better than nothing," she said to Neal.

Warrior removed the mask and flicked a switch beside his bed, and the hissing sound from the nebuliser stopped.

"That's better. Got my breath again."

"Take your time, Mr Warrior," Neal said. "You've been through an unpleasant experience. May I ask why you decided not to press charges against Mr Brand?"

Warrior sighed. "It was a frightening experience, I'll grant you. I've never seen Laurie like that before. He was like a man possessed. He and Gray were close and he thought I had been cheating on Gray. That and . . . well, I was thinking of Maxine."

"Were you?" Ava asked. "Cheating on Gray?"

"DS Merry, always a pleasure." Then, quietly, "Yes, I was seeing someone else. I suppose you'll want his name?"

Ava was ready with her pen.

"Godfrey Hardy," Leon said.

He spoke so quietly Ava had to ask him to repeat the name. "Address?" Ava asked.

He told her. "I was with him the night Gray died," Warrior said.

"So your trip to London was an opportunity to be with this Godfrey?"

" Yes," Warrior said. "I met Godfrey when he came on one of my ghost tours . He was dressed as a *Spacedrifters* character — mine, actually. He'd read about my return to Stromford and sought me out."

"Did Gray suspect?" Ava asked.

"I doubt it. Gray had a very trusting nature, bless him."

"When were you planning on telling him?" Ava asked.

Warrior pulled himself up, wincing in pain. "I wasn't. The thing with Godfrey would have run its course in a couple more weeks or months. Gray and I were for keeps. I don't expect you to approve, but don't judge me, Sergeant. Gay or straight, we all give into temptation."

Ava coloured, thinking of her own indiscretions. This Leon Warrior did not seem to resemble the distraught, inconsolable man of a couple of days ago. Either his grief had been exaggerated, false even, or he was very practised at controlling his emotions. He was an actor, after all.

"One more thing, Mr Warrior . . ." Ava began.

"Are you going to ask me not to leave town?" Warrior said. His tone was one of amusement, but it was forced and he looked drained. No doubt, like Brand, he was full of pain pills.

"Were you aware that Mr Mitchell had also been seeing a young man in the weeks before his death?"

Leon Warrior looked at Neal. When Neal did not correct his sergeant, Warrior closed his eyes.

"I'll take that as a no," Ava said quietly.

* * *

131

Back in the car, Ava asked Neal for his thoughts on Warrior.

"Hard to make out, isn't he?" Neal said. "I'm surprised he didn't succeed better as an actor — he certainly keeps the real Leon under wraps. On Monday morning I'd have judged him a broken man. Today — well, who knows? I think he's a vain man, certainly, self-centred, definitely. Sincere? Probably not, although he was right to point out that we are all susceptible to temptation. Some are more likely to succumb than others."

Ava couldn't help but take Neal's last words personally, given her behaviour in their last case. But she suspected that Neal was also getting in a dig about her encounter with Dr Agard.

"Capable of murder?" Ava said.

"Yes, but then all of us are."

"There doesn't seem to be any obvious motive, given that Leon probably knew nothing about Gray and the mystery man. He was clearly shaken when I told him, don't you think? Unless Warrior stood to benefit financially from Mitchell's death . . ."

"Hmm . . .Better add this Godfrey to the list of details to be checked out."

"Yes, sir." Ava risked a question. "Back when we were waiting to see Brand, you started to ask me something and then Dr Agard came over."

"It doesn't matter," Neal said. "Can you drop me here? It's closer to home than the station and it's already late."

Ava turned and pulled into a disabled parking space outside the library to let Neal out. With a brief nod, Neal shut the door and walked off. A passer-by shook her head at the sight of a police car parked in a disabled space.

* * *

Neal walked fast to improve his mood. It was late evening when he arrived home. Neal lived in the Uphill area of Stromford, with his ten-year-old son Archie and his younger sister, Maggie. Outside the back entrance, he kicked his feet against the wall to shake off the snow, his toes too numb to feel the impact. Archie was in the living room with a friend. Both were holding Xbox controllers and Archie gave Neal a wave as he passed the doorway. Archie's school had been closed for a second day because of a burst pipe. Since he had received the Xbox for his birthday, it had become his son's favourite pastime and Neal tried to limit the hours Archie spent on it. His son had already started asking to play more violent games 'because his friends played them.'

"Dinner's in the oven!" Neal's sister, Maggie, called to him from upstairs.

She cooked during the week and Neal cooked at weekends, if not busy on a case. After that it was takeaways. Sometimes Neal cooked extra meals to freeze so that Maggie wasn't unduly burdened. Maggie helped out enough with Archie. In return she lived with them rent free, but Neal was careful never to take his sister's contribution for granted.

"I'm off out with a new friend to see a movie. Only met her a couple of days ago, but we have a lot in common."

Neal asked what she was going to see.

"Oh, just some chick flick. You wouldn't like it. That actor's in it — the one you can't stand."

"Which one?" Neal called after her but Maggie was already out the door. Neal settled down to eat alone at the kitchen table. Perhaps he should get a dog, he thought. He could take it for long walks on the common and get to know some other dog walkers, maybe even female ones.

* * *

Maxine Brand walked into Accident and Emergency and scanned the people waiting there. Laurence was nowhere to be seen. Not knowing if that was a good or bad sign, she approached the helpdesk and was directed to a door protected by an intercom.

Eventually a nurse in pink scrubs let Maxine in and pointed to a cubicle with curtains drawn around it. Maxine slipped inside. Her heart lurched at the sight of her husband. Laurence lay fast asleep on the bed in his customary jeans and navy Berghaus fleece. His clothes were spattered with blood. She stared sadly at the bandages on his hands and the cuts and bruises on his face. She remembered that other time and place when she had been confronted with a similar scene — the man she loved lying in a hospital bed, hurt and vulnerable. She feared it would not be the last time she saw him like this.

"Oh, Laurie," she whispered, stroking his face gently. "Not again."

"Maxine?" She took his hand and sat on the edge of the bed.

"I'm here, Laurie."

"I'm so sorry."

She was silent.

"Leon isn't pressing charges."

Relief flooded through her. "You're sure?"

"The police have been. They told me. It's alright, Maxine."

For whom? Maxine thought. How generous her husband's victims were! Laurence could evoke sympathy in a psychopath. "You know they'll probably check your record anyway?"

Laurence nodded, miserably.

"We won't move this time, Laurie. *I* won't move." Maxine bent forward and kissed him on the lips.

He smiled at her, tears of gratitude welling up in his eyes.

* * *

After leaving the hospital, Maxine Brand went straight back to work. Helen Alder looked at her questioningly as she walked into the kitchen area. Normally the café would be closed by this time in the evening, but they were catering for a private function. Maxine was glad to be busy and around other people, especially Helen, whose support and discretion she knew she could rely on.

"Well?" Helen said. "How bad is it?"

Maxine sat down and let Helen pour her some tea. "Pretty bad." She sighed. "But at least Leon's not going to press charges. I'm just worried that the police might think Laurence had something to do with . . . what happened to Gray, or Caitlin. Oh, Helen, I can't believe what's been happening lately." At last she cried. It brought a welcome release. Helen held her, making soothing noises and stroking her back, telling her to let it all out.

"I love Laurie, but Stromford's my home now. I'm not starting over this time. I've told Laurie. No more running away."

"Good," said Helen.

She had never come right out and said it, but Maxine knew Helen thought she should never have given Laurence a second chance.

Chapter 13

Marcus Collins arrived and was seated in the interview room. Neal and Ava had been about to tuck into the bacon butties they'd brought in for breakfast.

"Thanks for coming in, Marcus," Ava began. "We're hoping that you can help us out with some questions." Again, she thought. It was only a couple of days since she had spoken with Marcus about Gray Mitchell's death.

The boy seated across the table from them looked utterly miserable — and hung-over. At nineteen, he was nearly eight years younger than Caitlin Forest, but Ava could see why a woman Caitlin's age might be attracted to him. He was not conventionally handsome, but he had a good physique.

"First off, Marcus, we know that you were seeing Caitlin Forest. We spoke with Laurence Brand this morning and he confirmed that you confided in him the night before last. He also mentioned that you'd spent time with Caitlin earlier yesterday and that she'd broken up with you. Like to tell us what that was all about?"

"We kept it a secret because that's what Caitlin wanted. I'm not sure why," said Marcus.

Ava nodded.

"When we saw each other after work yesterday, Caitlin told me she wanted to break up with me. I . . . I didn't want to. I tried to persuade her to change her mind."

"What did Laurence Brand advise you to do?"

"He said I should respect Caitlin's decision. He said Caitlin probably wasn't the one for me — plenty of other girls, you know, the sort of stuff anyone would say. I left feeing upset and decided to get wasted."

"You sent Caitlin a text. A pretty nasty one. Abusive, even," said Ava.

Marcus put his head in his hands. "I was wasted. I went to the pub, then the offie on the way home. I didn't even remember sending it till late this morning. I wouldn't have said those things if I'd been sober, you have to believe me."

"What time did you leave the pub, and which one was it? We'll also need the name of that off-licence you say you went to. I'm assuming you're going to say you went home and drank alone afterwards?"

"I did go home," Marcus said. "I drank some more, then texted Caitlin and then I crashed out." He gave Ava the name of the pub and the off-licence he'd visited. If the times checked out, he would have been home alone when Caitlin was murdered. Then he'd have no alibi.

"Okay, Marcus. You probably realise that sending an abusive text to someone is a serious business. Together with Caitlin's murder only hours after you sent the text, things look pretty bad for you. Do you understand?"

Marcus squinted at Ava. No doubt he had the mother of all headaches "Are you going to arrest me?"

"Not at the moment," Ava said. "But we will need to book you and take some fingerprints. You'll also be asked if you'll give your consent to a DNA test. I strongly urge you to do so. If you've done nothing wrong, you have nothing to fear. We'll be looking closely at any forensic evidence found at the scene that might put you there and it can only be a good thing if we fail to match it to you."

"I didn't hurt Caitlin, I promise," Marcus said, on the verge of tears.

"Take the test," Ava advised.

She and Neal stood up, leaving Marcus to ponder.

Chapter 14

Ava was curled up on her sofa with her fat cat, Camden, watching an episode of *Spacedrifters*. Science fiction wasn't really her thing, but she kept an open mind. The operatic opening credits seemed to last forever. They featured a whole parade of stars from the seventies and eighties, many of whom had disappeared without a trace.

Ava recognised Warrior immediately. He hadn't changed much in the years since the programme was made. He was dressed in a rather unflattering muddy green jumpsuit with flared trouser legs. It seemed to be a sort of uniform for the band of renegades of which he was a member. His acting was a bit hammy, his accent affected and unconvincing, but he was no worse than some other members of the cast.

The first half hour was boring. The action picked up when the band of renegades hijacked a spaceship and escaped their home planet pursued by government agents. Ava found herself rooting for Leon and his little band of rebels. She even watched the second episode and then the third. Around eleven, Ollie came downstairs to say goodnight. Ava was about to reach for the remote to turn the DVD off when a scantily clad woman on the screen caught her eye. She hit the pause button.

"Who's that?" she asked Ollie.

"That's Tara Smythe," her brother answered. "She was only in that one episode. I think she had an accident or something."

"Does she remind you of anyone?" Ava asked.

Ollie stared at the screen. "Nope."

"Don't you think she looks a bit like George Irons?"

Ollie looked again. He shrugged.

"Let me see that picture of you and George you've got on your mobile."

Ollie took out his phone. He found the picture he'd shown Ava a few days ago, of him and George goofing around at school. He stared at the picture, then at the screen again, and passed the phone to Ava. "Still can't see it."

Ava studied picture and screen until her eyes hurt. "I get it. It's not George Irons she looks like, it's his father, Ray. George looks a bit like both of them, that's why I thought of him first. They must be related."

Ollie stared again. "Nope, still don't see it."

"You never were much good with faces."

"I could ask George if a relative of his was in the show," Ollie offered.

"No, best not to. We can check it out." Ava looked at the clock, "Shouldn't you be in bed?"

"Had to finish another essay. Shouldn't *you* be in bed?"

"I'm just going to finish this episode."

"Told you it was good," Ollie said.

Ava was thinking that watching *Spacedrifters* might not have been a complete waste of her time after all.

"Night, Ollie," she said. She picked up the remote and Tara Smythe's pretty face came alive.

* * *

As soon as she met Neal the following morning, Ava announced her discovery. "Tara Smythe," she said. "Model and actress. Dated *Leon Warrior* with whom she appeared briefly in an episode of *Spacedrifters*. Sister of . . . wait for it . . ."

"Ray Irons?"

Ava looked so deflated that Neal added, "Lucky guess." It really had been, and he had no idea where it came from.

"I waded through three episodes of that drivel to make this discovery," Ava grumbled. "You could have held off for my big revelation."

Neal smiled. "Good work, Ava. Have you had a chance to follow it up?"

"I went Google mad last night, looking for information on Tara Smythe. There wasn't a lot — she died so young. She was dating Leon when he was in *Spacedrifters*, and it's likely he helped her get her role. Prior to that she'd been modelling, but nothing big time. Her career probably wouldn't have amounted to much, even if she'd lived to pursue it . . ."

Neal nodded.

"So. Here's the interesting bit. Tara died around the time Warrior was dropped from the show. I couldn't find a scrap of information to tie these facts together. Then Ollie told me that George Irons said Warrior had left the series because of some scandal or other. He remembered his father saying something about it. But if Ray Irons did know something, why didn't he go to the police? I guess he'd been in enough trouble with the police by that time. I'll pull up whatever I can on the investigation and see what else I can dig up." She paused. "Warrior's starting to look like a bit of a shit, isn't he, sir?"

"Hunt's given me a preliminary report on Caitlin Forest," said Neal. "Death occurred following multiple stab wounds to the neck and chest. Hunt thinks she probably knew her attacker. There were no defensive cuts to her hands or arms, indicating that she allowed him or her to get up close. She was probably taken by surprise, with no time to react. I'm convinced we're looking at a single killer here, yet the methods used are so different. One seemingly planned and the other risky and random."

"I suppose the killer could be the only factor in play," Ava suggested. "Like, the motives in each case were entirely unconnected, but the first killing unleashed something in the killer's psyche that had lain dormant — a desire to kill or simply seeing killing as a convenient way of getting rid of a problem, or getting what he or she wanted . . ." Ava tailed off.

Neal liked this sort of thinking aloud. He believed it was a creative process that set up new pathways in the brain. Connections could be made and coincidences rationalised.

"Maybe they'd killed before. Killing becomes a response, a solution to a problem, and the method depends on the killer's state of mind at the time. Controlled when there's no overpowering emotion or no sense of urgency, frenzied when strong emotions are involved." Ava hesitated. "Two people in one? Or one person who sometimes loses control . . . like . . . Laurence Brand?"

"Hmm," Neal said. "I'm all for getting into the psyche of the killer, but we're not trained forensic psychologists." Ava looked disgruntled. "Interesting theory, though. But let's just make sure we do the police work before jumping to conclusions."

"Let's see what PJ's come up with on Brand," he said.

Ava tapped on the glass to attract PJ's attention and signalled to her to come inside.

"He has a record," PJ confirmed. "Arrested on two separate occasions for assault. In both cases, he was let off when his victims refused to press charges. But he did submit to a psych evaluation which led to a diagnosis of

142

possible bipolar disorder, though not the severe type. Apparently there are degrees . . ."

"Details?" Neal asked.

"First time, he was in his early twenties. He had a sort of delusional episode and attacked a fellow student at his university during an exam. Apparently he became convinced that the student was reading his mind and stealing his answers. Second occasion was at his last school job. He leapt over the head teacher's desk and tried to throttle him. Two supply teachers managed to restrain him and the head agreed not to press charges as long as Brand resigned. That was five years ago. Brand resigned and was out of work for a couple of years. Then he moved to Stromford and set up his Roman tour business."

"What was the motivation for the second attack?" Neal asked.

"Apparently Brand was delusional again. He thought he was protecting a pupil whom he believed the head was abusing."

"Was he?" Ava asked.

"Not according to the pupil. He'd never even been in the same room as the head. There was no suspicion from any quarter that the head was guilty."

"Thanks, PJ."

"Wow," Ava said after PJ had left Neal's office. "I know, I know. It's not nearly enough to bring him in, but given his record and the fact that he has no alibi . . ."

"Let's not forget Marcus," Neal reminded her.

"No, sir." Ava made for the door. Neal called after her.

"Ava. I trust your date with Dr Agard went well last night?"

Ava coloured.

"PJ mentioned it this morning." Neal didn't add that in fact he had overheard PJ mention it to PC Winters at the water cooler.

"It was good," Ava said.

"Good," Neal said, and suddenly there it was again, that awkwardness between them. After Ava was gone, Neal sat, staring at his computer screen, until he roused himself to stab out an email to DCI George Lowe — an overdue update on the case so far.

* * *

Outside Neal's office, Ava made a face at PJ. "What's up?" her friend asked.

"You. Telling tales about my date with Joel."

"What are you on about? I never mentioned it to anyone — well, except Faye Winters."

"So how does Neal know about it?"

"He must have overheard. I seem to remember him hovering around the water cooler at the time we were talking. Hey, Ava, d'you think he's jealous?" Only a month ago, PJ would have hated the idea, but now she was slowly but surely being won over by Steve Bryce. The DS had been carrying a torch for her for as long as Ava could remember.

"Don't be an idiot, Peej. He's my boss. Even if he did fancy me, he'd be stupid to act on it. And before you say anything, no, I'm not interested in Jim Neal. So no blabbing, okay?"

PJ smirked. "Okay. By the way, I've got the artist's impression of the kid Faye's friend described."

Ava stood behind PJ as she brought the picture up. The face on the screen resembled no one she had come across in the investigation. It was certainly not Marcus Collins. It would be worth checking with Laurence Brand to see if it matched the face he had seen at Leon Warrior's bedroom window. And, of course, they needed Warrior to confirm whether the mystery boy was indeed his lover. It was important that they discover the nature of Gray's relationship with this young man as soon as possible.

"Thanks, Peej. We need to find out who this young man is."

"I'll get on it." They were interrupted by an urgent tapping at Neal's window. The DI was gesticulating at Ava.

"Better see what he wants," Ava said.

"I've just had a call from Gray Mitchell's sister, Carrie Howard. Her flight got in last night and she's eager to speak with us." Leon had already let them know that Mitchell's sister was coming. Apparently she was desperate to learn what had happened to her brother.

"She wanted to know if we could meet her at her hotel. She sounded a bit jet-lagged but insisted she was up to talking to us."

"She's not staying with Leon?"

"Not a big fan, apparently."

* * *

Carrie Howard was staying at a five-star hotel on the Long Hill.

Gray's sister was waiting for them in the bar, where she'd asked them to meet her. It was immediately obvious which of the women in the room was Carrie Howard. She bore no resemblance to her brother, but she was wearing a New York Yankees sweatshirt. She stood at the bar, pouring Budweiser into a glass.

"Carrie Howard?" Neal asked.

"That's me." She looked surprised.

"Inspector Neal. We spoke on the phone." He introduced Ava.

"Well, how d'ya like that?" Carrie said. "I saw you two walking through the door and would have bet my life you were a couple of lovebirds. I'm not often wrong about these things, y'know." She winked at Ava who didn't dare look at Neal.

"Now, can I buy you good folks a drink?"

"I'll get them," Neal said. He signalled to Ava to move Carrie Howard away from the bar.

"Let's have a seat over there," Ava suggested, nodding at an empty table. Carrie filled the double seat along the back wall, her backside too wide for a stool. Her belly pushed against the table and Ava politely pulled it out to give her room.

"I'm sorry for your loss," Ava said.

Carrie nodded, emptying her beer glass in a gulp. "Honey, I lost Gray the day he took up with that asshole, Leon Warrior."

"You didn't like Leon?" Ava asked, glancing at the bar, where Neal was failing to attract the attention of the barman.

"Let's just say we didn't get along," Carrie said.

"We? You mean it was mutual?"

"Uh huh, it sure was. From the minute I set eyes on that man, I knew he was bad news — and he knew I knew it too. I have a gift, you see, young lady. Ever see that movie about the kid who sees dead people?"

Ava's heart sank. "*Sixth Sense*?"

"That's the one. Well, I don't see dead people. I see live people."

"Oh. You mean like you're sort of good at reading people? Summing them up, kind of? Like a psychologist."

Carrie Howard stared at Ava. "I *see* them. You know, right into their souls."

"Ah." Ava hoped that Neal would be stuck at the bar for a bit longer. Long enough for Carrie Howard to stop talking nonsense.

"I have a kind of sixth sense about people, and I could tell Leon Warrior was a bad man. Just like I can tell that you're a good person, and that you're a little troubled right now." Carrie leaned forward. Her chins and neck merged. "On account of *him*." She jerked her head in the direction of the bar. Neal was finally handing a ten pound note to the barman. "He's a good person, too, by the way. That's all I'm sayin', honey. He's coming over."

She leaned back as Neal set down their drinks. Ava hoped the flaky part of their conversation was now over.

146

"How long are you here for, Mrs Howard?" Neal asked. Ava was wondering what Carrie would say next.

"Until after Gray's funeral. I got nothing to rush back for. I'm divorced and my kids are in college out of state."

"You're not staying with Leon Warrior?" Neal asked.

Ava kicked him under the table. "Carrie and Leon don't get on," she said. Then she asked, "Were you surprised that your brother was willing to move here to be with Leon?"

Carrie shrugged. "Gray was besotted. I knew there was nothing I could have said or done to stop him." She shivered. "Gray didn't like to be cold, and he must have hated the weather here after LA." It was the nearest Carrie Mitchell had come to being emotional.

"Were you and Gray close?" Ava asked.

"Used to be."

"Before Leon, you mean?" Ava prompted.

Carrie shook her head. "Before Gray decided he was a homo."

As jaw-dropping moments go, that one was right up there, Ava confessed to Neal later. Neither of them had seen it coming and they stared at Carrie in disbelief.

"I'm a Christian," Carrie said, as if that justified her bigotry. "*You shall not lie with a male as with a woman. It is an abomination.* Leviticus 18:22."

Her voice seemed to resonate around the bar and Ava looked around, embarrassed. To her relief, no heads were turning their way. Then it occurred to Ava that Carrie's words didn't chime with the fact that she'd travelled over five thousand miles to attend her brother's funeral. Though they did explain her dislike of Leon.

"When did Gray come out, Mrs Howard?"

"As a young man, back in the eighties. I warned him God would punish him and all his kind, and he did, didn't he?"

Ava stared at her.

"AIDS," said Neal, icily.

147

"Um . . . Mrs Howard . . ." Ava suddenly had no idea what she had meant to ask.

"Mrs Howard," Neal said. "Why did you ask to speak with us?"

"To tell you Leon Warrior killed my brother."

"Do you have any way of backing up that statement?"

"I know it in here," Carrie Howard said, placing a hand on her breast.

"You mean, in your heart?" Ava said.

"That's right, honey. Like I told you, I *know* people, and I know that man killed Gray."

Neal said, "Mrs Howard, I'd like you to know that we are conducting a thorough investigation into your brother's death. But as I'm sure you can appreciate, we need to be able to back up any accusation with solid evidence."

"You'll find it. The Lord will lead you to it, I know, Inspector Neal."

Ava felt there was little point in carrying on the conversation, but Neal plodded on.

"Were you in regular contact with Gray, Mrs Howard? Did he contact you recently and express any concerns about anything?"

Carrie Howard took a slug of beer and made an exaggerated show of thinking. "We didn't speak all that often. Gray and I had differences of opinion on a lot of things."

No surprise there, thought Ava. Carrie Howard made Ray Irons look tolerant. At least he was up front about his prejudices. Carrie justified hers with religion.

Carrie shook her head. "Nope, can't think of anything." She covered her mouth with her hand to stifle a belch, then yawned loudly. "I'm bushed. Must be jet-lag catching up on me."

More likely the booze, Ava thought.

"I need to use the bathroom," Carrie declared. "I'll get you guys another coke when I get back."

"That's alright, Mrs Howard. We have another appointment." Neal was already standing up.

"Guess I'll go get some shut eye, then. Is that cathedral worth a visit? Might as well do a bit of sightseeing while I'm here."

Neal and Ava assured her that it was indeed worth a visit.

* * *

The minute they were out of earshot, Ava murmured to Neal, "She does know, doesn't she? That her brother fell to his death from 'that cathedral'?"

"I suspect that's part of the attraction," Neal muttered. "Bloody waste of time that was. The woman's a bigot. Probably believes the world was created in six days and evolution's a load of bollocks. Beggars belief, doesn't it?"

Ava agreed. At the station, Neal was sometimes referred to as 'Red Jim,' because of his assumed political beliefs, which no one had actually heard him express. Jim Neal was a deeply guarded man. To Ava, it seemed that much of what was known about her colleague was a mixture of rumour and speculation. The rumours were based entirely on the small crumbs he scattered on the rare occasions when he'd had too much to drink. Even less was known about his personal life, except that he lived with his younger sister and his son. No one knew the truth about Archie's mother and no one dared to ask.

"I'm struggling to understand why she even bothered to come over," Ava said. "I mean, it sounds like there wasn't much love lost between them."

"No doubt she's hoping to profit in some way from Gray's death," Neal said. "I don't know if he and Warrior had a civil partnership. Unless Mitchell made a will, his sister might stand to benefit."

"They have a nice house," Ava said, "but neither of them were A-list actors, and they were running a ghost tour business. That doesn't shout big money to me."

"They weren't A-listers, but both had steady work, especially when they were younger. If they'd saved and invested well, they'd be financially secure. You saw the antiques in that house of theirs."

"Do you think money's a motive in this case?"

"We can't rule it out. If Warrior was tired of Mitchell and wanted him out of the way."

"That scenario makes it less likely that the same person killed Caitlin Forest. Why would Leon want her out of the way? Unless she knew something, but that's unlikely. She'd had plenty of time to speak to the police between Mitchell's death and her own."

Neal had no answers for Ava.

The opening bars of the song, 'Love is in the Air,' sounded out from Ava's pocket — Ollie had been at her phone again. Ava slipped it back unanswered. It was Joel Agard calling her, as he'd promised when they'd parted the evening before. Ava sneaked a look at Neal but he was staring straight ahead. His coat collar was turned up against the biting cold, concealing most of his face. She remembered the awkwardness between them when Joel's name came up earlier and had no desire to reawaken it.

"This case is full of your unknown unknowns, sir. There seems to be a lot of stuff we don't even know we don't know." She wasn't quite sure if what she'd just said made any sense.

Neal turned to her in surprise. "So you *were* listening."

"Don't I always?"

Chapter 15

Neal was feeling a little uncomfortable about interviewing Angie Dent again. She was likely to be still reeling from the death of her best friend, but since she might actually be a suspect, he had no choice.

He was hoping that, as Caitlin's friend, she might be able to offer some insights. He was particularly keen to see if Angie could provide information that would link the deaths of Caitlin and Gray Mitchell.

Neal had opted to interview Angie alone. Ava would follow up on her investigation into Leon Warrior's history with Tara Smythe and Ray Irons. He'd also tasked Ava with visiting Warrior and Brand again and showing them the artist's impression of the young man who had been seen with Gray Mitchell not long before his death.

Maxine Brand smiled faintly at Neal as he walked into the cathedral café. He had arranged to speak with Angie Dent informally at the café. Neal needed to speak with Maxine about her husband's history, possibly after he had talked to Angie Dent. Maxine poured him a coffee, the jug jerking in her unsteady hand.

Angie was fifteen minutes late. She didn't apologise, and even crossed over to the counter to pick up a coffee before joining Neal at his table. She had changed her hair, he noticed. A shorter style that a lot of famous female actors were sporting these days — a pixie cut, he thought it was called. The bubblegum pink was now a smooth, silvery blonde. She had a side parting and a fringe of hair falling over the left side of her forehead, softening the overall look. To Neal, she looked about sixteen, but it was hard to tell. Even when young women were make-up free, as Angie was today, it was difficult to tell how old they were.

"I'm sorry about what happened to your friend," Neal began. "I'm sure you must still be feeling upset and I'll try to keep this brief so that you can get back to work."

Angie nodded.

Neal wasn't sure whether her muttered reply was a "thank you."

"How long had you known Caitlin?" Neal asked.

Again, when she answered, Angie's voice was almost indistinct. Neal had to lean forward to hear.

"About a year. Since I started working in the gift shop. Caitlin came in one day and overhead me saying that I was looking for a place to stay. Her flatmate had just moved out. So I moved in."

"Would you say you got to know her well in that time?"

"Yes. We became good friends. I haven't had a lot of close friends because I moved about a lot when I was at school." She gave a sob and used her napkin to dab away a tear.

"Take your time," Neal said. He noticed the dark circles under Angie's eyes. "Couldn't you take a little time off work?" he asked.

Angie looked shocked. "Oh, no. I couldn't bear to be alone. Believe me it's much better to be around other people at a time like this — for me anyway."

Neal nodded. He asked Angie the usual questions about whether Caitlin had any enemies, whether she'd been behaving differently of late, whether she'd confided in Angie about any problems she was having. Angie's responses were laconic, offering him no new insights.

"You and Caitlin were part of a social circle that included the Brands and Helen Alder, Marcus Collins, Vincent Bone, Gray Mitchell and Leon Warrior, isn't that right?"

She flinched at the mention of Gray Mitchell's name. Neal reminded himself that Angie had lost two friends in less than a week.

"Caitlin had worked here for longer. She was friends with Vincent Bone and Laurence Brand and the rest of them and I sort of got included in their social get-togethers."

Another sob. Maybe Angie was contemplating her whole social network falling apart. Neal hoped she would manage to pick up the pieces, resist the urge she probably felt to pack up and move elsewhere.

Neal was interested in learning more about Caitlin and Gray's friendship. Their murders had been wildly different, yet they had occurred in the same time frame. It had to be more than just coincidence.

"Were Caitlin and Gray particularly close?"

"Yeah, I guess so. Caitlin was a sweet person. Everybody loved her. And Gray was a sweet guy. I think they just sort of recognised the goodness in each other, know what I mean?"

Neal nodded. It was obviously out of the question that Caitlin and Gray were involved in a sexual relationship.

"I think Gray felt sort of protective of Caitlin. He was sort of, not exactly a father figure, maybe more like an uncle?"

That would work, Neal thought. He had trouble forming a mental image of Caitlin. When he tried to recall what she looked like, only the incident room photograph of her dead and bloodied body came to mind.

"Do you think the same person who killed Caitlin, killed Gray?" Angie asked. She was spooning cream off the top of a dessert-style coffee. "Everyone's money's on that homophobic guy Gray had a run in with. But why would he want to kill Caitlin?"

Neal didn't answer.

"Did you know that Caitlin was seeing Marcus Collins?" he asked.

"Everybody knows about that."

"They do now. But did she confide in you?"

"Not exactly, but I guessed, and I think she knew I knew. I don't know why she felt she had to make a big secret of it."

Had Caitlin worried that Angie would disapprove of the relationship? That she would be jealous, perhaps?

He found Angie rather an elusive personality, not unlikeable, just a bit hard to categorise. The morning of Gray Mitchell's death she'd come across as quite an assertive type. Today she seemed almost retiring. And she looked guarded, but he was one to talk.

"I'm scared," Angie suddenly blurted out. "What if the person who murdered Caitlin comes after me too?"

It wasn't a completely irrational fear, Neal thought. He did his best to reassure her, knowing she would continue to worry.

"One more thing, Angie. Did you and Caitlin have a falling out at the party at Gray and Leon's house a few nights before Gray's death?"

Angie looked startled. "Not that I remember," she said.

"Don't worry about it. It's just that one of the other guests thought they saw you having a heated argument. They could have been mistaken."

"I really don't remember. I had quite a lot to drink that night and I felt unwell, so we left early. If someone saw us quarrelling, it was probably over something stupid, you know."

"Not over Marcus, then?"

"Why would we fight over Marcus? Do you think I was jealous or something?" Her eyes widened. "Oh my God! Please tell me you're not thinking I killed Caitlin over Marcus? I thought you were supposed to be a detective? That's the sort of stupid theory a kindergarten kid would come up with."

"It wasn't an accusation. You and Caitlin were friends. It wouldn't be the first time a relationship got in the way of a friendship." He wouldn't have persisted with this if Angie had not reacted so fiercely. She surely must have guessed that this question would be asked.

"I don't have an alibi for when Caitlin was killed. That's something else you can go to town on, isn't it? Why don't you just cuff me right now and be done with it?"

"That won't be necessary."

"Come to think of it, I was with Caitlin the night Gray died and she isn't here to vouch for me now, so why don't you just pin that one on me too?"

"Ms Dent . . . I think we're finished for now. I'm sure you'd like to get back to work."

"Yeah, right. Well, I won't be holding my breath waiting for you to find out who really killed Gray and Caitlin." With that, she stood up, her chair teetering, and headed for the door.

Neal hardly needed to look up. He knew he had an audience. Maxine and Helen Alder were staring at him, their faces both accusing and disapproving.

Maxine came over and sat down opposite him. "That young girl has been through the wringer since she found out her best friend was murdered. You had no right to come in here upsetting her."

"I'm investigating two murders, Mrs Warrior. How would you suggest I proceed?"

At that moment, Helen Alder ramrodded the swing door to the kitchen with a tea tray. She brought it over and plonked it down on the table, in front of Neal and Maxine. As well as tea, Helen had provided scones and cream — comfort food for Maxine, no doubt. Neal was feeling a tad hungry and he reached for a scone, avoiding the cream. He didn't feel want to put on the pounds. Unlike Ava, he was not a big fan of keeping fit.

"Laurie isn't a bad person," Maxine blurted out. "He wouldn't normally behave like that. It's just he's been under a lot of stress this week. Gray Mitchell was a good friend and his . . . murder upset Laurence greatly. My husband isn't a criminal, Inspector."

"We know about the previous incidents when your husband lost control, Mrs Brand. And about his condition." Neal spoke gently, but firmly. He watched her closely. He knew Maxine Brand was at least ten years younger than her husband. He wondered fleetingly what she had seen in Laurence Brand. Perhaps she had been attracted by his helplessness and vulnerability. There were people, nurturing types who were attracted by these characteristics. They were often drawn to the caring professions. Maxine had once been a social worker. It was obvious what Laurence Brand had seen in her. She was curvy, with luxuriant dark curls and a face that, back in Scotland, he would have described as 'bonny.'

"Laurie was stressed then too. I'm not making excuses for his behaviour, Inspector, but he really isn't a violent man. Sometimes he just gets things out of proportion."

"I think your husband has been fortunate that none of his victims pressed charges against him. Otherwise he would almost certainly have had a criminal record by now," Neal said.

Maxine stared miserably at the uneaten scone on her plate. "Laurie has . . . issues, but he's not bad. Gray Mitchell was bipolar too, you know. I think that's why they became such good friends. They understood each other."

She glared at Neal. "And they also understood prejudice, Inspector Neal."

Neal nodded soberly. He knew what she meant. The media was to blame for the general association of mental illness with violence. The truth was that people with these conditions were much more likely to harm themselves than the public.

"I am sympathetic, Mrs Brand. I know that people with mental health conditions are often unfairly treated."

"I suppose you think you're an expert because you've done a half day course on mental illness," Maxine said. From behind the counter, Helen Alder glowered.

"I don't consider myself an expert at all," Neal said. "I have had some training, yes, and yes, it was inadequate, but I also approach my work logically. I look at the facts. And the fact is that your husband has shown himself capable of violent behaviour."

Maxine Brand opened her mouth to protest, but Neal raised his hand. "That's why he is of interest to us. Whether or not he committed a more serious crime . . ."

"You mean did he kill poor Gray and Caitlin Forest?"

There was a pause, and then Neal continued. "Do you think your husband suspects Leon Warrior might have murdered Gray Mitchell? Do you think that's what this episode was all about? Not simply about Warrior having betrayed Gray by taking a lover?"

"I . . . I don't know. Maybe . . ." Maxine answered. "Yes, probably. Laurie's been getting more and more uptight about it ever since Monday morning. He'd probably convinced himself of Leon's guilt and let Caius take over."

"Caius?"

Maxine sighed. "Caius Antonius. Laurie adopts the persona of a retired Roman centurion for his tours. Sometimes, especially if he's stressed about something, Caius kind of . . . asserts himself."

"You mean your husband suffers delusions? He thinks he's a Roman centurion?" Neal asked, exasperated. Why was he only learning this now?

"Um . . . I suppose it could be interpreted that way. I prefer to think of Caius as an aspect of Laurie's personality. And it's not what you think."

"Tell me more about Caius," said Neal.

Maxine was clearly uncomfortable. "Well, Caius is sort of everything that Laurence isn't. My husband is not a very confident person and Caius is brash and a bit arrogant. Where Laurie is placid and perhaps inclined to be self-deprecating, Caius has the heart of a warrior."

Neal thought it was becoming a little clearer why Maxine found her husband attractive. He satisfied her need to nurture and, as Caius Antonius, it was likely that he satisfied her other, more physical, needs.

"Does your husband take his medication, Mrs Brand?"

"Yes. Only sometimes — again when he's unduly stressed — it needs to be reviewed to keep him . . . balanced. Please, Inspector, Caius can be naughty, but I know Laurie can keep him under control. He'd never let him kill anyone."

Naughty. Neal almost laughed out loud. Laurence Brand wasn't the only one who was deluded.

"Mrs Brand, were you aware that on the night she was killed, Marcus Collins asked your husband for advice about his break-up with Caitlin Forest?"

Maxine's hand covered her mouth. "No. Laurie didn't tell me anything about that. I knew something was wrong because Marcus left before his lesson was over. Normally he stays and chats to Laurie for a while afterwards. They kept that quiet, didn't they — Marcus and Caitlin, I mean. I had no idea."

"What was Marcus's emotional state when he left?"

"I didn't see him. Surely you don't suspect Marcus . . ."

158

"Just gathering information, Mrs Brand. You're part of a pretty tight-knit circle of friends, you and your husband. I understand that it's hard for you to imagine that any one of them might be capable of murder. However, it would be unwise to withhold information that might help identify the killer, out of a sense of loyalty. Unwise — and dangerous."

He paused to allow Maxine time to digest what he had said. "You were at Leon and Gray's soirée a couple of weeks ago weren't you, Mrs Brand? Did you notice Caitlin Forest and Angie Dent engage in a heated argument in the course of that evening?"

"No. I can't say I did. You think they were quarrelling over Marcus, don't you? You've really got it in for that boy!"

Neal ignored the comment. "Thank you, Mrs Brand," he said. "I hope your husband's condition improves soon." He tidied their plates onto the tray, gathering up the crumbs and brushing them onto a napkin. Then he followed Maxine to the counter where he handed the tray over to a hostile-looking Helen Alder. She snatched it from him with a curt, 'thanks.'

"Best scone I've had in ages." He was rewarded by a tight-lipped nod.

Outside the café, the weather was crisp and clear. There had been a slight thaw since the middle of the week but not enough to melt much of the snow. At least the Christmas market should go ahead as planned. Weather reports for the weekend predicted freezing temperatures but only a slight chance of more snow. Thankfully the ridiculous rumour about a serial killer on the loose had failed to gather momentum.

The setting for the seasonal market, in Stromford's historic Uphill district, was spectacular. Stalls selling crafts and food spilled out from the castle gates across the wide, cobbled esplanade and into the cathedral precinct.

Neal tended to give the market a wide berth. He disliked crowds as well as the ugly commercialism that seemed to have crept in in recent years. Thieves and pickpockets kept the Stromford police working overtime over the three and a half days the market lasted.

Thankfully the more commercialised area was confined to an area of parkland at the rear of the castle. It housed a children's play area, a pretty walled public garden and a conservatory with exotic plants and fish, which Archie still enjoyed visiting. During the Christmas market, the park was also the site of a sprawling funfair. Neal remembered that he had promised to take Archie this year. Maggie had told him that she'd be going with some friends.

When he reached the west side of the cathedral, Neal looked across at the spot where Gray Mitchell's body had been found under the snow. The only private residences overlooking the area were a row of five Georgian townhouses. The residents had all been questioned. No one had seen or heard a thing on the night Mitchell died.

What sort of noise did a body make hitting the ground at speed, cushioned only by freshly fallen snow? Would Gray Mitchell have had time to scream? Would he have been conscious as he made his terrifying descent? If so, how long had those final moments seemed to Mitchell?

Neal tried to imagine his whole life encapsulated in a few fleeting seconds and thought of Archie, his sister, his parents. And Ava. Abruptly, Neal brought his mind back into focus. There had been people who mattered to Gray Mitchell too. Had one of them killed him?

* * *

Ava had had a busy morning. She had visited Brand and Warrior at the county hospital to show them the artist's impression of the young man Mitchell had been seen with. She'd also followed up on her research into the circumstances surrounding Tara Smythe's death.

"No luck with the picture," she told Neal. "Brand and Warrior couldn't identify him — or they claimed they couldn't. If they were lying, they were pretty convincing. Neither of them showed any sign of surprise or recognition."

"Pity," Neal remarked. He rubbed his hands together. "Is there something wrong with the bloody heating in this place?"

"Er, it's just your room, sir. Cleaner noticed your radiator was leaking when she came in to empty the waste bin earlier, so it's been turned off. Someone was supposed to be bringing one of those portable heaters in."

"Aye, that'll be right." Neal remembered the promised electric fan that never arrived back in the summer.

"I hope your morning was fruitful, sir?"

"It was okay."

Ava whistled softly when he told her about Brand's alter ego, Caius.

"Angie didn't shed much light on anything. She was upset and jumped around a bit. She said she was scared she might be on the killer's hit list. I did get the impression she had some kind of feelings about Caitlin's relationship with Marcus, even though she denied it."

"I can't get my head around why they had to make a secret of it," Ava said. "I mean, two young people — why would they care if anyone knew?"

"Because they worked together?"

"Can't see that being much of a problem — in their line of work, anyway. I mean neither of them was the other's boss, were they?"

There was a short, awkward silence.

"Something to do with Angie, then? She said she and Caitlin were close, maybe Marcus — or Caitlin — thought she'd be jealous," Neal suggested.

"About Caitlin spending time with someone else, or because she had the hots for Marcus herself?" Ava mused.

"Maybe you could look into that?"

Ava nodded. "I've got a bit more info on Tara Smythe. D'you want to hear it now?"

Neal nodded.

"She was Ray Irons' half-sister. She went to the same school as Irons and Leon Warrior. She and Warrior started seeing each other about six months before she died. He got her the part in *Spacedrifters*. Before that, she'd done a few low-key modelling jobs — catalogues mostly."

"Wonder what Ray Irons made of all that?"

"Not hard to guess," said Ava. "Anyway, Warrior and Tara went out for a celebratory drink after winding up the episode Tara appeared in. Both of them were completely wasted when they left the bar. Leon declared himself to be 'rat-arsed' according to the barman, who reported seeing Warrior tossing the keys to Smythe. The barman suggested they leave the keys with him, but Smythe insisted she was good to drive. She wasn't even wearing a seatbelt, sir."

"Was Warrior?"

"Yeah, that's what saved him."

"What year was that?"

"1982."

"Wearing a seatbelt wasn't compulsory until 1983. Plenty of people didn't even bother strapping their kids in, back then," Neal said. "I expect Ray Irons blamed Warrior for his sister's death."

"Well, duh! Sorry, sir, but it's a bit of a no-brainer, don't you think?"

"He didn't need a further reason to hate Warrior, did he? The fact that he suspected Warrior of being gay was reason enough."

"D'you think Warrior dated Tara to get back at Irons for the bullying?"

"Possibly, or he may still have been questioning his sexuality."

"He would have been twenty-one by then. Is that likely?"

"In those days? More so than now, probably."

"It might be worth speaking with Irons again. Wonder why he didn't mention his sister before? I suppose he didn't want to give us any more reason to believe he would kill Mitchell to get at Warrior. He must have known it would all come out, though."

"Warrior wasn't in the next series of *Spacedrifters*, didn't you say? Did you have time to follow up on the reason he was dropped from the series?"

"As a matter of fact, I did," Ava said, smugly. "I managed to track down one of the producers on the show and phoned him. He was very forthcoming, considering he couldn't know if I was really from the police. Anyway, according to him Warrior was an alcoholic. He was becoming a liability. He showed up late on set, fluffed his lines and made a nuisance of himself with other members of the cast. The crash was the last straw. Warrior was very lucky that the whole thing wasn't all over the press. It would be now. He was a minor celebrity and Tara Smythe was a nonentity, so he managed to stay out of the papers. He headed for the US within weeks of the hearing into the crash."

"He must have cleaned up his act in the States, given that he managed to work out there for so long."

"Should we bring Irons in for questioning, sir? He's got motive and opportunity. He was at home alone the night Mitchell died."

Neal thought for a moment. "He's kept his nose out of trouble for the past twenty years. He looked after his sick wife until she died. And, don't forget it was Gray Mitchell who assaulted Irons, not the other way around."

"I suppose he's got more going for him than not as far as the defence would be concerned."

Neal rubbed his hands together again. "See if you or PJ can locate someone who knew Tara Smythe well. A former school friend, whatever. Preferably someone who also knew Warrior and Irons. And good work this morning, Sergeant."

"It wasn't all me," Ava said generously. "PJ helped."

"Then tell her thanks," Neal said, and picked up his phone. "Now, who do I contact about that bloody heater?"

Chapter 16

Marcus Collins stood outside the Brands' house, hand poised to knock, when the door opened inwards. Maxine ushered him in.

"I saw you from the upstairs window."

"How's Laurence?" Marcus asked. He shook off his jacket and handed it to Maxine. He followed her down the hallway, past the study where he had his Latin lessons with Laurence. Past the familiar framed pictures of classical sites. Marcus had stood in front of each one of them while Laurence told him stories about the site. It made Marcus long to visit them one day. In fact, Laurence had suggested that he come along with them next summer.

"He's a bit woozy," Maxine explained. "They're adjusting his medication and it takes time to get it right. I'm just glad to have him home. Oh, Marcus, he could have landed himself in prison!"

Marcus held her while she cried. "It's okay, Maxine, everything's going to be alright." Marcus knew all the right words to use — he had seen plenty of movies. But the words were sincere. He was as fond of Laurence and Maxine as they were of him. They had no children of their own and seemed to regard him as a surrogate son. They had even suggested that he rent one of their spare rooms for a nominal amount. Marcus had turned the offer down because he was seeing Caitlin, and she had insisted on keeping their relationship secret. Marcus thought of Caitlin and wept too. He clung to Maxine, needing her just as much as she needed him.

"I'm so sorry, Marcus," said Maxine. "Here I am hogging all the comfort when you've lost your girlfriend."

"S'okay," Marcus said. "We'd just split up. I sent Caitlin a horrible text message the night she was . . . the night she died and now the police think I . . . they think I . . ."

"Shush," Maxine said. "No one in their right mind would believe a thing like that. You wouldn't hurt anyone." She led Marcus into the kitchen and made him sit down while she poured them both a glass of brandy.

"I don't usually drink spirits," Marcus said, uncertainly.

"All the more reason to drink it now," Maxine said. "It'll calm your nerves." She downed hers in a single swallow, indicating that Marcus should follow suit.

"You know the police suspect Laurie too, don't you? I know they're just doing their job, but it's ridiculous. They should listen to people who know their loved ones and stop wasting their time running around trying to invent stories about innocent people."

"I don't understand how they could suspect Laurence. He's the gentlest person I know."

Maxine reached across the table and took Marcus's hand.

"Bless you," she said. Then she told him about Laurence's past 'episodes,' including some that the police didn't know about.

"Wow," Marcus said when she had finished. "I can't imagine Laurence doing anything like that. And the whole

Caius thing? I thought it was all a bit of a laugh, not part of an illness."

"Well, I like to think of my husband as a bit eccentric rather than delusional. Reducing a person's personality to a syndrome is demeaning, don't you think? I'm also convinced that Laurie is actually stronger than Caius. He'd stop him going too far."

Marcus was feeling a bit overwhelmed, but he understood that Maxine needed someone to sound off to. Who better than another suspect?

"I'm sorry for going on, Marcus. I've already had a heart to heart with Helen and she's coming around this evening. She's a good friend. I don't know what I'd do without her."

As if on cue, the doorbell rang and Helen Alder's voice boomed down the hallway. "Alright if I come in?"

Before Maxine could answer, Helen burst into the kitchen. She stopped and raised a questioning eyebrow. Marcus and Maxine were still holding hands. The bottle of brandy sat on the table next to their empty glasses.

"Come and join us," Maxine said. "I'm starting a new society — friends of the unjustly accused."

"Maybe I should go and see Laurence now?" Marcus stood up.

"Of course," Maxine said, also getting to her feet — a little unsteadily. Evidently she had needed more than one glass of brandy to calm her nerves.

"It's okay," Marcus said. "I can find my way."

"Second door on the left," Maxine said. "Take a look at the one on the right as well. It's the one we were offering to rent to you."

Marcus nodded and made his way upstairs. He tapped softly on the door to the Brands' bedroom. There was no response. He pushed the door open a crack to peer inside.

Marcus was expecting darkness, but the bedside lamp on Laurence's side of the bed was on and tilted towards Laurence. It lit up his face, as well as the book that had slipped from his hand. "Laurence?" Marcus whispered. He wasn't sure whether to wake his friend. He stood, taking in the high ceiling and wide bay and the mirrored wardrobes running along one whole wall. There were more pictures of classical scenes on the walls and a replica Greek vase overflowing with flowers on a dresser by the window. Perhaps it would be worth having a peek at the spare room, Marcus thought.

Laurence stirred. "Maxine, is that you?"

"It's me, Marcus. I've come to see how you are."

Laurence pulled himself up. He was wearing striped pyjamas and had a tasselled dressing gown around his shoulders. His thinning grey hair was sticking out at all angles.

"You look like Einstein," Marcus said, grinning.

"I look a bloody mess and I'm the meds they've given me. But at least I've lost the impulse to chuck a brick at Leon Warrior, so I suppose that means they're working."

"I didn't know . . ."

"That I'm a nutter?" Laurence said. "Certifiable lunatic. Shouldn't be allowed out. I could have killed Leon."

"But you didn't."

"No, I didn't. By the time the police arrived I was coming to my senses. A brick to the side of the head will do that to you."

"Was it just the brick?"

"You mean, was I in control? Not when I threw the brick, but I don't think I would have caused Warrior any further harm."

"Why . . ?"

"I got all worked up after seeing Warrior with that boy and thinking he'd cheated on Gray. It kind of escalated to convincing myself that Leon killed him. I meant to confront Leon and get him to admit the truth. I didn't mean to harm him."

"I believe you."

"And I believe you had nothing whatsoever to do with Caitlin Forest's death. All we need to do now is convince the police that we're telling the truth."

"Easier said than done," Marcus said. "Does it hurt?" He pointed to the dressing on the side of Laurence's head.

"Not as much as my pride, and not as much as I deserve. So, Marcus, where did you go after leaving here that evening?"

Marcus explained. Laurence shook his head when Marcus told him about the message.

"Mobile phones are a blessing and a curse. Alcohol and texting are a toxic mix."

"I wish I could take it back. Not because it makes me look guilty, but because of what happened to poor Caitlin." Marcus choked.

"*Errare humanum est* (to err is human)," Laurence said softly. Wearily.

"We know we aren't killers," Marcus said fiercely. "So we need to help the police find the real killers. But how?"

Laurence squinted at his pupil. "Promise me you won't go getting yourself into trouble, lad. Let the police do their job." Laurence's words were slurred now. His head was nodding and his eyelids were beginning to droop.

Marcus sighed. He went downstairs. Through the half-open door to the kitchen, he could hear Maxine and Helen talking. Not wishing to disturb them, Marcus pulled his jacket from the coat stand and let himself out.

The more Marcus thought about his last meeting with Caitlin, the more he became convinced that she had not, in fact, grown tired of him. She couldn't have just switched off her feeling for him that abruptly, unless she had been pretending all along. He and Caitlin had been together for only a few months. Even if it was simply sexual attraction, she should have wanted him for longer than that.

Okay, there was the age gap, but Caitlin hadn't cared about that. Relatives and friends had always commented that Marcus was older than his years. Look how well he got on with Laurence Brand and Gray Mitchell. He had always preferred the company of older people. Girls his own age had always seemed silly and immature — all that giggling and shrieking.

He had fancied Caitlin for weeks before he'd plucked up the courage to ask her out. Then he had asked so quietly that she had had to ask him to repeat his words. He had almost lost his nerve. And she knew very well what he had said. It was the only time he could remember her being cruel, until she had broken up with him in the gardens of the Applewhite.

Now that she was dead, Marcus felt that he had betrayed her. It wasn't just because he sent that cruel text message. He had allowed Laurence to convince him that he should accept the situation and move on. Now he felt that if he had gone to Caitlin, pleaded with her to tell him the real reason why she wanted to end their relationship, she would still be alive. Marcus was convinced of this.

Marcus tried to think of reasons why Caitlin would want to finish with him. He thought about it until his head hurt. In the end, he decided to draw up a list: Either Caitlin had never fancied him (unlikely). Or she really had tired of him that quickly (again, unlikely). Or he had done something to put her off him (nothing he could think of). Or — and this was the most plausible explanation — some unknown person or thing had come between them.

What then? The age difference? Another man or woman? Fear? Was she trying to protect him? This one intrigued him. Who would he need protecting from? Someone Caitlin knew would be the obvious choice. But who?

How well had he known Caitlin, really? She disliked speaking about her past and never mentioned her childhood. If Marcus pressed her for details, she would talk about her schooldays in a vague way, as though they had taken place in another country.

"The past is a foreign country; they do things differently there." It was a favourite quote of Laurence's. Marcus wasn't sure he understood it completely, but it seemed to resonate with Caitlin's accounts of her childhood. When he asked her about school she would say something like, "Oh, I don't remember anything except the cold. It always seemed to be snowing then."

Marcus couldn't remember that much snow when he was a child. When he was five years old, Caitlin would have been twelve. Marcus had received a toboggan that Christmas and it seemed like there was hardly ever enough snow to use it. To hear Caitlin, you'd think it had snowed for months on end every year of her childhood.

Still, memory was shaky and unreliable. Marcus knew this from talking with Laurence and Gray, Vincent and his other older friends. How many times had he listened to Laurence and Vincent Bone argue about when a certain song had been 'top of the pops' (whatever that was). When Marcus googled the facts on his smartphone he had proven both of them wrong.

Marcus began to think he might be catching some of Caius's anger. He resented being considered a suspect. If the police weren't going to act, maybe he should do some investigating of his own.

* * *

The downstairs window of Leon Warrior's house had been repaired. Maxine had asked him to send the bill to her but Leon had paid cash. Maxine had visited him in hospital, full of apologies and explanations and excuses for her husband's behaviour. Leon had reassured her that he did not intend to press charges. He said that he was sympathetic to Laurence's condition, having lived with a man who suffered from bipolar disorder. He had known, of course, about Laurence's illness. Unlike Gray, Laurence had not been open about his illness. Gray had suspected that he was ashamed of it. He had been counselling

Laurence to be more accepting of his condition. Gray had dealt with his own illness in the same way as he acknowledged his sexuality. It was simply a part of who he was. Bless him, he had never complained, Leon thought. He looked at the beautiful boy sleeping beside him. One day, probably quite soon, the boy would find someone younger and more attractive.

Leon had been shocked to hear that Gray had been seen in the company of a young man. The thought that his lover might have been unfaithful was more painful than he could ever have imagined. Leon had often been unfaithful over the years. Only now did he understand what it felt like to be betrayed. With a start, Leon realised that he had never loved anyone the way he had loved Gray. That beautiful, gentle man had truly been the love of his life.

Leon wished he could ask for forgiveness. His young lover stirred and rolled onto his back. He looked at Leon's tears, reached out and touched his cheek, then slowly, seductively, licked his wet, salty fingers. He placed his other hand on Leon's thigh.

A sudden rage took hold of Leon. "Get out!" he screamed.

The young man withdrew his hand and looked at him.

"Get. Out." Leon turned away so that he would not see Godfrey slipping, naked, out of his bed and gathering his discarded clothes from the floor. He did not want his resolve to weaken.

Leon stayed in bed until he heard the door slam shut downstairs and the garden gate squeak once on its rusted hinges — the young man did not bother to close it behind him. Leon hauled himself up and took a long, hot, purging shower.

All morning Leon skirted around the drinks cabinet in his living room. After all these years, he was discovering the truth that an alcoholic was never really cured. Then, just as he was about to grab the bottle, he changed his mind. He needed to find out more about Gray's mystery man.

The police had searched his house thoroughly in the days following Gray's death. They had found nothing. It occurred to Leon that he was much better placed than the police to uncover any signs of Gray's secret life. He let go of the scotch bottle.

Leon went upstairs and began a systematic search of Gray's possessions, beginning with his clothes. By the time he was finished, their walk-in closet resembled the aftermath of an upmarket rummage sale. All he had discovered were a few Hershey bar wrappers in the pocket of a jacket Gray hadn't worn since they left California.

He turned his attention to credit card receipts and bills, all of which the police had already examined meticulously. The police had informed him that Gray had met with his mystery man at the Barley Inn. If so, he must have paid with cash and thrown away the receipts. All Leon managed to come up with was a ticket stub for a play at the Tithe Barn. This was puzzling, but not damning.

After a couple of hours of fruitless rifling, Leon was ready to give up. At least his rummaging had kept him away from the bottle. As he reached once more for the scotch, the doorbell sounded. He sidestepped around the furniture, holding close to the wall in case another brick came crashing through the window. He didn't dare approach the window in the hallway either, so the unwelcome sight of Gray's sister, Carrie Howard, floored him completely.

"Carrie. What a surprise . . . Er, come in."

"Hello, Leon. I've told at least three people I'm coming here and they all have instructions to call the police if I'm not back at my hotel by two o'clock this afternoon. So don't go thinking you can just go bumping me off like you did my brother." Carrie stomped into the hallway.

"What on God's earth are you talking about, Carrie?"

"And you can quit with the toffee-nosed English accent, Leon. It never worked on me. You're no more upper class than I am."

"What do you want, Carrie?"

"Drink would be nice," Carrie answered. "I'll have what you're having."

"I don't . . ."

"I can smell it on you, Leon. Besides, it takes one to know one." She tapped her nose.

Wordlessly, Leon led her into the living room and poured them both a scotch.

"So?" Carrie demanded.

Leon raised his eyebrows.

"Why'd you do it?"

"If by 'it,' you're insinuating that I killed Gray, then you're even wackier than Gray said."

"You're full of shit, Leon Warrior. I know Gray would never bad mouth me. Too full of the milk of human kindness or whatever bullshit he used to come out with when he was rehearsing his lines." She downed her drink and held out her glass.

"Same old Carrie."

"You betchagoddamlife I am! A leopard don't change its spots." She stared pointedly at Leon.

"I didn't kill Gray."

"The hell you didn't."

"Believe what you like, Carrie. Why the hell would I kill the person I loved more than anything in this world?"

Carrie laughed. "You haven't lost the person you love more than anything in this world, Leon. He's standing right in front of me."

"I'll ask you again, Carrie. What do you want?"

Carrie reached into her handbag and extracted a white envelope addressed to her.

Leon recognised Gray's writing instantly. "What's this?" he asked, resisting the urge to snatch the envelope from her. He didn't need to. Carrie handed it over.

"You might want to sit down before you read it."

Leon ignored this. He saw from the date on the envelope that Gray had posted the letter two weeks before his death — just before Leon had taken his trip to London.

"Surprised he kept in touch with me, are you? I never approved of Gray's sexual leanings, but he was still my brother and I loved him. It was natural he'd turn to me in his hour of need and, as a good Christian I couldn't turn my back on him."

Leon's legs began to quiver and the paper shook in his hand. Leon understood immediately why Gray had chosen to communicate via snail mail rather than email. Gray had not been so trusting after all. After a couple of paragraphs of news, Gray revealed the true purpose of his letter:

> *For reasons I do not intend to go into now, I have decided to leave Leon and return to the States. I recently received an invitation from my old acting friend, Melissa Carter, to join her travelling theatre company as assistant director and actor and . . . I have a favour to ask of you . . . buying land . . . transferring the payment to your account . . .*

Leon could scarcely believe what he was reading. Only the sight of Carrie Howard's sneering face stopped him from sinking to the floor and burying his head in his hands. It took every scrap of his acting ability to try and conceal his feelings. Even so, he could not control the physical signs. A slow smile was overtaking the sneer on Carrie's face.

"I can see you weren't expecting that." She held out her a hand for the letter. "Gray finally came to his senses and saw you for the phoney rat you are."

For the second time that day, Leon yelled, "Get out!"

But Carrie Howard wasn't finished. "This house, all your savings, everything. It's all going to be mine when you're arrested for murdering my brother." She had moved close to Leon. Instead of throttling her, he repeated his order to get out. She stuffed the letter back in her bag and turned on her heel.

Leon watched her lumbering down the pathway to the still-open gate. She didn't close it behind her either. Leon ran outside and slammed it shut so violently that the whole fence shuddered.

* * *

Neal and Ava drew up outside Ray Irons' house for the second time in as many days. This time the snow had all but disappeared and the path to his doorway was less treacherous.

Irons answered his door sporting a festive jumper with a picture of a red-arsed Santa pissing against a Christmas tree.

"Classy jumper," Ava whispered to Neal.

Ripper was barking from the kitchen and Irons asked if they minded if he let the dog in. He assured them his pet wouldn't hurt a fly. The dog was surprisingly well-trained. After some initial tail chasing and a couple of attempts to sniff Ava's crotch, he followed Irons into the living room and settled down at his feet. Uninvited, Neal and Ava also sat down.

"What can I do you for this time?" Irons asked, stroking the dog's muzzle.

"Why did you not tell us that Leon Warrior once dated your sister, Mr Irons?" Ava said.

Irons shrugged. If the question made him uncomfortable, he didn't show it. "Never thought it was relevant."

"We've seen the reports of the accident Tara and Warrior were involved in. Mr Irons, did you blame Leon Warrior for what happened to Tara?"

"You're kidding me, ain't you? Who else would I blame?"

On the journey to Irons' house, Ava had wondered why Irons had taken no action against Leon Warrior. He had not been charged with threatening or assaulting Warrior. He had also failed to make a statement at the hearing into Tara Smythe's death. There had to be a reason. Irons wasn't the sort of person to let something like that go.

"Why didn't you confront Warrior about your sister's death? You already hated him for going out with her. I can't believe you would just let Leon off the hook if you believed he was responsible for Tara's death."

"My sergeant's right, Mr Irons," said Neal.

"What did Leon Warrior have on you?" Ava said.

"What are you getting at? That poofter had nothing on me."

Ava saw that now Irons seemed more afraid than angry. All of a sudden she thought she knew the reason.

"We can always ask Leon, Mr Irons. *He's* completely at ease with his sexuality."

Ava could see Neal's astonishment. She didn't blame him. It had only just occurred to her. Irons' obvious discomfort convinced Ava that she was on the right track. Ray Irons was deeply in denial about his own sexuality. She had heard that homophobes are often repressed homosexuals, in deep denial about their own sexuality.

"Leon Warrior knew, didn't he? I bet he used that knowledge to his advantage at school when he realised that you weren't able to cope with your feelings for other boys. Leon told people that he was bullied. He told Gray that you had bullied him because of his sexuality, and maybe that was true, but I suspect Leon was a bit of a bully himself. Am I right, Mr Irons?"

Irons just stared at her.

Neal threw in something else. "Did he catch you engaging in some kind of sexual act with another boy? Or did you and Leon—?"

Neal never finished his sentence. Irons was out of his chair in a flash. Ripper gave a yelp of pain as his master stood on one of his paws. It was only Irons' concern for his pet that prevented him moving on Neal before he could dodge out of the way. As it was, Irons landed on the sofa beside Neal and lunged in his direction. Ava winced as Neal deflected a punch with his forearm. He yelled at Irons to back off. All the while, Ripper was growling and tugging at the leg of Neal's trousers.

"Can we have a bit of calm here!" Neal said.

"Ripper. Here." Irons commanded. The dog quieted immediately and sat by its master. "Good dog." Irons stroked the little terrier until it calmed and lay down at his feet. It was almost touching.

"Want me to cuff him, sir?"

"That won't be necessary, Sergeant. As long as Mr Irons restrains himself and keeps his dog under control."

"You bloody provoked me, mate! You was totally out of order."

Neal paused, then cautioned Irons for using abusive language to a police officer.

"Typical, ain't it? I'm the one who's a victim here and I get a warning for defending myself."

Ripper emitted a sympathetic whimper.

"But I think my sergeant was right, wasn't she, Mr Irons? Unless there's some other reason why you didn't go after Warrior?"

Ava braced herself for another stream of invective, but Irons seemed to be exhausted. He leaned back in his soft leather sofa.

"I could've had him put away for manslaughter," he said, a tell-tale quiver in his voice. "That bastard boasted he was fondling her tits and distracted her so she lost control of the car."

Ava and Neal exchanged looks. "He actually confessed that to you?" Ava said. "Why would he do that?"

"Getting back at me for the bullying, and because he knew I wouldn't say anything. Anyway, it would have been his word against mine if I'd tried to make anything of it."

He stared at Ava, and she knew she had been right.

"Satisfied?" Irons said.

Ava felt a pang of sympathy for him then. She saw that he too, was a victim. Then again, he had done some very bad things.

"You taking me in, then? Only I need to make arrangements for Ripper."

"If it was Warrior dead instead of Gray Mitchell, I might consider it," Neal answered. He stood up. "Ripper's safe for the time being."

Back outside, Ava said, "You don't think he did it, do you?"

Neal didn't answer until they reached the car. "As I've said countless times, what I think doesn't matter. It's what can be established from the evidence and the facts that counts. And for now, that's not a great deal."

Chapter 17

"Angie!" Marcus called.

Angie Dent was leaving the workshop for her afternoon break. "D'you fancy a walk?" Marcus said. "I thought we could talk about . . . you know?"

"Caitlin?"

"Yeah. I know you're missing her a lot and I thought maybe I could, you know, kind of . . . help." This wasn't going well. He should have rehearsed what he wanted to say instead of trying to wing it.

"I'm still finding it a bit weird that you two couldn't have told me you were seeing each other. I mean, I was Caitlin's best friend."

"Yeah, well, I'm sorry about that. It was just that we didn't want too many people to know, what with us working at the same place. We thought it might have been kind of awkward."

"I'm not 'many people,' Marcus. You guys were my friends."

Although Angie hadn't agreed to a walk, they had fallen into step together. Marcus steered them towards the cathedral. It didn't take long to reach the spot where Gray's body had been found.

"I walk past here every day," Marcus said. "First Gray, now Caitlin. Do you think there's any connection?"

Angie shrugged. "Who would want to kill either of them? Gray was a lovely man and Caitlin . . . well, you loved her too, so I don't need to tell you what Caitlin was like."

"We broke up," Marcus said. "The day before . . . Caitlin died . . . she told me she didn't want to go out with me anymore."

Angie stopped dead. She placed a hand on Marcus's arm, "I'm sorry, Marcus. That must be hard. I'm sorry for being selfish. We've both lost someone we cared about." She gave a sniff.

"Hug?"

"Okay." T

hey held tightly to each other. To anyone passing by they would have looked like a couple of lovers in a happy embrace. When Marcus released her, he was aware of Angie's reluctance to be let go. They shuffled apart, both standing awkwardly, hands stuffed in their jacket pockets.

"Thanks," said Angie. "That helped."

"It helped me too," Marcus said, smiling at her. Angie smiled back.

She looked much prettier without her pink hair, Marcus thought. Caitlin had told him that Angie would be jealous if she knew about their relationship. She was a possessive friend and she fancied Marcus herself. Marcus had sensed it, of course. Angie had flirted with him on many occasions, often when Caitlin was around. Sometimes he'd even flirted back, but for some reason it amused Caitlin rather than upset her. It was as though she was having a laugh at Angie's expense. Or had it been at his? Marcus had to admit that when he'd begun his apprenticeship at the cathedral and met Caitlin and Angie, he'd liked them both.

Marcus generally considered women to be savvier than men, particularly when it came to all that touchy feely stuff about emotions and relationships and the like. So he had accepted that Caitlin knew what she was talking about, and that she had sound reasons for keeping their relationship a secret. Now Marcus wanted to know why it had been such a big deal. Angie Dent seemed to him to be the obvious place to start. Trouble was he needed to get to know her better. He cleared his throat.

"I know this is going to sound a bit weird, Angie, but I was wondering if maybe we could go for a drink later and have a chat?"

Angie stared at him. She was clearly surprised and Marcus worried that she might think he was making a move on her. They had walked all around the cathedral and were almost back at the workshop.

"You want to talk about Caitlin," she said quietly.

Marcus was sure he could detect disappointment, resentment even, in her tone. "Caitlin and I broke up. She made it pretty clear she didn't want to see me again. Even though I'm grieving, I'm feeling kind of conflicted. She told me she didn't have any feelings for me anymore."

Marcus made what he hoped was his best wounded puppy face. The girls at school had always found it cute and irresistible. Angie wavered, looking at him closely, shifting from foot to foot and clearly feeling unsure herself. Then she put her hand on his cheek.

"Okay. But, just for a talk. You're still on the rebound and I don't want to be your temporary fix."

Marcus covered her hand with his and nodded. At that moment, Vincent Bone appeared at the door to the workshop. He frowned, and reminded them that their break was over, something he almost never did. Marcus felt embarrassed. He didn't want to lose the respect of a man he held in high regard. While everyone now knew about his relationship with Caitlin, he was pretty sure they didn't know that Caitlin had dumped him the night she was killed. He was also pretty sure that the police hadn't told anyone about the text he'd sent to Caitlin.

"Call me," Angie whispered, and pulled her hand away.

* * *

Saturday morning. It was eight thirty. Neal turned into the leisure centre car park and glanced in the rear-view mirror. Archie was sitting in the back seat, frantically pressing buttons on his 3DS.

"This isn't looking good," Neal said.

"What? Oh." The car park was empty. The few vehicles in sight were turning around and heading for the exit. Usually on a Saturday morning the place would be swarming with vehicles coming and going as parents brought carloads of kids for their swimming lessons.

"Is the pool closed?" Archie asked, yawning.

"Good deduction, Sherlock. Sit tight while I ask the guy by the door."

He returned a couple of minutes later. "Boiler's broken. Pool's lukewarm at best and there's no hot water in the showers. Apparently they put something on their website about it last night."

"Aaaw maaaan!" Archie groaned. He enjoyed his Saturday lesson.

"We could go to the pool at the Academy."

"I hate that pool, and the changing rooms are rubbish. There's no cubicles." Archie was just beginning to be self-conscious about undressing in front of others. "Anyway, it's always lessons at this time on a Saturday morning. We wouldn't get in."

"Breakfast?" Neal said. It was their other Saturday morning ritual. Breakfast at one of the cafés at the bottom end of the Long Hill, usually after Archie's swim. Later in the day Neal would be working but he always tried to keep this part of the weekend free for Archie.

Neal drove along Greenwell Road, one of the main routes on the north side of the city. At this time of the morning there was hardly any traffic. To avoid the city's hefty car-parking charges, Neal left the car at the top of the hill and they walked in the direction of the cathedral. As they passed the west front, Archie asked Neal to show him the exact spot where Gray Mitchell's body had landed. Neal pointed at the grassed area and reminded Archie to be respectful.

"Remember that cool medieval jousting tournament that we saw back in the summer holidays?" Archie said.

They passed through a stone arch leading to the cobbled square between the cathedral and the castle. Neal smiled, remembering his son's enthusiasm for the event.

"Where are we eating this week?" He always left the choice to Archie.

"Mattie's?" Archie said. The café was on a side street near the bottom of the Long Hill where the High Street began. It had been Archie's choice for the previous three weeks.

"They'll be surprised to see us so early."

The morning delivery was arriving just as they came in the door. Neal and Archie headed for their usual table, stopping at the counter to say good morning to the manager. Susan was standing on a steep ladder leading down to the basement storeroom. Neal suspected that this was what attracted his son to Mattie's café. The first week they had visited, the morning delivery had been late and they had seen the trap door to the basement lifted up for the first time. Archie had shown so much interest that Susan had allowed him and Neal to climb down and take a look at the basement, which was as big as the café upstairs. Neal was already familiar with it. A couple of years ago, when Mattie's had been a butcher's shop, he had climbed down the same ladder to view the butcher's body, which was lying in a pool of blood and sawdust, a meat cleaver embedded in his chest.

"I'll be with you in a jiffy," Susan called, disappearing down the hatch. She was telling the delivery man that she'd just got back from a fortnight in Alicante and was reacclimatising to the cold.

At last she was ready to take their order. Neal ordered coffee and a croissant for himself and a big breakfast for Archie.

"Shocking business all these murders, isn't it, lovey?" Susan remarked when she brought their order over. "So close to the Christmas market, too."

She had no idea Neal was a police officer and he wasn't about to enlighten her. He glared at Archie, to indicate he shouldn't give him away.

"He came in here sometimes, Mr Mitchell, the man they found up at the cathedral. Nice man, very polite. He liked my coffee. He used to come in with a young man, a young acting hopeful, I think. He was telling me he was in a play at the Tithe Barn Theatre. Gray was giving him some acting tips. They liked to sit upstairs where it was quiet and they had a view of the street."

Neal stared at her. He knew for a fact that one of his uniformed officers had crossed Mattie's off during the door to door search of places likely to be visited by Gray Mitchell. But Susan had been on holiday. She wouldn't have seen the artist's impression of the young man Mitchell had been seen with at the Barley Inn.

As soon as Susan moved away from their table, Neal whipped out his phone and sent a text to Ava. He asked her to send him a copy of the artist's drawing and to obtain programmes for recent plays at the Tithe Barn. Even if there was no picture of Gray's mystery man on the programme, they should be able to find someone at the Tithe Barn who could identify him from the artist's impression.

When Susan returned with their food, he showed her the picture.

"Is this the young man you saw with Mr Mitchell?"

"That's him," Susan said. She looked at Neal. "Are you a policeman?"

"He's a Detective Inspector!" Archie piped up.

"Is that young man the killer?" Susan asked, alarmed.

"No, just someone we need to talk to," Neal answered quickly. "I can't tell you anything more."

"That's alright. My brother's a copper. He's in the Met. I know all about being discreet." She beamed at Neal. "You let me know when you've finished that drink, lovey. It's bottomless coffee for you from now on."

"Good choice of eating place," whispered Neal to Archie when Susan moved away from their table.

Archie grinned. No doubt he thought Neal was referring to the food.

* * *

Neal dropped Archie at home at lunchtime and drove straight to the station. He couldn't wait to speak with Ava.

He found her at her desk, surrounded by theatre programmes. "Any joy?"

"Yes, sir. I called round at the Tithe Barn just after I got your text this morning. I showed the front of house manager our picture and she recognised our mystery man immediately."

"Did you get a name?"

Ava nodded.

"Nathan Elliott. Seventeen years old. Doing A levels at the grammar school, would you believe? Ollie knows him. He's a friend of George Irons, Ray Irons' son."

Ray Irons. Again. The man's name kept coming up, yet Neal still resisted seeing him as their killer.

"What else did Ollie say?"

"That's all. But . . ." Ava paused. "Nathan's coming over this afternoon. Ollie rang him up and asked if he could come over and help with a maths problem. We can go there now and ask Nathan a few questions."

"Nice work, Sergeant."

186

"Hell, yeah!"

Neal half-expected her to try to high-five him the way Archie was always doing. He was relieved when she restrained herself.

"I'll take my own car, then you don't need to come back here afterwards . . . I'm sure you have plans for the evening." Neal managed not to make it sound like a question, but he was fishing and Ava wasn't likely to miss the implication.

"I'm seeing Joel. He's off until Sunday evening, so we thought we'd drive to the Wrenwood and stay over."

Neal forced a smile. It was difficult. The Wrenwood was a country house built at the turn of the twentieth century in the style of a Jacobean mansion. Neal had dined there once, with Jock Dodds. They had sat in a glorious oak-panelled dining-room with views over acres of gardens and woodland.

"Ready, sir?"

"Aye," Neal said, quietly. "I'll see you there."

* * *

Ava's lonely cottage was four miles out of Stromford and set back from the road in a copse with only a few other cottages. None of these were less than a quarter of a mile away from Ava's. The last time Neal had visited he had arrived to find her trying to staunch the blood flowing from the neck of a suspect she'd just stabbed with a pair of kitchen scissors. He was counting on less drama this time around.

Through an avenue of trees leading to Ava's cottage, Neal saw his sergeant's new Ford Fiesta already parked near her front door. He pulled in and parked alongside it.

Ava had left the door open and Neal walked inside to a delicious aroma of baking. Ava had told him that Ollie was a keen cook. Neal thought it an unusual hobby for a boy his age. Maggie was a big fan of *Bake Off* but Neal found the nation's enthusiasm for the show perplexing.

Now there was no one bleeding out on Ava's sofa, Neal had time to take in her living room. The décor was a mixture of the contemporary and the traditional. The sofa was new, he noted. He wondered if she had claimed for it on her house insurance. It would have made for an interesting claim. All that blood.

Ava emerged from the kitchen. "Make yourself at home, sir. Can I get you a drink? Ollie, come and say hi."

A young man popped his head around the opening and gave Neal a wave. If Neal hadn't known they were brother and sister, he would have thought they were unrelated. Chalk and cheese, his mother would have said. Nor did the difference end with their appearance — one dark, one fair. Ollie seemed to lack Ava's confidence and self-assurance.

"Tea, please." Neal made for a long oak table that seemed to be a hub for police work and homework. There was a laptop at either end and a collection of textbooks and papers opposite what Neal recognised as Ava's notebooks. He positioned himself somewhere between the two.

"Nathan will be here soon," Ava said, handing Neal a mug of tea and a slice of cake. "Ollie's been baking." She shouted into the kitchen. "What's this one called again, bro?"

"Chocolate and vanilla marble loaf cake! It's Mary Berry's recipe."

Ava shrugged. "It's a cake. I'll eat it." She took a generous bite.

They heard the sound of a motorbike outside and Ollie came out of the kitchen, dressed in a striped chef's apron.

"That'll be Nathan," he said, heading for the door. Neal and Ava exchanged glances. A lot was riding on what Nathan Elliot would have to say.

Ollie and Nathan high-fived each other on the doorstep and spoke for a few minutes. A couple of times

Nathan looked over at Neal and Ava and nodded his head. Neal wasn't sure how much Nathan knew about the real purpose of his visit. He hoped it wasn't a complete ambush.

"Ollie's already told him why we're here," Ava said.

The introductions over, Ollie and Nathan sat down opposite Neal and Ava. Neal opted to let Ava do the interview.

"Nathan, we know that you were acquainted with Gray Mitchell, the man who was murdered a couple of weeks ago up at the cathedral." Nathan nodded. "Can you remember the last time you saw Gray?"

"On the fifteenth. We went to Mattie's . . . I, er, didn't want to risk any of my friends seeing me with Gray."

Neal was interested that it was that way around. He'd thought it had been Mitchell who didn't want to be seen.

"Why was that, Nathan?" Ava asked gently.

Ollie, Neal noted, was staring at his hands.

"Because, well, you know, because . . ." Nathan looked to Ollie for support, but Ava's brother said nothing.

"Because Gray Mitchell was gay?" Ava prompted.

"I'm not prejudiced," Nathan said hastily.

"It's alright. Everything you say to us is completely confidential." Ava looked at Ollie, who nodded. "How did you meet Gray Mitchell?"

"George Irons introduced us."

"And how did George Irons know him?"

"He got in touch with him after Gray decked his dad."

This was intriguing. Now Mitchell and Irons were connected in an entirely new way.

"Was Gray Mitchell counselling you about your sexuality, Nathan?" Ava asked, again very gently.

Nathan blushed bright red.

"Yeah." He looked sideways at Ollie, who shrugged in a 'no big deal to me' manner.

"George wanted to apologise to Gray for his father's behaviour, even though his dad was the one who got hurt. George was angry at his dad — he thought he was totally out of order having a go at Leon Warrior. George is nothing like his dad."

"I take it George mentioned that he had a friend who was confused about his sexuality and Gray volunteered to help?"

"Yeah. George is a good mate. We've known each other since junior school."

"And you and Gray met — how many times?"

"About five or six times, in coffee shops mostly. Once we went to the Barley."

"Who else knew that you were meeting Gray?"

"No one. I didn't want anyone to know and I asked Gray not to tell anybody, not even his partner, Leon."

"Okay. So you never met Leon or any of Gray's friends?"

Nathan shook his head.

"I need to ask you something a little delicate, Nathan. Is it okay if Ollie stays or would you prefer him to go upstairs?"

"He can stay."

"Okay. I need you to understand that you should not talk about this with anyone else, alright?" Ava looked from Nathan to her brother. They both agreed.

"Did you ever tell Gray that you were feeling depressed or suicidal, Nathan?"

Nathan stared at her. Then, very quietly, he answered, "Yes."

Ava nodded.

"The first time we met I told him I was ashamed and scared and that I didn't know if I could face living either as an openly gay person, or as a person who had to pretend to be something he wasn't. I was pretty fu . . . messed up. George was worried about me."

"And Gray helped?"

190

Nathan smiled for the first time. "Yes. He was awesome."

"Good. That's great. I'm glad someone was able to help. We're nearly done, but there's just one more question I need to ask."

Neal knew what that question was.

"Nathan, on the night Gray was killed, did you send him a text saying you were thinking of taking your own life?"

The look of shock on Nathan Elliot's face was confirmation enough, but they needed to hear him say it.

"No! Is that what you think happened? Did someone pretend they needed Gray's help, then kill him? Someone pretending to be me?"

"Yes. That's exactly what we think."

Someone had known about their meetings. Someone in Gray Mitchell's small circle of friends had taken advantage of this vulnerable young man to appeal to Gray's inner goodness and lure him to his death. Another known known, thought Neal, but there were still too many unknowns.

* * *

Ava saw Neal to his car while Ollie and Nathan played on Ollie's Xbox. Neither of the boys felt like maths problems after the conversation they had just had.

"So who knew that Gray was counselling Nathan?" Ava asked. "Leon Warrior? Laurence Brand? They seem like the most likely candidates. Whoever it was, he or she could have sent that text to Mitchell, knowing he'd think it was a cry for help from Nathan."

"There's also Ray Irons," said Neal. "He could have overheard George talking about it. He might even have misheard or misconstrued and thought his son was seeing Gray Mitchell. I can imagine him being outraged enough to want to kill Mitchell for that, especially after Mitchell had humiliated him that time."

"That's an interesting one," Ava said. "And he'd be getting back at Warrior. Killing the man Warrior loved — or so Irons thought. As we know, it was all a bit more complicated than that."

"Aye, it nearly always is."

"Where does Caitlin Forest fit in? Is there some connection we haven't looked for? I can't think of a single plausible reason why any of our principal suspects would want to kill her. Or isn't there a connection? Maybe we should be investigating Caitlin Forest's death independently of Mitchell's."

"We already are. You know that. Every murder is given equal weight. But it won't do any harm to look at Forest's background. Find out who she was. Look for anyone or anything that would tie her to Mitchell or another member of their circle. You're checking that, aren't you?"

"I'll get onto it."

"Monday will do," Neal said. "Take tomorrow off and enjoy your date."

"Thanks, sir. I will," Ava said. "Do you have plans for the evening?"

Neal shrugged. "Movie with Archie, then more of Breaking Bad with Maggie. Perhaps a quiet read if I get the chance."

"Have good one. And say hi to Maggie from me."

A thin film of ice had formed on Neal's windscreen. His headlamps illuminated Ava's lonely, tree-lined drive. A cat bolted across the path in front of him and Ava scooped it up, scolding Camden for his poor road sense.

As Neal pulled away, Ava began to think about her date, and what she would wear. There wasn't a whole lot of choice. Her wardrobe consisted overwhelmingly of clothes that she could wear either to work or on weekends. There wasn't much there in the way of glamour. Last time she had worn her favourite dress, it had been drenched with Christopher Taylor's blood. But Ava's looks required

192

very little embellishment. She was zipping up a little red dress that she'd bought at an end of summer sale, when her mobile buzzed. It was a text from Joel. There had been an accident on the city bypass and all hands were needed in A&E, probably for the rest of the weekend.

Ava pictured the beautiful room awaiting them at the Wrenwood, and the night of passion that wasn't to be. The zipper never got past half way. She shook off the dress and slipped into a tracksuit, intending to go for a run.

Downstairs, Ollie and Nathan were busy stealing cars and toting guns in their video game. Ollie shot her a guilty look. At least Nathan looked relaxed and happy. Not for the first time, Ava wondered what kind of world this was that could persecute decent people for not conforming to the norm.

Chapter 18

Laurence was anxious. Marcus had not turned up for his Sunday morning lesson, nor had he phoned to say that he wasn't coming. More worrying still, he had failed to answer any of the messages Laurence had left for him. Maxine Brand tried to convince her husband that Marcus probably thought Laurence still wasn't well. Or else he'd had a late night and was sleeping off a hangover. Laurence was unconvinced. Marcus never stood him up. He was certain that the boy would have called with an excuse or an explanation.

Laurence declared that he was going to call by Marcus's place, just to make sure the boy 'hadn't come down with something.' Maxine did not try to dissuade him. She knew that her husband would only fret until he found out why Marcus hadn't shown. She was also running late for work.

"Call me if there's a problem," she said as she left the house. "But I don't expect to hear from you."

An hour later, Laurence arrived at the terraced house Marcus shared with a couple of other lads. There was no reply at first, but after Laurence had knocked three or four times, the door was opened by a bleary-eyed man in his mid-twenties. He had that gaunt look about him that Laurence associated with drug addicts. Marcus had told him one of his flatmates was a bit of a junkie, and Laurence guessed he was looking at him now.

"I'm looking for Marcus Collins. He does live here, doesn't he?"

"Dude," the young man said.

Laurence wasn't sure if this was supposed to be a greeting. No clarification was forthcoming, so he asked, "is Marcus home?"

"Dude?" A question.

"I'm Laurence Brand, Marcus's Latin teacher. Maybe he's mentioned me?"

The man shook his head. "Dude."

"Well, anyway, perhaps you could check whether he's at home," Laurence asked.

The man shouted up the stairs, "Dude!"

Another twenty-something male appeared on the upstairs landing. "What's up?" he asked. Flatmate one shuffled out of the frame and disappeared through a door in the hallway.

"I was up till two in the morning and I never heard him coming in," the man upstairs said. "His room's next to mine. I'll just check for you."

He did not invite Laurence inside. Laurence waited, shivering in the raw morning air. He heard the sound of knocking, then heard Marcus's name called. Then the young man reappeared at the top of the stairs and shook his head. "Not here! Wanna take a look for yourself, mate?"

Laurence stepped inside. The murky hallway held an unpleasant odour — a toxic mix of unwashed armpits and unflushed toilets, decaying rubbish and stale cigarette smoke. The stair carpet was sticky and as Laurence drew nearer to the open toilet door, the worse the unflushed toilet smell became.

"Scuse the smell. Dude stunk out the toilet earlier," his host said.

"His name is Dude?"

"No, it's Shane. We all call him Dude because that's pretty much all he says these days. This is Marcus's room."

From somewhere down the hallway a woman's voice called and flatmate two disappeared, leaving Laurence to explore Marcus's room alone. Laurence was surprised to find that the door had no lock. If what he had heard about drug addicts was true, then surely Marcus should be more security conscious? But then he saw that Marcus possessed nothing that would be of value to the other two. He had two shelves of books and very little else. Even his wardrobe, whose door gaped open, revealed only a couple of changes of clothing.

Unlike the rest of the house, Marcus's room was clean and tidy. But Laurence was staring at the bed. It was made. Marcus had not slept in this room overnight. Laurence knew that Marcus had an Ipod and an Ipad, which he normally carried around with him. They were nowhere here. Laurence couldn't see his mobile phone either. He did not feel comfortable searching through Marcus's drawers. He was about to leave when he spied a green sticky note in the shape of a leaf on the table next to Marcus's bed. Laurence picked it up. Angie Dent's name and phone number were written there, encircled several times in red ink. Outside the circle, Marcus had doodled a red question mark. Laurence frowned. On an impulse, he stuck the note in his trouser pocket.

From next door came the sounds of vigorous lovemaking, and a headboard banged rhythmically against the wall. Laurence listened for a moment or two before heading down the staircase. He didn't bother to let Dude know he was leaving.

He mustn't panic. It was Sunday morning. Plenty of people nowadays spent Sunday mornings with someone they had only met the night before. Marcus had been through a lot, first being ditched by Caitlin, then becoming a suspect in her murder investigation. Who could blame him if he'd gone out and had a good time, ending up in Angie Dent's bed? In a corner of his mind, Caius nodded, knowingly. Laurence checked his phone. Still no reply from Marcus.

Leon would know Angie's address. Caitlin had given Leon Warrior her contact details when she was working on his stained-glass window. Laurence hadn't spoken with Leon since he had attacked him with the brick. His finger hovered over the keys of his mobile phone for a while before he found Leon's number. The conversation that followed was punctuated by apologies and awkward pauses. It took a while, but Laurence went some way towards repairing his relationship with Leon. He also obtained the address of the flat that Caitlin Forest had shared with Angie Dent.

Laurence debated with himself whether driving round to Angie's place to search for Marcus was a rational course of action. He knew very well that his previous actions had seemed perfectly sane at the time. Only later had he realised that they were unquestionably deranged.

In the end, he concluded that if he were deranged now, he would not be in any doubt. Therefore, driving round to Angie's place to check up on Marcus was the action of a concerned friend, not someone in the grip of a delusion. All the same, he didn't tell Maxine what he was doing.

* * *

Caitlin Forest's name was still on the intercom list, he noticed. Of course there was no answer. Had he really expected there might be? Laurence wandered around to the back of the block. He saw with a pang, the police tape around the recycling shed where Caitlin's body had been found. Then he returned to the intercom and pressed a number at random. A voice answered — female, sleepy.

"I'm a friend of Angie Dent's. Would you mind letting me in? She's not answering and I'm worried about her. She's been a bit depressed since her friend died."

To his astonishment, without a word, the entrance door clicked open. Hadn't the police warned the occupants there was a killer on the loose? Marvelling at the stupidity of some people and his own good fortune, Laurence closed the door behind him. He climbed the two flights of stairs to Angie's flat. He stood outside her door feeling like a stalker, even pressing his ear to it, but there was nothing to hear.

He knocked, gently at first, then more insistently. No reply. Laurence was beginning to feel foolish. What did he think he was doing checking up on Angie and Marcus? No, not Angie, just Marcus. He was inordinately fond of the boy, he realised, and loved him like the son he'd never had. It was love, he concluded, not madness, that was making him behave this way.

Unable to think what else to do, Laurence tried ringing Marcus's number again. Inside the flat came a sound that caused his heart to jolt. Marcus's ringtone.

Then Laurence heard voices on the stairs and a uniformed police officer suddenly appeared in the corridor. He was accompanied by what at first glance appeared to be a giant teddy bear. As they drew nearer Laurence saw that it was a young woman dressed in a brown fluffy onesie with ears. She pointed at Laurence. "That's him. That's the man I saw wandering around the back of the block, the one who buzzed my number asking about Angie."

Laurence opened his mouth to explain. Before he could say anything, the young police officer marched up to him and demanded to know his business.

"I . . . I'm looking for Marcus," Laurence stammered.

"Who the hell's Marcus?" bear woman asked. "He said he was looking for Angie Dent."

"I think it would be a good idea for you to come downstairs with me, sir. I'd like to ask you some questions and run a quick check."

"But . . . but I haven't done anything wrong!" Laurence protested. "His phone's ringing in there. Why isn't he answering it? If he's gone, he would have taken it with him. You need to break the door down or something." Laurence was aware of the familiar storm mounting inside him.

"Nobody's going to be kicking in any doors," the young officer said, moving the bear woman behind him protectively. "If you'll just accompany me quietly, sir." He gripped Laurence by the elbow.

The storm surged to the surface. "Get your bloody hands off me!" He shrugged himself free of the officer's grasp.

"Marcus!" Laurence shouted. He began to bang on the door to Angie's flat. "Marcus! Are you in there? It's me, Laurence Brand. Let me in! MARCUS!" Without realising it, Laurence had raised his voice until he was yelling Marcus's name over and over, all the time hammering harder and harder on Angie's door. Along the corridor, doors were opening, heads popping out.

"Sir, I advise you to calm down and stop banging on that . . ."

Suddenly the storm erupted. Before he knew what he was doing, Laurence spun around and punched the policeman in the nose. Bear girl screamed. A couple of men ran down the corridor towards them. Laurence resumed shouting and banging. The copper laid a hand on his shoulder. "Right, dat's it," the officer said, through his bloody nose. "I'b arresting you for assaulting a police officer."

Laurence was manhandled to the ground by the policeman and the two men. They held him still while the police officer cuffed him. Laurence continued to shout Marcus's name until he was hoarse.

* * *

"Sooo, tell me everything, girlfriend," PJ said.

"Nothing to tell. Joel had to work. Haven't seen him all weekend," Ada replied.

"Poor you," said PJ.

"How about you? How's it going with Steve?" Having forgotten Jim Neal, PJ was now seeing the young police sergeant who had hankered after PJ all this time.

"It's going great. Steve's so romantic. You'll never believe what he did for our six month anniversary—"

At that moment, Neal appeared in the doorway of his office and beckoned to Ava.

"Tell me later."

"It looks like Leon Warrior could be in the clear," Neal said by way of greeting. He seemed tense. Neal didn't often greet people with a smile, but he was normally polite enough to say 'good morning.' But Ava was becoming accustomed to his moods.

"How so?"

"We followed up his reports of what he was doing on the night Mitchell was murdered. He was caught on CCTV outside a club in Soho, at two in the morning and again at a filling station at five. Godfrey Hardy was with him. It's all but impossible for him or Hardy to have killed Mitchell."

Neal went on. "We've got the digital forensic report on Mitchell's laptop back and I've got printouts of his email and search activity."

Ava leaned forward.

"Mitchell corresponded with his sister quite a bit. Considering her attitude to his sexuality, he was remarkably forgiving."

"He was a good person. Everyone we've spoken to says the same. Words like 'kind' and 'generous' and 'lovely,' kept coming up when people described what he was like. I know we're trained to look for the darkness in people. Normally I'd be suspicious as hell if someone

200

came across as too good to be true, but it really seems that Gray Mitchell was practically a saint."

"Ray Irons might not agree with that," Neal said.

"Hmm . . . even then it was Mitchell's sense of injustice that made him act. He was furious about how Irons had bullied Leon."

"I've raced through the reports. I'd like you to go through them in more depth. Look for connections, anything that might be significant."

"I'll get right on it, boss." Ava stood up.

Neal cleared his throat. "How was the Wrenwood?"

"No idea. We had to cancel. Joel was working all weekend."

"I'm sorry," Neal said. His voice was gruff.

Ava shrugged. "C'est la vie."

"Aye. Get back to me as soon as you can on that. We've eliminated one suspect this morning, but we're still a long way from solving this case."

It was a long, slow morning, propped up by so much caffeine that, by midday, even Ava was starting to feel jittery. She wondered if she should go for a quick run in her lunch break, but instead she asked PJ to bring her a sandwich. She carried on working at her desk, staring at the forensics reports and copies of Mitchell's emails and Internet searches until her neck and shoulders ached and her concentration was splintering. Even then, she continued well into the afternoon. She discovered his fondness for silly cat videos and his passion for the theatre. He supported, not just gay rights, but other humanitarian causes as well. And then, at the dog end of the afternoon, something incongruous came up. Mitchell had done a series of searches for crimes that had occurred in the Midwestern states of the US in the early nineties. It was as if Mitchell had been searching for something specific but couldn't quite pinpoint what it was.

Like most inexperienced researchers, Mitchell seemed unaware of how to refine his searches. Time and again, he had typed in a vague or too general search term. Ava rubbed her tired eyes and turned her attention to Mitchell's email correspondence. She decided to start with his sister, Carrie, and she spent the next hour ploughing through their recent exchanges.

In the final paragraph of an email dated a few weeks before his death, Ava found something that seemed to tie in with his true crime searches. Mitchell was asking his sister if she could find out about a crime that had been committed somewhere in the Midwest around twelve or thirteen years previously. It involved the murder of a teenage girl. He'd remembered hearing about it when he was touring in the Four Corners region.

Ava did a quick Google search and discovered the Four Corner states were Colorado, Arizona, New Mexico and Utah. She was momentarily distracted by pictures of visitors to Four Corners. They placed themselves at the spot where the four states met and contorted their bodies so as to be in all four states at once.

Mitchell couldn't recall which of the states the crime had occurred in. All he remembered was that there had been something unusual about the crime, or the perpetrator, but he couldn't remember what it was.

Ava sifted through more emails, keeping an eye out for Carrie's replies to Mitchell's request. A few emails later, Ava thought she had uncovered something promising, but it was only a link to a newspaper archive. Ava sighed. She had a vague sense that she was somehow in transit from an unknown unknown to a known unknown, even if she still had no clue what it might be.

At times like this, Ava regretted that she wasn't a computer geek. She rubbed her tired eyes. She was about to look in on Neal with what little she'd unearthed, when PJ signalled her over to her desk. She was on the phone and wanted Ava to listen in.

Minutes later, Ava knocked on the window of Neal's office. He looked up from his report to hear what was so urgent.

'I've just had a call from the duty officer in the nick. Laurence Brand's got himself into trouble again."

"What's he done now?" Neal asked, wearily.

"Assaulted a police officer. Guess where?"

"Well?"

"Outside Angie Dent's flat."

"And?" Neal asked.

"He was looking for Marcus Collins. Apparently, the lad didn't turn up for his Latin lesson yesterday and Laurence was concerned."

Neal was all attention now. "Why would he go to Angie's place looking for Marcus Collins?"

"No idea, boss, but Brand's asking for us."

"Let's go."

On the way, Ava told him what she had learned from trawling through Gray Mitchell's correspondence with his sister.

"I don't see how we could obtain information through any of the main police databases. Bit too vague, I think. I imagine there are truckloads of cases over there that would fit that description. It might be worth speaking with Carrie Howard again. She might have come up with something, but I can't see that it would be relevant to our case," said Neal.

"If it's okay with you, I'll speak to her again, sir."

"Rather you than me," Neal said. "Go ahead, by all means."

* * *

The duty officer showed them to Brand's cell. Brand rose stiffly, from a bare wooden bench.

"Thank you for coming, Inspector. Sergeant," he said, looking from Neal to Ava. "They said I could make a phone call and I asked for your number. The duty officer kindly said he would let you know so that I could use my phone call to speak with Maxine."

Neal nodded. He was trying not to gag. It was always the same when he came down here. An evil stench of urine, faeces and vomit permeated the air, overwhelming him. He glanced over at the rank-looking stainless steel toilet two few feet away.

Next to him, Ava was wriggling her nose.

"I'm sorry to drag you down here to such insalubrious surroundings," said Brand.

"Mr Brand, can you just get on with it," Neal said. "You asked to see us and here we are, but we haven't got all day. What were you doing at Angie Dent's flat?"

"I was looking for Marcus. I've been worrying about him since he failed to turn up for his Latin lesson yesterday morning."

"Aye, we already know that. Why did you think he'd be at Angie's?"

Laurence handed Neal a screwed up piece of paper that he'd retrieved from his trouser pocket. It was green. Unfolded it resembled a leaf. Someone had written Angie Dent's name and number on it in and encircled it in red, adding a red question mark outside the circle.

"So? What's this?" said Neal.

"I found it in Marcus's room yesterday morning. Marcus hadn't been home. His bed hadn't been slept in, so I . . ."

" . . . You thought he might be at Angie's house because he'd written her name on a post-it?" Neal's question dripped sarcasm.

Laurence Brand looked at Ava, but there was no encouraging smile. "I . . . that is . . . Marcus and I talked the other night. We both knew we weren't guilty . . . and before you ask how we could possibly know that, Inspector, it's a matter of trust. Marcus was determined to show he had nothing to do with Caitlin's death. He was very fond of her, you know."

"Funny way of showing it — sending her a hate-filled text," said Ava.

"He was drunk and feeling hurt. It's not in Marcus's character to do something like that normally," Laurence said.

Neal rolled his eyes. Every vitriolic troll on the Internet used alcohol as their defence.

"I said to Marcus that we had to prove our innocence," Brand said. "I think he took me literally. Maybe he saw Angie as a potential suspect."

"What makes you think that?" Neal asked.

"I . . . I . . . don't have a tangible reason. Call it a hunch, but maybe Angie was jealous of Marcus's relationship with Caitlin. I saw the way she looked at him sometimes. Marcus didn't say much, he's not the type to gossip, but he did once say that Angie manipulated Caitlin. Then, there was that row between Angie and Caitlin at Gray and Leon's soirée. The more I think about it, the more I wonder if Angie had just found out about Caitlin's relationship with Marcus. Maybe Caitlin was a bit drunk and got up the courage to broach the subject with her? I know this is what you people call speculation, but what if I'm right?"

Neal sighed. The row again, the one that no one but Laurence seemed to have noticed. "I'm sorry, Mr Brand, but I can't help feeling you're building up a story around your conviction that Angie's dangerous. You have nothing to back this up and you do have a bit of a track record of . . . distorting reality."

Brand looked dejected. "Please. If you do nothing else, at least check whether Marcus is okay. That boy is like a son to me . . ." His eyes welled up and he turned away. "I'm truly sorry I hit that policeman. I was so worried about Marcus I couldn't control myself."

"Aye, well you need to learn to think before you act, Mr Brand. I doubt that the arresting officer will be as forgiving as Leon Warrior, and maybe that's not such a bad thing." Now it was Neal's turn to look away, unable to bear the sight of Brand's abject misery.

As he and Ava turned to leave, Neal said, "We'll check into Marcus's whereabouts, if only to stop him doing anything stupid." He took out his mobile and called Vincent Bone. Neal asked Vincent if the boy had turned up for work that day. Then he asked if Angie Dent had been in the shop. He waited while Vincent checked.

"They weren't there, were they?" Brand asked.

"It doesn't mean something sinister is going on, Mr Brand. Quite the opposite, in fact. Mr Bone saw the two of them together on Friday and from what he said, it seems likely that Marcus and Angie are finding consolation in each other. Seems to me that Caitlin had good reason to feel jealous of Angie. Marcus obviously wasn't heartbroken enough to be deterred from making a move on her best friend."

"Oh."

Neal was at the end of his patience with Brand. "If anything turns up regarding Marcus, we'll let you know, but I don't expect you'll be hearing from us soon."

Ava gave Brand a sympathetic smile as she hastened after Neal. "Another minute in there and I think I'd have had to vomit," Ava said outside the cell door. "You must have been gagging, sir." She wriggled her nose.

Neal was aware that his intolerance for unpleasant smells was legendary. Someone had let off a stink bomb at the pub once and he'd made the mistake of covering his nose with a handkerchief, to the amusement of his colleagues.

"Where are you at with looking into Caitlin Forest's background?"

"I gave PJ some information to follow up."

"Chase her up," he said.

"D'you think Brand's delusional again?"

"Possibly. But jealousy is a powerful emotion. It's been a motive for murder since time immemorial. Have you never read Othello?"

"Totally different scenario, sir. If I remember rightly, Othello had that other bloke, Iago, wasn't it, feeding him false information."

"Something like that."

"Is it okay if I go see if Carrie Howard is at her hotel? I might as well see if she can shed any light on Mitchell's interest in an old murder case he could remember nothing about."

Neal considered this a waste of time, but he nodded. His sergeant was fidgety and needed to be doing something other than staring at a computer screen.

"Let me know if she says anything worth repeating."

Chapter 19

Marcus Collins yawned and stretched, then gazed down at the woman lying next to him, remembering the amazing sex they'd enjoyed the night before . . . and the night before that . . . and much of the previous day. They'd spent the time in the Premier Inn, with the Do Not Disturb sign hanging on the outside door handle.

How had this happened? Only a week ago, Marcus had been pleading with Caitlin not to break up with him. Now here he was, in bed with Angie Dent, and randy as hell.

Angie stirred and woke up. She was always wide awake in an instant. They were both naked. His desire was making a tent of the sheet, but when Marcus reached out for her, Angie slid out of bed.

"We have to go to work today, Marcus," she said. "We didn't even phone in sick yesterday. People are going to be asking questions."

Marcus sighed. He watched Angie head for the shower, then slid out and joined her. "One for the road," he said hopefully. Angie didn't object when he stepped in beside her.

* * *

Marcus and Angie left the hotel separately. Another secret romance, Marcus thought, but Angie said it was only temporary. It was so soon after Caitlin's death that their affair would be seen as disrespectful. Was he doing the right thing? And if so, why did he feel guilty? Laurence Brand had assured him that there were plenty of other girls who would jump at the chance of dating him. He was following Laurence's advice, wasn't he? Getting back out there. But — Angie of all people.

* * *

Marcus walked into the stonemasons' workshop.

"What happened to you yesterday, Marcus? We even had the police phoning up asking if you were okay," Vincent Bone said.

"I'm sorry. I know I should have called, but I felt really unwell," Marcus lied, clumsily. "Literally couldn't get out of bed."

"No," Vincent said dryly. "Must be catching. Angie Dent was unwell yesterday too. Seems she couldn't get out of bed either."

Marcus avoided Vincent's eye. "I'll get to work, then," he said.

"Marcus, did you speak to Laurence Brand over the weekend?"

Marcus reddened. He had meant to apologise for missing his lesson on Sunday, but somehow he'd never got around to it. "No. Why? Is Laurence okay?"

Vincent made a face. "Not exactly." He told Marcus where Laurence had spent his Sunday night, but was unable to tell him what had happened. All he knew was that Laurence had assaulted a policeman.

"Take an early break," Vincent said. "Go see Maxine in the café and find out what happened. It was something to do with you, I think. Laurence thought you'd gone missing or something."

"Thanks, Vincent." Instead of going straight to the café, Marcus took a detour to the gift shop. Angie was pricing decorations and hanging them on a Christmas tree. She didn't seem overjoyed to see Marcus, and she already knew what he had to tell her.

"You don't know the half of it," Angie said. "Your nutjob friend was arrested outside the door to my flat. He was yelling your name over and over."

"Why? Why would he do that?"

But Marcus knew the answer already. When he had visited Laurence after his release from hospital, they had talked of doing some investigating of their own. It might help clear both of them of suspicion. It was the reason Marcus had approached Angie in the first place. It seemed that Laurence had homed in on Angie too and convinced himself she was the killer. Marcus kicked himself for missing his Latin lesson without informing Laurence. He had set Laurence on another course of reckless behaviour.

Angie's fingers tightened around a bauble and it broke in her hand.

"Shit! Look what you made me do." Angie's hand was bleeding.

"Here." Marcus passed her his handkerchief.

She threw it back at him. "Just go and see your 'friend,' Marcus. I think he's after your ass."

"Are you jealous?" Marcus tried to slip his arm around her waist, then withdrew it. Angie wasn't in the mood for teasing.

* * *

Maxine saw him the minute he walked through the door to the café, and came towards him.

"I'm sorry I didn't call on Sunday, Maxine. Was it my fault Laurence got locked up?"

Maxine looked as if she was about to hug him. She patted him on the arm instead. "Of course it wasn't your fault. Laurie was worried about you and got it into his head that Angie had kidnapped you and meant to do you harm. It was a classic case of Laurie's imagination taking him to places no one else would think of." She looked Marcus over. "You *are* okay, aren't you?"

Unexpectedly, Marcus gave her a bear hug. "You guys are so sweet, the way you care about me. I wish I'd called Laurence on Sunday." He was grateful that Maxine did not ask where he had been.

Maxine related the woeful tale of Laurence's arrest. "He's going to be charged this time, I'm afraid, but I don't think they'll lock him up. He's still adjusting to his new meds. They'll take that into consideration." She sighed. "I'm going to make sure he stays safely indoors for the time being."

"I'll call him," Marcus said. "Can I do it here?"

"Go into the alcove. I'll bring you a cup of tea."

When Marcus sat down to make the call he discovered he didn't have his mobile. He and Angie had called at her flat before going to the Premier Inn. He must have left it there. He had not missed it during his weekend of wild sex. He borrowed Maxine's mobile and called Laurence. His friend was so pleased to hear that Marcus was okay that his voice broke. Marcus apologised for missing his lesson without calling. Then he asked, "why did you think Angie would hurt me, Laurence? Surely you don't think she had anything to do with Gray or Caitlin's murder?" A long pause. "Laurence?"

"I . . . to be honest, I don't know, Marcus. I went to your flat-share and found a piece of paper by your bedside with Angie's number on it. Then my thoughts started to race. Before I knew it, I was banging on her door. By the time the police arrived, I'd convinced myself you were in there, bleeding to death or worse."

Marcus reddened. "I'm sort of seeing her."

"Yes," said Laurence. "I can't say I'm happy about that, but I may be overreacting — it does seem to be a weakness of mine. I'll apologise to Angie. I just wish this whole unpleasant business was over. I can't bear the thought of the police thinking you or I had anything to do with it."

"I know," Marcus said. "Feel better, Laurence." Marcus, too, was choking up a little.

"Thank you," said Maxine when she brought his tea.

Marcus looked at her.

"For caring about him too," she explained.

* * *

"How are you getting on with tracing Caitlin Forest's next of kin?" Ava slumped into the chair next to PJ, invigorated after her early-morning swim. She had not, after all, been able to track Carrie down the day before and was hoping PJ might have come up with something on Caitlin.

"Good morning to you too."

"Sorry. I'm getting impatient with this case. I was just hoping you'd come up with something."

"Well, I haven't. Not really. Still haven't been able to track down any relatives. I contacted the head of the school where she did her GCSEs, and she confirmed that Caitlin's parents died when she was seventeen. She remembers because it was such a tragic event. Caitlin was meant to stay on at her school to do A levels, but after her parent's death, she quit and left her home town of Saffron Walden. The head did contact Social Services to try to find out what arrangements had been made for Caitlin, but was told she'd already gone. Her parents died in the summer holidays and by the time the head found out, Caitlin had just disappeared."

"Great," said Ava. "So there's a whole, what, three years of her life unaccounted for before she moved to Stromford."

"About that."

"What happened to her parents?"

212

"They drowned. Trying to rescue her eight-year-old brother. He was swimming in the sea with Caitlin and got caught in a rip current."

"Jesus, how unlucky can one family get?" Ava thought for a moment. "I'm assuming you've checked all the usual channels for the time after Caitlin left Saffron Walden?"

"Yes, ma'am," said PJ. "No tax or insurance records for those three years. No nothing in fact. It's like she was living off the grid during that time. Bet she went to London. That's where most runaway kids make for."

"Well, she wasn't a runaway and she wasn't exactly a kid, but you're probably right. She might have got some sort of job off the books, lived with people she'd met there . . . Jeez, we've got hardly any chance of building up a back story for her. Might be worth speaking to Marcus and the others in her circle. Maybe she spoke to them about her pre-Stromford life."

"D'you think she might have met Gray Mitchell in London and he learned something about her, or did something to her that would make her want to kill him?"

"Maybe," Ava said. "That wouldn't explain why she was killed though."

"Revenge? For Mitchell's death."

Ava wondered who would want to avenge Mitchell's death. Leon — maybe — but he'd been cheating on Mitchell. Ray Irons? To pay Leon back for his part in Tara Smythe's death, or for humiliating him in front of his son, George? Or was it Marcus, the spurned lover?

It occurred to Ava that it was not simply motive and opportunity that made a murderer. These people all had reasons for killing, some more urgent than others. Ava was convinced that it was some element of the personality that predisposed a person to kill — a darkness inside that had to obtain release. Laurence Brand, with his mild-mannered, inept, almost bumbling character was an unlikely murderer. His alter ego, Caius, was a different character altogether, and one whose passions could cause him to lose control.

But how far would Caius be prepared to go before Laurence reined him in? Too many unknowns, Ava thought.

Neal didn't think Irons was capable of murder. Irons had lived his whole life denying his true nature. It seemed that his worst deeds were all in his past, as far as physical violence was concerned. But he was still a bigot.

* * *

"I'd like to drive down to Saffron Waldon," Ava announced to Neal when he returned from his morning briefing. "I might be able to find some information on Caitlin from people who knew her when she lived there. I could speak with neighbours, old school friends. What do you think?"

Neal did not answer immediately.

"Are you okay, sir?"

"What? Yes. I was just wondering if I would have time to come with you. It's probably over two hours' drive away, isn't it?"

"Thereabouts."

Neal sighed, consulting his watch.

"I promised I'd take Archie to the Christmas market this evening. Doubt I'd make it back in time."

"Bit risky, with the roads still being bad and the extra traffic at this time of year with all the Christmas shoppers."

"Bloody Christmas market. Okay, you'd better go alone. Or take PC Jenkins with you, if you like. She's taking her detective's exam soon, isn't she? Be good experience for her, working with you."

"I'll take that as a compliment, sir. Have a mince pie and a glass of mulled wine for me tonight," she said cheerily as she left his room. She didn't need to look back. There was a scowl on Neal's face.

* * *

"This is nice. I don't get out of the office that much," PJ said, as they cruised down the A1. "D'you think we could stop at a service station or something for a pee? I'll treat you to a coffee."

"There's a Little Chef coming up on this side in a couple of miles. I'll pull in there. I'll have a large Americano, no milk, one sweetener." Ava thought of the journeys she'd made with Neal. She would have risked damaging her bladder rather than suggest they stop.

They pulled in to the roadside restaurant about ten minutes later.

"Well, *hello ladies*!" called out the driver of a carload of young lads as Ava and PJ stepped out of their car.

"Is there anything we can help you with today?"

"You tell me," Ava said, flashing her badge. "You can start by showing me your licence. I'd like to check you're old enough to drive."

"Aw. Serious? You're cops?" The driver lifted his rear to retrieve his wallet from the pocket of his jeans.

"Seriously, you're nineteen?" Ava said, glancing at his licence.

"I know. It's my baby-face good looks." He grinned.

"Get on your way before I decide I need to run a check on that car you're driving."

"Don't worry, we're going. Nice to meet you ma'ams."

As he drove off, all four lads blew kisses in Ava and PJ's direction. Ava whipped out her notebook and pretended to write down their registration number.

"He was kinda cute," PJ said, watching the departing car.

Ava rolled her eyes, but she had to admit that the driver, at least, was not bad.

* * *

Twenty minutes later, they were back on the road.

"I really didn't need that Danish," PJ sighed. "I've got Weight Watchers tonight. It's not fair. You never put weight on, Ava."

Ava was about to ask how many lengths PJ had swum before work that morning, but decided to say nothing. PJ was the sort of person who would always believe that some people were just naturally thin. Maybe sometime Ava would show her pictures of what she had looked like at school, before she began to exercise. Losing weight had been a by-product of achieving peak fitness, which, for private reasons, Ava considered a survival strategy. That's why she ran and swam and trained — so that she would never have to go down without putting up a fight. She said none of this to PJ. She just pointed out that she wasn't skinny. She had plenty of muscle.

The medieval market town of Saffron Walden was in the north-west of Essex.

"Pretty town," PJ commented as they drove through the busy main street past the market square, empty of stalls today.

They had called ahead and arranged to meet Mrs Jane Raeburn. She was the former head of the school that Caitlin Forest had attended until she left Saffron Walden for who knew where. Mrs Raeburn's detached mock-Tudor bungalow was located in a quiet residential street on the outskirts of town. She came out onto the drive to greet Ava and PJ.

"Would you like some tea?" she asked. She ushered them into a pleasant sitting room with William Morris wallpaper and a sagging sofa on which lay a giant bloodhound with a velvety, wrinkled forehead and lugubrious brown eyes. He raised his weary eyebrows as they entered the room, but didn't move.

"Get up and let our visitors sit down, Sherlock," said Mrs Raeburn.

He gave a snort and grudgingly got off the sofa.

"Now entertain our guests while I make some tea," she told him.

Sherlock was already settling into an armchair by an exquisitely decorated Christmas tree and looked too weary to provide much in the way of conversation. He did, however, perk up when Jane Raeburn returned with a tray with tea and a plate of cakes.

"Lucky you didn't arrive a few days ago. We were practically snowed in," she remarked.

They looked out at the front garden where mounds of packed snow still lingered under the darkest corners. There followed a few pleasantries but it was obvious that Mrs Raeburn was keen to get to the point.

"I'm retired but I'm busier than ever," she explained. "I'm on the board of governors at a school near Braintree and there's a meeting this afternoon. You wanted to know about Caitlin Forest, didn't you?"

Ava nodded, her mouth full of Victoria sponge.

"I was so sorry to hear what happened to her. I always hoped she'd managed to get over the terrible tragedy of losing her family, and find some way to get on with her life."

"She did," Ava said. "She was working as a stained-glass restorer at Stromford Cathedral. Did you know that?"

Mrs Raeburn shook her head. "I'm glad. She was good at art. Got an A star in her GCSE."

"What sort of girl was she, Mrs Raeburn?"

"I thought you'd ask me that. It's hard to say, really. Caitlin wasn't particularly academic but she was a competent, if not gifted, artist. She wanted to do A levels in art and photography. But you don't want to know all that, Sergeant."

Ava was thinking that Jane Raeburn must have been a formidable head. She exuded confidence and calm and her eyes were intelligent and inquisitive behind her rimless glasses.

"I'm afraid I don't really know what she was like." Mrs Raeburn looked apologetic. "She was a bit of a loner, I think, and some of my teachers thought she lacked empathy. One or two expressed doubts about her. She was sometimes caught out in rather elaborate lies."

"How about friends? Did she have many?"

"I think that was one of the concerns about her. Caitlin tended to be somewhat controlling, I believe. She was rather good at getting other students to take the blame for her transgressions, particularly the younger ones. I won't go as far as to say she was a bully, but then again, it's distinctly possible that she found some way of dissuading other students from speaking out about her behaviour. She was rather good at manipulating people."

Mrs Raeburn thought for a moment. "One of my teachers hinted that Caitlin showed signs of psychopathy, but he was an English teacher and rather prone to flights of fancy. He left my staff to write books about serial killers, I believe."

Ava nodded. Beside her on the sofa, PJ was scribbling away in her notebook. Ava had a sense that Mrs Raeburn was trying to think of the right words to use.

"There was one incident I remember. A girl Caitlin took under her wing. Her name was Beatrice Connor — everyone called her Bea. Bea was a lovely girl, but rather shy, not very confident or self-assured, unlike Caitlin who was bossy — or should I say assertive? Why is it that girls are always 'bossy' rather than 'assertive?'"

Ava tilted her head.

"Bea had never been in trouble previously, then, all of a sudden she seemed to be forever in my office for some misdemeanour or other. It was usually to do with starting a malicious rumour about a classmate or member of staff. Then, one day, Bea came to my office all upset, saying that Caitlin Forest kept trying to persuade her to do things that she knew were wrong. Apparently Caitlin was able to convince Bea that she was right and Bea was wrong. Poor Bea was in a complete muddle over her morals."

Ava stared at Mrs Raeburn. PJ was on her second slice of cake. She put her plate down and hastily picked up her notebook.

"How did you deal with that?" Ava asked.

"I called Caitlin's parents in and we talked. They were nice people — not loud, like some Americans can be. They agreed to speak with Caitlin, and I made sure that Bea's timetable was changed so that her lessons didn't coincide with Caitlin's."

"Mrs Raeburn. Did you just say that Caitlin Forest's parents were American?"

"I'm sorry, I thought you knew. Though thinking about it, Caitlin did try to disguise her accent. Children tend to mimic their peers, not their parents. They like to fit in."

"Can you think of anyone else we could talk to who might remember Caitlin well, or who might be able to think where she could have gone after leaving Saffron Walden?"

Mrs Raeburn looked over at Sherlock as if for inspiration. He cocked an eyebrow and looked back. Ava doubted whether he would be as helpful as his namesake.

"A lot of her contemporaries are scattered across the country now," said Mrs Raeburn. "I suppose you could speak with the people who lived next door to the Forests, Ian and Maria Scott. But I believe they're at their house in Spain until January. I could find out their contact details for you, if you like. I don't really know them but my cleaner also cleans their house and she'll have been told how to get in touch with them in case of an emergency."

"Thanks," Ava said, I'd like to thank you for the information you've given us, Mrs Raeburn. It's been really useful."

"Perhaps you could do me a little favour in return, Sergeant Merry?"

Ava was sure she knew what Mrs Raeburn's request was going to be. She was right.

"Get in touch with me again when you find out who murdered Caitlin. I'd be interested in hearing the outcome of your investigation."

Ava thanked Mrs Raeburn again and she and PJ drove back into the centre of town. They parked next to the common and walked to the market square looking for somewhere to have lunch, choosing the first pub they came to that looked like it would be warm inside.

PJ ordered fish and chips, Ava chose a vegetable curry. The bartender gave them a wooden spoon with the number thirteen on it, saying he hoped they weren't superstitious.

"That was a good morning's work," Ava declared as they settled in at a table with a view of the street. "Neal's always harping on about the need to uncover as much detail as possible about the victim's past life — you never know what might be relevant."

"D'you think it's significant that Caitlin Forest was American?" PJ said. "Given that Gray Mitchell was also from the States?"

"Food for thought, isn't it? Could be a piece of the puzzle, or it could just be coincidence. It certainly gives us a new slant to consider, as well as a possible connection between them. I think Gray grew up somewhere on the East Coast before he moved to Los Angeles. Be interesting to see what part of the US Caitlin's family lived in."

"Want me to email ahead and get someone checking out the neighbours' contact details in Spain?"

While PJ took out her smartphone and composed an email, Ava checked her inbox. She was hoping to see a text from Joel but there was nothing. Admittedly, they both had busy working lives, but if neither of them had time to text each other, what chance did they have of getting it together to form a relationship? With a sigh, Ava returned her phone to her pocket. The waiter brought their meals over and the women chatted about other things as they ate.

"Do you mind if I have a glass of wine?" PJ asked. Ava had half-hoped that PJ would offer to drive back to Stromford, but she told PJ to go ahead. Somewhat to her surprise, PJ came back from the bar with a large glass of white wine.

"You planning on knocking yourself out for the boring journey home?" Ava was only half joking.

PJ shrugged. "It's cheaper to go large."

It was late afternoon by the time they arrived back in Stromford. PJ had been heavy-lidded before they left the pub and Ava had endured her snoring for most of the journey. It was a tedious drive and she'd listened to the radio to amuse herself, switching between channels in search of something interesting. At one point, she tuned in absent-mindedly to a phone-in discussion about victims of serious crime. It made for depressing listening.

Ava sighed. Discussions like this only reaffirmed her belief that she had made the right choice in pursuing a career in the police. Her decision had been precipitated by an incident in her fresher's week at university that had resulted many months later in a tragedy that still haunted Ava. It was the reason why she dropped out of her degree course.

* * *

"Wake up, sleeping beauty." Ava and PJ pulled into the car park behind the station.

"Wha . . . we back already?" asked a startled PJ. "I feel crap."

"Drinking in the afternoon will do that do you," Ava said smugly.

Jim Neal looked up when they came into his office. Ava filled him in on what they had found out. He congratulated them on doing good work.

"Follow up on this Mrs Raeburn's info immediately," he said.

As if Ava needed to be told.

"I'm taking Archie to the market and the fair this evening, as I told you, so I'll be leaving a bit earlier than usual."

Ava smiled. "Should be fun."

"You're not going? Is Dr Agard working?"

"Fraid so, and Ollie's not bothered — he's not fond of crowds. I might go tomorrow if Joel's finished in time."

As she closed the door behind her, Ava had the distinct impression that Neal had been fishing. She broke into a smile, which she immediately pretended was aimed at PJ.

"I've tracked down the Forest's neighbours and they're willing to speak with you on Skype. Do you want me to set it up for you in one of the side rooms?"

"Just let me grab a coffee."

Five minutes later, Ava was sitting in front of a tanned and healthy-looking couple in their mid-fifties. They were sitting on a balcony with a sea view in the background.

"Mr and Mrs Scott, I'm Detective Sergeant Ava Merry. I understand my colleague has already briefed you on the reason for our call?"

The Scotts nodded in unison. "I'd like to begin by asking you how long you knew the Forests?"

Mrs Scott cleared her throat. "The Forests lived next door to us for just over a year before the tragedy. I'm afraid we didn't get to know them terribly well. They were very quiet people, not at all how you might expect Americans to be. They were pleasant enough but they didn't reveal much about themselves. We had them over for drinks a couple of times, hoping to get to know them better. They'd make small talk but whenever you asked anything about their life in the States they'd just sort of brush you off. They said they'd come to Britain because they wanted a quiet life. Ian and I used to joke that they were in some sort of CIA witness protection programme. But it didn't seem so funny when the Forests and their little boy died in such tragic circumstances."

"Did they work in Saffron Walden? Do you know what either of them did for a living?"

Mrs Scott answered, "He was a teacher at a comprehensive in Braintree. She was a 'stay-at-home mom,' as she called it, but she had been a teacher too, back home. Kindergarten, as they say."

"And what about their daughter, Caitlin? What sort of girl was she?"

The Scotts exchanged glances. This time it was Ian Scott who spoke. "My wife and I were both sad to hear about what happened to Caitlin's family. The news your colleague just gave us about Caitlin's fate was truly shocking."

Ava waited, sensing a but.

"But," Mr Scott said, "in my opinion, Caitlin Forest was a deeply disturbed young woman and I'd be lying if I said I was sorry about what happened to her."

As if affected by Ian Scott's assertion, the Skype connection broke up. For a few seconds an image of Scott's solemn face was frozen on the screen.

"Dammit," muttered Ava, hoping the connection wouldn't fail completely.

Then Scott came back to life, continuing to speak as if unaware that their conversation had been interrupted.

"Sorry to speak over you, Mr Scott, but you froze for a bit there. Would you mind repeating what you just said in case I missed something important?"

"Well, I don't know if it's important in terms of your present investigation, Sergeant Merry, but I imagine it might provide you with some background information on Caitlin's character. I said that Caitlin Forest tried to kill my wife."

It was Ava's turn to freeze. "That's, er, that's quite an allegation, Mr Scott. D'you think you could give me some more details? What did Caitlin do, exactly?"

Maria Scott, who had initially given an impression of being an assertive woman, was now deferring to her husband completely. She allowed him to do all the talking, and she seemed to have shrunk beside him.

"Maria was out walking our dog, Amble, one evening when she caught Caitlin bullying — assaulting actually — a school friend. She was concerned enough to intervene. Caitlin kicked my wife on the shin and called her an 'interfering bitch.' Maria had a nasty bruise for days afterwards. Maria told the Forests about it and they promised to deal with Caitlin themselves. They all but begged Maria not to report the incident to the school. They said they were sure it was a complete one-off and that the other girl had been teasing Caitlin for weeks over her American accent."

"And how did they deal with Caitlin, do you know?"

"She was 'grounded,'" Ian Scott said, making air quotes. "And she apologised to Maria. Claimed she'd been 'off it' because of her period, or some such nonsense."

Is that all? Ava thought. She remembered her own teenage years — the mood swings, the impulsive, sometimes wayward, behaviour that she had attributed to her hormones. She thought Ian Scott was being slightly over-dramatic in saying Caitlin had tried to kill his wife. She was about to say so, when he continued.

"Two days later, Maria was involved in a near-miss. The Forests' car rolled down their drive and almost knocked her over. Mrs Forest had just got out of the vehicle and Caitlin was still inside. Caitlin claimed her mother left the handbrake off and she couldn't get to it in time from the back seat. I know what you're thinking, Sergeant Merry," Ian Scott said as Ava raised a hand to interrupt. "It was an accident, and, yes, Mrs Forest did insist that it was her fault, that she'd forgotten to put the handbrake on." Ian Scott looked at his wife, who was now visibly upset. She held onto her husband's arm.

"You didn't believe her?" Ava wished she was in a real face-to-face interview instead of an online one. It was harder to read faces when you couldn't look someone in the eye. Skype eyes were eerily devoid of emotion.

"Tell her what you saw," Ian Scott said to his wife, covering her hand with his own.

Maria Scott cleared her throat. "Caitlin winked at me afterwards. It was the most chilling thing. I knew then that she'd released the handbrake deliberately. What I don't know is if her mother knew it too, and was covering up for her."

"Mrs Scott. I hope you don't mind me asking this, but were you actually hurt?"

"I could have been."

"You didn't see the car rolling towards you?"

Maria Scott looked embarrassed. "Not immediately. I was bending over to clean up after Amble. She'd pooped at the entrance to the Forests' drive. She saved my life by barking."

"I see," Ava said, slightly lost for words. Was this something or nothing? A genuine accident or an act of malice?

"There was something not right about that girl," Maria Scott said, "something . . . unwholesome. Our chocolate lab, Amble, always gave her a wide berth and that dog loves everyone."

"Thank you for your help, Mr and Mrs Scott," Ava said. She wondered whether the Scott's dog could be relied upon as a credible judge of character.

"One thing before you go, Sergeant Merry," Mr Scott said, quietly. "My wife and I have never come right out and said it, but we could never understand how Caitlin managed to survive when the rest of her family drowned."

Ava nodded. "I understand what you're implying, Mr Scott, but of course I can't comment. I don't know any of the details of that case." Ava looked at her watch to indicate that she had to bring the call to a close.

For a few moments after the connection terminated, Ava stared at the screen. She couldn't decide whether the Scotts were credible or a bit bonkers. Their suspicions about Caitlin seemed far-fetched and groundless. A bruise to the shin, a near-miss accident and their pet dog's disapproval. Caitlin may well have been a bit of a problem teen but that didn't mean she had graduated into a killer.

Ava thought over possible motives for Caitlin killing Gray Mitchell. Both were Americans, which might be of significance. Caitlin had been only fourteen when she arrived in the UK. Was there some connection in their past that had given her a motive for killing Gray? It was disheartening to think that their investigation might hinge on something that happened long ago and in another country. An unknown unknown.

Ava thought again about Gray Mitchell's Internet search history and his emails to his sister concerning an unusual crime about which he seemed to know very little. Had his interest in that crime been triggered by something, or someone, here in Stromford? By Caitlin Forest, perhaps? It seemed unlikely, given that Caitlin was so young when she lived in the States. Something to do with her parents, then?

Ava texted Carrie Howard. Within seconds, she obtained a response that the American woman was free and willing to meet her, although, of course, she was intending to go to the Christmas market later on.

Ava wasn't looking forward to another encounter with Carrie Howard. Ava had no reason to hope that Carrie had undergone a personality change since they last met. She was meeting Carrie in the bar of her hotel. Where else? There was a cashpoint machine near Carrie's hotel and Ava made the slight detour to withdraw some cash. She knew she'd be expected to stand Carrie a drink or two for the pleasure of spending time in her company and pumping her for information.

Ava stared in dismay at her account balance. Her sergeant's pay was more than adequate to meet her own needs, but since Ollie had moved in there had been a lot of extra expenses. Their mother seemed to have abrogated any financial responsibility for her son when he left home. Ava was left to pick up the bill for all her brother's worldly needs. She continued to be astounded by how much a teenage boy could eat. Ollie's interest in cooking was a further drain on her finances — he tended to favour upmarket, expensive ingredients. Ava was now having to make adjustments to her own spending to keep within budget. Ollie was apologetic and had offered to look for a part-time job, but Ava knew how much his studies meant to him and how much he wanted to get into a good university, so she had assured him that she could cope. The rewards of having Ollie live with her could not be measured in monetary terms.

As expected, Carrie was warming a seat at the bar, her more than ample buttocks spreading out to fill the space around her like a giant, brushed denim peach. Ava perched on the stool beside her and asked what she was drinking.

"Since you're buying, I'll have a double," Carrie said. "Scotch on the rocks."

The bartender was already hovering nearby. He needed no encouragement to come over. Ava ordered Carrie's scotch and a sparkling water for herself.

"He didn't serve me that fast," Carrie complained. "Guess your ass is more appealing than mine." She grinned at Ava. Her perfect, white, North American teeth glinted.

"So, what can I do you for this time, Detective? I thought we established last time we met that there wasn't much I could help you with. You any closer to proving Leon Warrior killed my brother?"

Ava sighed deeply.

"I'll take that as a no. Thought as much."

"I'm not sure if it has any relevance," Ava began, "but I've been looking through your brother's emails and I noticed that he'd asked you to look into unusual crimes in the area he'd been touring with his Shakespeare troupe about twelve years ago."

"Yeah? So?"

"Well, I was wondering if you'd been able to pinpoint what he was thinking of. I know his email was a bit vague . . ."

"Nothing vague about it," Carrie said. "Not for someone who has an interest in true crime stories. Gray knew he was consulting the right person."

Ava was surprised to learn that Carrie Howard had an interest in anything other than booze.

"Plus, my ex was a cop and we're still on good terms. He made a few calls to his buddies in the region and we came up with some cases that Gray could sift through. If you're gonna ask me why Gray was interested, you're gonna be disappointed. He didn't say and I didn't ask."

Ava had been through scores of email messages and she wondered if she'd overlooked the crucial one.

"Kurt — that's my ex — was over here about a month ago on holiday and he met up with Gray. Said he'd let Gray know what he had."

Ava's heart sank. "So you never emailed any details to your brother?"

"Nope." Carrie was looking down at her empty glass. Trying not to think of her bank balance, Ava ordered her another double scotch.

"Carrie, can you remember what cases you came up with?" Ava was not harbouring much hope. Then again, she was beginning to think Carrie Howard was sharper than she would have people believe.

"Sure can," Carrie answered.

Ava waited.

"Fact is there ain't that many serious crimes that are all that unusual. I guess you have the same thing here? Lot of domestics, the odd gang-related homicide, that kind of thing? Run-of-the-mill type homicides."

Ava nodded.

"There were a couple murders that had a ring to them, you know, kinda out of the usual. One was a serial thing, some deranged psycho who was mistreated by his ma and pa when he was a nipper took to chopping up young women in the Colorado region. The FBI finally gunned him down someplace outside of Boulder."

Another encouraging nod from Ava.

"The second case involved two teenage kids — girls who took a dislike to one of their classmates and threw her off the roof of a parking garage, what you guys call a multi-storey car park. This was in a town in Colorado where Gray spent a week performing — what was it now, oh some Shakespeare play or other. One of the girls had wealthy parents who hired them fancy lawyers and they got off on some kind of psychological defence. You ever hear the term, *folie à deux*?'"

Carrie's pronunciation of the French words was execrable, but Ava was familiar with the term and knew what she was talking about. She frowned. Folie à deux was a rare phenomenon, and not uncontroversial. Also known as 'shared psychotic disorder,' it occurred when one person shared the delusions of another. Often one of the two suffered from a genuine psychiatric disorder — schizophrenia or some other disorder that induces psychosis in its sufferer. The second person, often the weaker, more submissive one, comes to share the same delusion.

There had been cases where people had become so caught up in the delusion that they committed a murder together. But why would Gray Mitchell be interested in such a case? Was it worth pursuing? Had Mitchell simply become an aficionado of true crime like his sister? Or had something in his personal life provoked his interest? Ava had forgotten all about Carrie for a moment.

"Well? You know what it means, then?" Carrie asked.

"What? Oh . . . yes I've heard of it. Do you know what happened to the girls?"

"Like I said. They got off. One of them, the one they thought was the real nutjob, she was sent to a psychiatric facility for a few years. No idea what became of the other. Maybe Gray followed it up, I don't know."

Ava was experiencing a familiar, tingling feeling that she often had when she thought she'd discovered something significant. She didn't know what that something was yet. Her brain needed time to synthesise all her thoughts and make the right connections.

"Thanks, Carrie. You've been really helpful. Would you be able to give me your ex-husband's contact details, preferably his phone number? I'd like to speak with him as soon as possible."

"Sure. Got a pen?" She wrote the number in Ava's notebook, then lowered her empty glass to the bar with a sigh.

Ava got the hint. She was grateful enough to stand the woman another drink, but she also had Ollie's next meal to think of. Ignoring the hint, she thanked Carrie and slid off the bar stool. Carrie, obviously disgruntled, snapped her fingers at the bartender.

Ava calculated it would be around noon in Kurt Olson's part of the world —an acceptable time to call. She found a quiet café, tucked herself into a booth and called the number. Olson answered on her second ring. There was the din of some kind of heavy machinery in the background. Mercifully it stopped abruptly when Ava introduced herself, which she had to do all over again when it was quiet.

"Sorry about the noise," Olson said. "I was drilling a hole to put up a picture."

After enquiring about Carrie and expressing his sadness about his ex-brother-in-law's death, he asked how he could help. Ava explained the purpose of her call.

"I'm interested in a case that Mr Mitchell might have been researching at the time of his death. It was a case he'd asked his sister for information on, and I believe you were able to help?"

"Are you talking about the *folie à deux* case?"

"Yes," answered Ava. "Anything you can tell me about it would be useful."

"Sure, no problem. Always happy to help our boys and girls in blue across the pond. You thinking this has something to do with Gray's murder, Sergeant?"

"I'm not sure. It's a bit out of the box, but I'd be interested in hearing any information you might have on the case — and why Gray was interested in it."

A pause. "Well, it involved two schoolgirls who murdered another girl at their school. They lured her to the top floor of a parking garage with the promise of alcohol, and pushed her off. Shocking case, really."

"How did they get caught?"

"Well, the girls didn't leave things to fate — they bashed the poor kid over the head several times with a couple of vodka bottles before they pushed her off. And they'd been caught on camera entering the parking garage. It wasn't a sophisticated crime, Detective. They were kids who had no idea what they were doing in terms of planning and risk assessment. Unlike their trial, which was a piece of work."

"How so? Do you mean the verdict? Do you think it was contrived?"

Kurt Olson snorted.

"Those girls were inseparable friends, but hell, how many girls of that age have — what is it they call it nowadays — BFFs?"

"Best friends forever."

"What you just said," Kurt replied. "How many of them go crazy and commit murder together? There was that case in New Zealand in the fifties . . . sixties? Coupla schoolgirls beat the mother of one of them to death with a sock fulla rocks. They made a movie out of it, I think, with that Brit actress in it. You know; the one who was in *Titanic*?"

"Kate Winslet," Ava said. "I know the film you're talking about. It was called, *Heavenly Creatures.*"

"Something like that. Anyway, one of the girls had wealthy parents who hired a big-shot lawyer to get his daughter and her friend off. You'd have expected an unusual case like that to create a sensation, but for some reason it didn't. Didn't even make the national news and there wasn't a lot of local coverage either. Guess it pays to have the right connections, right?"

There was no arguing with that.

"Why did they do it, do you know, Mr Olson? What was their motive?"

"Sheer wickedness, if you ask me. Officially, it was claimed their victim had been bullying them, accusing them of being lesbians, but if that had been the case, no one knew of it. The police questioned teachers and other kids but couldn't verify it one way or the other."

"Do you remember the girls' names, Mr Olson?" Ava held her breath.

"Give me a minute, Detective. Once upon a time I could have told you straight off, but my memory's not as sharp as it used to be.

It took only a couple of minutes for Kurt Olson to find the information.

"Thanks, Mr Olson," Ava said. Her hand shook as she wrote the names down on a napkin — all she had to hand.

"No need to thank me, Detective. You just make sure you nail whoever killed my brother-in-law, though I don't know how his death is related to those girls in Colorado.

Gray never did get around to telling me why he was so interested in that case."

Ava paid for her coffee and grabbed her coat. She texted Ollie to let him know that she would be late home. She was going to the Christmas market after all.

Chapter 20

"Bloody Christmas market," Neal muttered to himself as he changed into jeans and the Jack Wolfskin winter jacket Maggie had bought him for his birthday.

He would have avoided the market altogether if he hadn't promised to take Archie this year. Archie was excited about the funfair, and particularly the big white Ferris wheel that looked like Stromford's version of the London Eye. Maggie had been on it the year before and waxed lyrical about the magical views.

It wasn't that Neal disliked the market per se. It was just that the logistics of policing it were something of a nightmare. It killed any enjoyment he might have had. Still, tonight he was off duty. He would make an effort to take off his policeman's hat for once and try his best to absorb the wonderful atmosphere that everyone kept telling him about. He might even fill himself up with Christmas cheer, he thought glumly.

"See you later — maybe?" Maggie called to him. She was going to the market with a group of friends and from the sound of it, they were planning to eat and drink their way around the stalls.

Stromford was twinned with a German town, and the first Stromford Christmas market had been modelled on the traditional German ones. It had been a small affair then, but over the years it had grown to fill the whole of the cultural quarter around the castle and cathedral. Opening night was said to be quieter, and the locals tended to think of it as their night — before the coachloads of visitors arrived the next morning. Nevertheless, it would still be crowded and busy, with plenty of opportunities for pickpockets.

"Are you nearly ready, Dad?" Archie asked, appearing in his bedroom doorway.

"I'm ready. Let's go," Neal said, ruffling his son's hair affectionately. "Have you got your wallet in your inside jacket pocket, like I told you?"

They set off, walking in the direction of the cathedral. It dominated the skyline in all its floodlit glory, the perfect backdrop to the event. Neal had suggested they take a look at the stalls first, and then head for the fair. They walked down the cobbled street to the castle's east gate, past festive stallholders dressed in Victorian costumes, and welcoming market marshals with luminous green waistcoats pulled over their outer coats. A rich blend of enticing smells beckoned them forward — chestnuts roasting on hot coals, mouth-watering hog roasts, and the spicy aroma of mulled wine wafted on the night air. Neal began to relax, thinking that perhaps this wouldn't be so bad, after all.

They hadn't eaten yet. Maggie had had said they should try out the street food on offer. Neal and Archie queued at a stall selling German sausages, and ate them strolling through the grounds of the castle, pausing to admire the crafts and other goods on sale.

Neal had to force himself not to survey the crowds for possible miscreants. From time to time he nodded at a colleague in plain clothes. He was surprised at the number of faces he recognised in the crowds, people he'd come across in shops, businesses, or social events. That was the thing about living in a city like Stromford. It was more of a town, really, its city status deriving from the cathedral rather than the size of its population. Stromford was on a small enough scale for its inhabitants to lose a little of the anonymity of larger cities.

"Inspector Neal!"

Neal spun round and came face to face with Leon Warrior, a long, black cloak gathered around him. He was wearing a top hat and carried a cane. Warrior bowed and tipped his hat at Archie and Neal introduced his son. Warrior handed Archie a card advertising his ghost tour.

"Wow, Dad. A ghost tour. Can we do it?"

Warrior smiled.

"Maybe," Neal said and they moved on.

They had hardly gone any distance when they bumped into Laurence and Maxine Brand with Marcus Collins. More introductions for Archie and the promise of a Roman tour this time. *They're all out tonight*, thought Neal. Which of the suspects in the murder enquiry would they bump into next?

"Jimmy!" His sister Maggie's voice soared over the sound of a group of carol singers. "Hey, Arch. Having a good time?"

She came over to join them and ruffled Archie's hair. Archie made a face. Neal made a mental note not to ruffle his son's hair in future. Maggie was tipsy. She called her friends over and introduced them one by one, saying, to Neal's mortification, "What do you think, girls? Told you he was a looker."

He hoped his sausages hadn't left a film of grease around his mouth. One of Maggie's friends looked familiar under her red beanie hat. It was Angie Dent. She gave Neal a half-smile and he nodded, surprised to see her with his sister. Maggie had mentioned a new friend a few days ago — hadn't they been going to the cinema? Neal was

236

sure he would have remembered if his sister had told him her new friend's name was Angie Dent.

"Cheers, bro," Maggie said, toasting Neal with a plastic cup of *gluhwein*. See you at the fair, Archie."

Neal wondered what state of inebriation his sister would be in by the time she got there. He watched her until she disappeared into the crowds. After all, he was not his sister's keeper.

They were well into the grounds of the castle now, stalls to the left and right and all the way down the middle. For the next hour, father and son strolled from stall to stall, browsing, and occasionally making a purchase — some German biscuits, or Christmas decorations. Archie bought a star engraved with Maggie's name, which he planned to hang on their tree as soon as they got home and see how long it took for his aunt to spot it. Christmas lights twinkled all around them and the tinny sound of a group of carol singers alternated with that of a brass band playing carols over the loudspeaker system. Neal found himself being drawn in by the festive atmosphere and even beginning to enjoy himself.

Suddenly he felt his mobile vibrating in his inside jacket pocket. He pulled it out and peered at the text on his screen. It was from Ava, asking if she could meet him. Neal glanced at Archie with a twinge of guilt. It was his night off and he was supposed to be spending it with his son. Ava was aware of this and wouldn't have called him unless it was urgent.

Neal drew his son aside and told him he needed to make a call. They retreated to a relatively quiet spot behind a row of stalls. Ava answered immediately.

"Sir, I'm sorry to disturb you when you're with your son, but there's something I need to talk with you about urgently." There was excitement in his sergeant's voice.

He sighed. "This had better be good, Sergeant. Where are you?"

"Just by the back of the castle. You know where the drawbridge is, there's a stall selling Christmas lanterns. I'll wait there."

Neal looked round. Archie had taken out his phone and was playing a game.

"Arch, I've just had a call from Sergeant Merry. I need to meet her for a couple of minutes. That okay?"

"We're still going to the fair, right?" Archie looked crestfallen.

"Aye, we're going to the fair." Neal hoped he would be able to keep his word.

Ava was waiting for them across the drawbridge beside a stall lit up with candles flickering prettily in an assortment of containers. She was wearing skinny jeans tucked into those boots — the sheepskin ones that Maggie also liked. She was also wearing some kind of animal hat, but it looked entirely normal here. Half the people milling around were wearing some sort of silly headgear. Or maybe not so silly, Neal thought, feeling the chill of the frosty December night nip his ears.

Ava greeted Archie with an enthusiastic high five. They had met before when Neal had invited Ava to go bowling with his family in an attempt at bonding with his new partner. Archie was a big fan.

"There's a school just round the corner where they're doing teas and coffees in the sports hall. It'll be warmer there," Ava said. Her nose was red with cold and from the way she was moving from foot to foot, it appeared that the boots were not up to their task. Neal nodded.

They followed Ava to the primary school and into the hall, where school dinner tables had been laid out and set with plates of mince pies. There were those utilitarian green cups and saucers that always seem to appear in schools and village halls whenever refreshments are called for. Neal bought tea for himself, instant coffee for Ava and a hot chocolate for Archie. Mince pies came with the drinks. They managed to find an unoccupied table and

Archie took out his phone. In a low voice, Neal asked Ava what was so urgent that it couldn't wait.

Neal glanced at his son from time to time throughout Ava's account of her meeting with Carrie Howard and her subsequent conversation with Carrie's ex-husband. Unable to resist a melodramatic flourish, Ava produced the crumpled napkin inscribed with the names of the girls who had been involved in the *folie à deux* case twelve years ago in the US. She placed it face down on the table, provoking an impatient scowl from her DI.

The two names were not entirely familiar.

"Evangeline Dent. Katrin Forest," Neal read aloud.

Ava met his eye, cocking her head to the side. "Not a leap, is it?" she said.

"Give me your thoughts," said Neal.

"They killed Gray Mitchell," Ava said. She glanced in Archie's direction and lowered her voice. "They'd killed before. The method was similar — they worked together to lure their victim to a quiet place. They must have found out that Gray was counselling Nathan Elliott and texted Gray, pretending to be Nathan. What I don't know is whether Angie and Caitlin knew Gray in the States twelve years before. My guess is that Gray posed some kind of threat to them, so they got rid of him. Remember Laurence Brand's claim that Angie and Caitlin fell out at Gray and Leon's soiree? It's possible it had something to do with Gray — something he said, maybe?"

"And Caitlin. Who do you think killed her?"

"Angie?" Ava said, more uncertainly. "We need to bring her in for questioning, sir."

Neal sighed. His evening with Archie was slipping from his grasp. Suddenly his face darkened.

"What is it?"

Neal leaned across the table and whispered, "Angie Dent is with my sister."

Chapter 21

He enjoyed the Brands' company, but Marcus Collins kept thinking that he could be having more fun with Angie. He finally made his excuses to leave them and go in search of her. Laurence gazed at him protectively. Marcus knew that Laurence was still suspicious about Angie Dent, but he couldn't let his sympathy for Laurence spoil his chance of having a good time this evening. Maxine, as always, had stepped in to reassure her husband. She also told him that his obsession with Angie had to stop.

Marcus weaved through the crowds, looking for Angie. She'd told him she was going to the market with some friends. He didn't want to call her. He was looking forward to sneaking up behind her and encircling her waist, surprising her and hoping she'd be pleased to see him. She had been a bit off with him over the incident with Laurence Brand, and he was anxious to repair their relationship. If it could be called a relationship.

Marcus had assumed that finding Angie would be easy. He had not banked on the crowds. Everyone looked alike in their dark-coloured winter coats, but he knew that Angie would probably be wearing her red beanie hat. He hadn't seen her outdoors without it since the cold snap started.

Leaving the castle via the drawbridge, Marcus caught sight of the detectives who were investigating Gray Mitchell and Caitlin's deaths. They were walking in the direction of the primary school, with a young boy in tow. Marcus wondered briefly if they were a couple, envying DI Neal his luck.

The market stalls spilled out across the street and into the parkland, where they were gradually replaced by long white marquees selling local produce and crafts. The area beyond that was occupied by the funfair and game stalls. Marcus headed there, reasoning that by now, Angie and her friends were most likely hitting the rides.

It wasn't long before Marcus caught sight of a red beanie hat spinning round and round in a giant yellow teacup. As the ride slowed down, he made out Angie's face looking a shade pinker than those of her companions. He waved to her as she stepped down, calling her name over the loud music.

Angie seemed pleased to see him. She introduced her friend, Maggie, and they became a trio. The other girls in the group claimed that the rides were making them queasy. They declared they would be in the Stag if anyone cared to join them later.

"Been on the Ferris wheel yet?" Marcus asked.

"I promised to go on with Maggie," Angie said. "Sorry."

Marcus was disappointed, but he followed them to the spot where the giant white Ferris wheel dominated the fairground. He decided to wait and go on with Angie next time around. He took his mobile out, ready to take pictures.

* * *

Angie and Maggie climbed into a car together. Maggie felt slightly nervous but bolstered by Dutch courage. The wheel began to turn, and within seconds they were soaring above the marketplace, looking down on the fairground — the gardens and the castle, the floodlit cathedral, and a seething mass of people below. Their car moved slowly, stopping every now and again so that those at the top could enjoy the view. As they neared the apex, Maggie's mobile rang.

"That's Jimmy's ringtone," she said, laughing. "Hi, Jimmy, where are you?" Then, "I'm on the big wheel with Angie. It's amaaazing!"

Maggie smiled at her new friend. They'd met only a few days ago and already Angie had made her feel special.

As she listened to what her brother had to say, Maggie suddenly went quiet. She turned to face Angie, who was watching her closely from her side of the passenger car. Maggie wished she wasn't feeling so drunk, then, she might have managed to conceal her shock from the woman sitting beside her, her leg touching hers. But she was drunk and her horror at what her brother was telling her was written all over her face. Angie only had to look.

* * *

Ava listened as Neal asked Maggie where she was. She could see the fear in his face. She hoped that Archie, engrossed in a game on his phone, wouldn't look up and see it too. Was it a mistake for Neal to tell his sister that she might be in danger? How would Maggie react, particularly if she'd had a couple of glasses of gluhwein?

He was telling Maggie to get off the ride as soon as it stopped and make some excuse to get away from Angie. There was a pause. Neal looked at Ava and she was appalled at his stricken expression.

"Tell me," she pleaded.

"Angie knows," he said, not even bothering to lower his voice. "She just pulled a knife on Maggie."

"Oh no!"

"Who's pulled a knife on Auntie Maggie?" Archie asked. "Dad, what's going on? Is someone going to hurt Auntie Maggie?"

Neal looked at Ava, dismayed.

"N . . . no, no Archie. Auntie Maggie's fine, but Sergeant Merry and I need to check on her. I'm going to need you to stay here for a bit. Is that okay?" He said to Ava, "Go outside, grab the first uniform you come across and tell them to come in here and watch Archie."

Ava was on her feet and out the door in seconds. The market was well-policed and she spotted a couple of community police officers immediately. She showed her badge and explained that there was an emergency, and one of them quickly followed her inside. Neal handed over Archie to her care. His face was streaked with tears.

It was a two minute walk to the fair from where they were, but the crowds made running impossible. Ava called for back-up as they pushed their way through the press of people, shouting, "Police! Move aside!"

As they neared the slow-moving Ferris wheel, they could hear screams. Neal was shoving people out of the way.

As soon as they approached the big wheel they could see that something had happened. The crowds had cleared a space around a small group of people beside the gate leading to the passenger cars.

"Maggie!" Neal yelled, sprinting over towards the gate.

"Police! Out of the way!" Ava shouted, but she could already see that they were too late. The small group round the gate made way, revealing a prone figure and another, stooped over it. A third figure knelt by its side.

Ava slowed her pace. She dreaded finding Maggie Neal lying injured on the mud and grass. In front of her, Neal had slowed too. He was almost upon the stooped figure, ready to drag him out of the way. Ava covered her mouth, stumbling forward.

243

And now Neal was on his knees beside the stooping figure. It was Marcus Collins, and his hands were covered in blood. Ava looked down in horror, but the blood on Marcus's hands did not belong to Maggie Neal. Lying on the ground, bleeding from a wound in his chest, was Laurence Brand.

"Oh, my dear boy," Brand was saying, as Marcus tried to help him. "I told you that young woman was trouble."

From somewhere in the distance sirens wailed — police back-up, an ambulance. Ava was awash with relief and dismay at once. Looking at Neal she could see the same mixture of emotions on his face.

"Sir?"

Neal looked around, bewildered. "Where did they go?"

Maxine Brand, at her husband's side answered, "They tried to stop her — she stabbed Laurie."

"Which way?" yelled Ava at Marcus. The boy lifted a shaking, bloody finger to point their way forward.

* * *

Maggie Neal stumbled through the crowds. Angie Dent was gripping her arm and pressing the blade of her knife, covered with Laurence Brand's blood, into Maggie's side. Maggie's head was reeling with the horror of what had happened — her brother's phone call on the Ferris wheel, and then Marcus Collins stepping towards her as Angie dragged her out of their car, knife at her throat.

Then an older man had pulled Marcus back by the hood of his parka, and thrust himself in danger's way instead.

Angie had slashed at him, finally managing to thrust her knife into the man's chest as Marcus lunged forward to drag him to safety. Maggie had had her chance then, while Angie was lashing out wildly, but her head was still befuddled with alcohol and she didn't react. When she thought what to do, it was too late.

By then, Angie had grabbed her arm, stuck the knife against her ribs and pushed her away from the scene. She had whispered in Maggie's ear to keep moving or she'd do her, like she'd done the others. Within moments, they had disappeared into the throng of fairgoers, two young women seemingly out enjoying the Christmas festivities. Except one of them was a vicious killer.

They were heading out of the fairground now, passing through the park gates and along a street lined with houses. The curtains were open, Christmas lights twinkled at the windows. Maggie caught a passing glimpse of an elderly couple sitting at their window, smiling at passers-by, a tall Christmas tree winking behind them in the corner of their living room.

"You could get on quicker without me. I'm only holding you up."

"Shut up, bitch!" Angie's voice was entirely different now. Her shifting, indefinable accent had become unmistakably North American.

"Who the hell are you?" Maggie asked.

She winced in pain as Angie pushed her roughly into a shop doorway to let a crowd of market-goers pass by. Maggie was afraid to move or call out. Finally, when the road ahead was clear, Angie prodded her with the knife, drawing a squeal from Maggie as the blade scratched the surface of her skin. They stepped out of the doorway and turned the next corner, leading to the car park, where Angie had left her car. Maggie realised with dismay that the exit led away from the cathedral quarter. Away from the market with its lights and people, and the chance of Jimmy finding them before it was too late.

"Please, let me go," Maggie pleaded. "You can get away now. There's no need . . ."

Angie pushed her towards the car. Maggie knew that if she got in that car, she would never get out of it alive. Angie had killed two people already — three if Laurence Brand had been fatally wounded. She would not hesitate to kill again. And if she managed to get out of Stromford and safely away, she would have no more need of a hostage . . .

They had reached the car now. Angie pushed Maggie up against the door to the driver's seat. Maggie felt the pressure on her ribs relax as the knife withdrew. She gasped. Was Angie going to let her go? Then she felt the cold steel blade press against her neck and tears pricked her eyes. "Please . . ." She looked into Angie's pale, impassive eyes and saw no hint of feeling there. Maggie thought of her brother, her nephew, and all the people she cared about. She wondered if she would see any of them again.

* * *

Neal and Ava beat their way through the crowds. Angie and Maggie had only a few minutes' head start. At the junction of two streets, they paused, unsure which way to go.

"The car park!" Neal said, panting. "Angie picked Maggie up in her car. They were going to park in the car park off Thornbush Avenue."

Ava nodded. As Neal bent double for a second to recover his wind, Ava sprinted on ahead. By the time he caught her up, she was running across the car park towards a woman who was apparently propping another one against the side of a car.

"Police!" Ava yelled, nearly upon them.

"Wait!"

Ava froze. Neal knew that she would have thrown herself headlong at Angie without a thought, but it was not her call. Neal came to a halt beside Ava and looked into Maggie's anguished eyes. They pleaded with him to help her. He had never let his 'wee sister' down and he wasn't about to now.

"Let her go, Angie," Neal said. "You can't win here. If you harm her, we'll be on you in an instant. You can't drive and hold a knife to her throat."

Neal bit back his words. Angie couldn't drive, but she could hold a knife to Maggie's throat and force her to drive. He waited, tormented, for her to say as much or to shove Maggie into the driver's seat. But Angie seemed to be in no hurry. He reminded himself that she had done this before, murdered in cold blood. Her lack of response prompted him to speak again. If he could get her talking there might still be a chance to get a hold on the situation. Beside him, Ava was tensed, wound tight. He knew that every instinct in her was screaming 'act,' but he needed her to be still, to wait.

"You killed Gray," he said, his tone flat. "You and Caitlin, or should I say, Kristin?"

That got a reaction — a tic, a flash of anger, but Maggie suffered for it. Slowly, deliberately, no hint of emotion in her cold eyes, Angie scratched her captive's throat, drawing a bead of dark blood. Maggie's eyes widened in pain and fear, but there was another emotion in them too now — concern for her brother's safety.

"You think you know it all, don't you, *Inspector* Neal? All about Caitlin and me. Well, you don't know shit."

"Your real name is Evangeline. You grew up in a small town in Colorado. You met Caitlin in high school. You were best friends. You did everything together, including killing your classmate. Then Caitlin's parents betrayed you, didn't they? Her parents were wealthy, they got her off completely, took her out of the country to start a new life in the UK. They took her away from you."

It took every ounce of effort he could summon for Neal to keep his voice steady, reassuring. He was winging it now, inventing from the crumbs of information Ava had fed him as they raced from the school hall.

"But you didn't get off as lightly as Caitlin, did you? Caitlin was the quiet, subservient one and you were the dominant one. That's what they argued, wasn't it? And you were the one they punished. What happened to you,

Angie? Did you do time in prison or in a psychiatric facility? That must have really hurt."

Beside him, Neal could almost hear Ava's heart pumping adrenaline through her veins. He knew she must be straining every muscle to stop herself rushing forward and grappling the knife from Angie's hand. No doubt she was convinced she could do it. It was all a matter of misdirection and timing, she would insist. Neal extended a hand, fingers splayed as a signal for her to wait. She had to trust him.

Neal kept talking. His voice was calm, the lilting, almost hypnotic rhythm of his Scots accent belied the tension in his body, the fear gripping his heart.

"I think they were wrong, weren't they, Angie? Caitlin was just as much to blame, if not more. She was the one who convinced you that your classmate was possessed, not the other way around. She made you do it, didn't she?" Angie's mouth opened and closed, but she didn't speak.

"Did she contact you, Angie, or did you come looking for her? You must have missed her. One minute you have this beautiful, intense relationship, this love — am I right? You loved Caitlin, didn't you? Then she's gone and you're left utterly alone, as if she'd died. How does a person recover from something like that, Angie? How did you cope?"

No reaction, no relaxation in Angie's grip on the knife, or her hold on Maggie. Neal feared that his attempt at engaging Angie was failing. He kept talking, aware only of the danger to his sister. He needed to chip away at the carapace surrounding Angie Dent's heart.

"Did she forget about you, Angie?"

"No!" Angie cried suddenly, "Never! She would never have forgotten me. They wouldn't let us get in touch. They said we shouldn't see each other ever again. They didn't even let us say goodbye."

Angie was feeling something, at last, but whether it put his sister in more or less danger, Neal had no way of knowing.

Neal gave Angie a slow, encouraging nod.

"I came the minute they let me out of that place," Angie said. "She said she missed me, that she needed me."

"What did she need you for, Angie? Was it to help her kill Gray Mitchell?"

"Gray Mitchell was evil. Everyone thought he was so kind and gentle, but Caitlin was the only one who saw him for what he really was. When she told me what he was really like, I could see it too. He wanted to kill her. Us. We had to stop him."

"I don't think you're telling the truth, Angie. I think you wanted to share Caitlin's belief, but you couldn't. You felt alone, didn't you, Angie? Like you felt when you were separated from Caitlin all those years ago. You thought you had her back when you arrived in Stromford, but you didn't. Angie, listen to me. The reason you felt that way was because you'd changed. You were no longer the young girl who was so unconfident, so unsure that she willingly fell into her best friend's fantasy world. I think you helped Caitlin lure Gray to his death but I think you did it because you were afraid of being alone again."

Neal's thoughts were racing. He needed to keep thinking fast. He was afraid that if he stopped talking, the spell would break and Maggie would die.

"Then I think you killed Caitlin because you knew she would never stop killing, never stop wanting you to help satisfy that need in her and you no longer believed her, did you? She told you Gray was evil but you could only see what everyone else saw — a good man."

He was trying desperately to interact with Angie. He wanted Angie to believe he was on her side. Angie stood, poker-faced, still pressing the knife to his sister's throat.

"Sir?" Ava said, quietly, urgently, needing a signal to act, but Neal wasn't finished. He still felt he had time to win Angie's trust and turn things around.

"You don't want to kill again, Angie. Now that Caitlin's dead, there's no one to manipulate you. You can stop. There's no need to hurt anyone else."

Angie had been moving her gaze back and forth from his face to Ava's. Now, suddenly, she looked him straight in the eye.

For the briefest moment, Neal felt a stirring of hope. He thought he had made a connection, hit at some truth Angie could relate to. By the time he realised his mistake, it was too late.

Angie laughed. "You really don't get it, do you?" she said. "You were right about one thing, though. I did miss Caitlin. She was the only other person I've ever met who understood me, and killing her was the hardest thing I've ever done in my life."

Angie looked directly at Neal. "So much harder than this," she said, and slashed the knife across Maggie's throat.

Time stopped for Neal. He was aware of a protracted "Noooo!" rising from deep within him as he lunged forward, too late to catch his sister as she fell, blood pouring from the gaping wound in her neck. Then he was there on the ground beside Maggie, trying to stop the blood that seemed to be gushing everywhere — onto his hands, his coat, his trousers where her head lay cradled in his lap.

* * *

Ava stared at the scene before her, sickened and dismayed. For an agonising moment she hesitated, torn between helping Neal and his sister and going after Angie. One look at Neal told her that he was in no state to give direction and Angie was already sliding into the car. Ava took control of the situation, instantly pulling out her mobile and yelling for back-up. At the same time, she hurled herself at the car, managing to yank open the rear door just as Angie revved the engine and the car jerked to life.

"Get out, bitch!" Angie screamed at Ava. Abandoning her attempt to start the car, she twisted out of the driver's seat and scrambled over the gearstick to launch herself into the back seat beside Ava. Ava raised her arms instinctively as Angie lunged at her with the knife. For a brief moment Ava was afraid. Then she shifted resolutely into survival mode.

Ava wrestled with her attacker, dodging the knife and struggling to gain the upper hand. She grasped Angie's wrist and strained to keep the knife at arm's length. Somehow, Angie managed to force Ava down until she was sprawling across the seat. Then, in a single, deft move, she straddled Ava, pinning her down. Ava still had a grip on Angie's wrist and she tensed every muscle in her right arm to keep the knife at bay as she lashed out with her left.

Time slowed and Ava felt a mounting sense of horror as her tired muscles trembled under the strain and she saw the weapon in her attacker's hand inch closer. She couldn't hold Angie off for much longer. Ava mustered everything she had and with it came a sudden, electrifying burst of adrenaline.

Ava's left arm shot out and she seized Angie by the wrist. Now grabbing onto Angie's knife arm with both hands, Ava yanked Angie's wrist to angle the weapon sideways and pulled Angie towards her. Using her opponent's weight as leverage, she pulled herself upwards to smash her skull into Angie's chin. Angie yelped and a trickle of blood dripped from her mouth but still she held onto the knife. Even so, the balance of power had shifted. Ava twisted Angie's arm backwards and there was the sickening sound of bone breaking. This time, Angie screamed in agony and the knife dropped from her hand, narrowly missing Ava's face.

Ava shoved Angie off her and slammed her hard into the door of the car, ready to fight unrestrainedly now, no weapon to hold her back.

Then, suddenly, the door of the car opened outwards and Angie tumbled out. Ava scrambled out after her and landed on top of Angie. She dragged her to her feet and handcuffed her roughly.

"Angie Dent. I am arresting you for the murder of Caitlin Forest…"

As she recited Angie's rights, Ava looked over to where Neal was still tending to his sister. Maggie Neal was lying deathly still.

"Sir?" Ava said, but Neal did not seem to hear her. Oh no! Ava sank back against the car, all the triumph of overcoming Angie stolen away from her by the shock of seeing the impossible amount of blood on the garment Jim Neal was pressing to his sister's throat.

Chapter 22

A concerned paramedic wrapped a blanket around Ava's shoulders, urging her to accept a lift to the hospital in his EMS vehicle. His partner was trying to persuade Neal to do the same, but he was insisting on riding in the ambulance with Maggie.

Feeling slightly hysterical with cold and shock, Ava sank into the back seat of the car and watched as two police constables shoved Angie Dent none too gently into the back of their squad car. Now that her adrenaline-fuelled burst of strength had subsided, Ava was beginning to shake. She took a step towards Neal, then stopped. It wasn't that she did not wish to speak to him, only that she had no words to offer that could take away his pain. She suspected he wouldn't have heard her anyway. So, with regret, Ava allowed herself to be bundled into the EMT vehicle without a word of comfort or goodbye for her DI.

* * *

Neal was aware of Ava's absence as soon as the emergency medical car pulled away. Her departure left him feeling adrift, even though he could not have faced speaking with her at that moment. He was too full of self-recrimination and guilt. The way he saw it, all the responsibility for his sister's injury lay squarely at his feet. He would never forget it.

He had misjudged the situation, precipitated the unthinkable by letting emotion cloud his ability to think. On their mad dash from the school hall to the car park, Ava had fed him some facts about Caitlin's past and he'd concocted a whole flawed theory based on this meagre information. He'd literally talked Angie into cutting Maggie's throat as surely as if he'd wielded the knife himself.

"Come on, mate," the paramedic said to him again. Neal turned and stumbled up the ramp of the ambulance. The sound of Maggie's ragged breathing filled the space. He had done his best to save his sister's life, now it was up to the experts. He sat quietly by while the paramedics did their job. It was only when they pulled out of the car park that he remembered that Archie would still be waiting in the school hall with the community police officers. Neal pulled out his mobile and made arrangements for his son to be brought to the hospital. How would he break the news to Archie if his beloved aunt did not survive?

* * *

Ava Merry sat at her desk, staring through the glass into Jim Neal's empty office. It was three days since the events leading to Angie Dent's assault on his sister. Maggie Neal was going to live. Her brother's prompt action in staunching the flow of blood, and an emergency tracheotomy performed by the paramedics had saved her life. Ava had spent much of those three days unravelling the circumstances, past and present that had culminated in the near tragedy.

At the heart of the investigation had lain that 'unknown unknown,' the thing they didn't know they didn't know. How could they have known it? Who could have known that the key to finding the person who had

254

lured Gray Mitchell to his death lay in the story of two young girls who had formed an intense and murderous bond a dozen years ago in another country?

Ava was still grappling with the concept of a *folie à deux*, a phenomenon now less romantically described by psychiatrists as 'shared psychotic disorder,' in which two people can become caught up in a common delusion. In the case of the two adolescent girls, Evangeline and Katrin, as they were then known, their shared delusion had taken the form of an irrational belief in the demonic possession of a fellow classmate, whom they also believed was trying to drive a wedge between their passionate, possibly sexual, friendship.

Together, they had hatched a plan to lure Melanie to the roof of a multi-storey car park where they had plied her with vodka, then attacked her with the empty bottle, before pushing her off the roof.

The girls' lawyer had argued that Angie had been the dominant personality, pulling Caitlin into her dark fantasy world. Hired by Caitlin's wealthy parents, the lawyer had succeeded in negotiating clemency for the girls on the grounds that they were victims of circumstance, and because of their age. If they had never been classmates and formed a friendship, they would never, individually, have been capable of committing murder.

As a condition of their lenient sentence, it was ordered that they should be separated. Caitlin had walked away from court free to leave the country with her family. Angie had been committed to a psychiatric facility where she had spent the next seven years of her life. After her release it had taken her a long time to work out where Caitlin was living, but when she did, she made immediate plans to seek her out.

Ava had listened to the story unfold, sitting in the interview room with DSI George Lowe. From time to time in the course of the long hours spent questioning Angie, Ava glanced up at the two-way mirror in the room.

She knew Neal was standing there, riveted by every word of the proceedings. She half-expected to see his angry fist come splintering through the painted glass at any moment.

"Caitlin was my best friend. We were closer than sisters," Angie had begun. "We were connected on a level that transcended the physical. Each of us understood what the other was thinking, feeling."

"Whose idea was it to kill your classmate, Melanie Ingalls?" Lowe asked.

Angie, after a whispered exchange with her legal representative, refused to answer. That was past history and she knew she could not be judged on it here.

It wasn't that Ava didn't believe any of it was true. It was difficult to get her head round the possibility that a delusion could be spread from person to person like an infection, but she accepted the wisdom of those more expert about psychiatry than she was. After all, whole ideologies had thrived on shared beliefs, sometimes with tragic results. History was peppered with examples of people who were prepared to kill or die for what could be interpreted by others as mere delusions. Still, Ava was reluctant to believe that Angie and Caitlin had ever been caught up in a common fantasy.

They were two people who should never have met. That's what the judge had said in her summing up in their original trial. That had been twelve years ago. Ava could not help but wonder at the opportunities now open to people who 'should never have met,' courtesy of the Internet.

Turning to the present day, George Lowe had asked, "Why did you kill Gray Mitchell?"

"Gray Mitchell was evil," Angie said. She held Lowe's gaze, as if trying to mesmerise him into accepting that this was what she truly believed. "I didn't see it at first, but Caitlin convinced me. He was planning on killing us. We had to act."

"I don't buy that," Ava said. "I think that this time around — maybe last time too, if you ask me, it was an act of evil, plain and simple. The only delusion you and Caitlin shared was that you could get away with murder."

Angie shrugged. Prove it, she seemed to say.

Ava had spoken with Carrie Howard's ex-husband again. He had been doing some detective work himself and discovered that the travelling theatre company that Gray Mitchell had belonged to had performed Shakespeare's 'Othello' at the girls' school back in 2001, the same year they had killed Melanie Ingalls.

"One of you thought Gray Mitchell might remember you and reveal your true identities, didn't you?" Ava leaned forward as if trying to stare into Angie Dent's mind. "Was it at the party at his and Warrior's house? Maybe he came up to one of you and asked if he had met you before? The thought of being discovered made you physically sick, didn't it? Caitlin had to take you home and together you devised a plan to kill him."

Angie scarcely flinched, but Ava felt that she was right.

George Lowe felt it too. He said, "We know that you knew that Gray Mitchell was counselling Nathan Elliot about his sexuality. We showed Nathan your picture and he confirmed that he'd met you once when he was with Gray, and Gray had introduced you. You and Caitlin used that knowledge to lure Gray Mitchell to his death with that desperate text, which you knew he'd assume was from Nathan."

Angie's bland stare left them both frustrated. Ava could almost feel Neal's tension bleeding through the two-way mirror.

"Why did you kill Caitlin? The other killings make a kind of sense, but why would you kill her?" Ava asked.

At first, it seemed that she was not going to answer. Then, with an apologetic look at her legal adviser, Angie shrugged and said, "She was supposed to be my friend."

* * *

"I can understand why they killed poor Gray, but I don't get why Angie would kill Caitlin," Maxine Brand said, shaking her head. Ava looked around the small gathering of people in the Brand's homely kitchen. Laurence Brand was present, still recovering from his near-fatal stabbing. And Marcus Collins who now occupied the Brands' spare room. Also, Helen Alder, Vincent Bone and Leon Warrior. They were all sitting around the Brands' kitchen table as though assembled for a social gathering. At Maxine's question, all eyes turned to Ava.

"Love turned to hate," Ava answered. "Angie spent seven years in a psychiatric unit because Caitlin's wealthy parents bought their daughter's freedom with a fancy lawyer who was able to persuade the judge that the girls suffered from a shared psychosis. They believed Melanie Ingalls was possessed by the devil, allegedly. Unknown to Angie, Caitlin had been carefully tutored to paint Angie as the dominant personality, the one who had communicated her delusion to Caitlin, a susceptible and naïve middle-class girl."

"So was it a true *folie à deux* or not?" Laurence Brand asked.

Ava shrugged. "Maybe first time around there was an element of that in it. As to who influenced whom, I don't think we'll ever know. My money would be on Caitlin, but I'm inclined to believe they fed each other's fantasies. It's now suspected that Caitlin had a hand in her family's drowning. It's likely she hated her parents for separating her from Angie."

"She seemed so . . . normal," Helen Alder commented. "Caitlin, I mean — and Angie too. Just two ordinary young women. Who would think they had such an extraordinary secret in their past, or such a capacity for evil." She looked around the table.

Most heads were nodding. Ava thought she caught Maxine and Laurence exchange a knowing look.

Perhaps the couple understood more than the others how fluid the definition of 'normal' could be.

"She loved her work and she was good at it," Vincent Bone said. "She created beautiful stained-glass designs of her own." He shook his head.

Ava remembered the conversation she had had with him in the stonemason's workshop, about the grotesques and gargoyles, how to the medieval mind their ugliness represented evil. Evil was ugly, she thought, just not on the outside.

"I'm sorry for all the trouble I caused," Laurence Brand said.

Ava smiled. "No harm done."

"I don't know how to feel about Gray's murder," Leon Warrior said, with self-pity in his voice. He had been silent until that moment. "He was going to leave me, you know. Go back to the States. I wish I'd had the time . . ."

No one turned to him with sympathetic murmurings. They still counted Leon as a friend, one of their close-knit little social circle — what remained of it — but their compassion was diminished by their loyalty to Gray Mitchell's memory.

"How is DI Neal?" Maxine asked.

"He blames himself for what happened to Maggie." She had not seen her boss for a couple of days. At their last meeting, she had tried again to convince him that he wasn't to blame, but he had retreated behind a wall of self-recrimination and was not yet ready to dislodge a single brick. She hoped it was not a permanent structure.

Ava thanked the Brands for inviting her to their gathering. Maxine saw her to the door. The biting cold outside was a stark reminder that they were still in the grip of a particularly bitter winter. Ava pulled her woolly hat out, the owl one that she knew Neal thought slightly ridiculous. She tugged it over her ears and walked down the street. According to the weather forecast, there was more snow to come. It would wrap the city in its cold beauty again, hiding whatever ugliness lay beneath.

THE END

Thank you for reading this book. If you enjoyed it please leave feedback on Amazon, and if there is anything we missed or you have a question about then please get in touch. The author and publishing team appreciate your feedback and time reading this book.

Our email is jasper@joffebooks.com

www.joffebooks.com

ALSO BY JANICE FROST

DEAD SECRET

Made in the USA
San Bernardino, CA
25 February 2016